Life After The Undead

By

PEMBROKE SINCLAIR

United States of America

Copyright 2011 PEMBROKE SINCLAIR
All Rights Reserved

Cover Artist: Jerrod Brown
Byline and Title Design: Suzannah Safi, www.design.suzannahsafi.com

All rights reserved. No part of this book may be reproduced in any form or by any electronic or mechanical means including information storage and retrieval systems -- except for brief quotations embodied in critical articles or reviews -- or transmitted in any format or by any means without express written consent from the publisher.

First Publication.

ISBN: 978-1-937809-01-0

Published in the United States of America
Published by
eTreasures Publishing, LLC
4442 Lafayette St.
Marianna, FL 32446
http://www.etreasurespublishing.com

This book is entirely fiction and bears no resemblance to anyone alive or dead, in content or cover art. Any instances are purely coincidental. This book is based solely on the author's vivid imagination.

Acknowledgments:

A special thanks to Jerrod Brown, horror artist, for creating the awesome cover.

I would also like to thank Dax. I couldn't have done it without you.

My gratitude goes out to Wendy Davy for editing this story, and to Martha and Patricia, as well as everyone else at eTreasures, who made publishing this book possible.

CHAPTER 1

I will never understand peoples' fascination with the apocalypse. Why would you waste so much time and energy worrying about something you can't change? Besides, most of the time, it never comes to fruition anyway. Remember Y2K? What a hullabaloo that was. People were so afraid computers were going to fail and throw society back into the Dark Ages that they were stockpiling supplies and moving into the wilderness so they could get away from technology. Why would they move to the wilderness? If technology was going to fail, wouldn't they be just as safe in a city? I guess they were afraid when technology failed, everyone would go crazy and start killing each other. Either way, it didn't happen. I wonder how those people felt afterward.

Then, there was the whole 2012 scare. This one was supposedly based on ancient prediction, so you know it was reliable. Are you kidding? Even the Mayans didn't believe their own ancestors' "vision." What happened was there had been a tablet that had the Mayan calendar carved into it. The end was broken and faded, so no one knew what it said. Our culture, being the pessimistic lot that we are, automatically assumed it was an end-of-the-world warning. But, again, nothing happened on December 21, 2012. Christmas came and went, and I think everyone, everywhere, even the skeptics, had a little something more to be thankful for. Life went on as usual, and all those doomsayers faded into obscurity.

The day the world *did* end was pretty nondescript. By that I mean there was no nuclear explosion or asteroid or monumental natural disaster. There weren't even any horseman or plagues to announce the end was coming. The world ended fairly quietly. I couldn't even give you a date because it happened at different times depending on where you were. It was never predicted, and I'm sure a scenario that no one even considered. Who really thinks the dead are going to rise from the grave and destroy the majority of the population? No one but Hollywood, and we all know those are just movies. But that is exactly what happened. Those of us that survived were left wide-eyed, mouth agape, trying to figure out what to do next.

There were a few who were able to pull their heads out and organize those left behind. They made sure the populace had food, shelter, and protection. They were saviors, the United States' heroes. Life wouldn't have gone on without them, and it was pretty difficult those first few years after the zompocalypse.

Sometimes it's difficult for me to remember what life was like before the rise of the undead. I was a teenager, though I hesitate to say normal. I wasn't deformed or anything, but my classmates thought I was strange. I had a fascination with the dark, the macabre, but I wasn't a Goth or Emo. I read books and magazines about serial killers. I didn't idolize them or want to be like them—hell no—but I was fascinated with how evil and black a human's soul could get.

I wanted to be a psychologist and work with the criminally insane, maybe figure out why they did what they did. Apparently, when you're 15, your friends think you're weird if you have desires to help someone other than yourself. While they were worried about becoming popular and getting the right boyfriend, I was trying to figure out how to make society better.

Of course, those dreams will never come true. Society doesn't exist. Everything I once held dear is gone. I lost my parents to the horde, like a lot of kids. Unlike some of the others, mine weren't taken by surprise or in some freak accident; they were taken because of their own stupidity. Some days I miss them a lot, but others I believe they got what they deserved. I might sound callous and uncaring, but what about them? Why would they abandon their 15 year old daughter? It used to keep me up at night, trying to find the answer to that question, but I've given up asking it. No reason wasting time on things that could've or should've been.

As I stare out the passenger side window of the semi, I'm reminded how bleak the future has become. The truck rolls down a once heavily traveled highway that has been reduced to a cracked trail. Gas stations and towns dotting the landscape have been abandoned and are crumpling into the weeds that are taking them over. There are a few areas that still resemble pre-zombie destruction, and these are the military outposts set up along the road, used for protection and refueling. I use the term "military" loosely because there is no formal military anymore. It's a rag-tag group of men and women who were lucky enough to get guns. I chuckle to myself. It's been two years since I was last out in the world, and a lot has changed since then. I still remember the day the zombies attacked. It's as clear as if it happened yesterday.

* * *

I sat on the bench, my head bobbing and feet tapping to Korn's "Freak on a Leash" as it pulsed through my eardrums. I mouthed the words until movement caught my eye, then turned. Carmen and her friends walked toward the school bus stop where I sat. Carmen walked by and for a moment our gaze met, then she flipped her long blonde hair and huffed, averting her gaze to the sky. I smiled and turned up my iPod.

Carmen and I used to be friends back in grade school. She used to be shy and awkward, like me, but when we got to Junior

High, she broke out of her shell. She started making new friends, ones that apparently weren't as weird as me. She quit talking to me. I guess I embarrassed her. I called her friends the Baa-Baa Twins because they followed Carmen mindlessly and did everything she told them to do without question—like sheep.

I stared at my feet, which once again started tapping to the beat. Someone bumped me. The other students made their way to the curb. Some of them believed they had to have the "right" seat on the bus, so they wanted to be first through the door. I remained seated. The bus was a little ways down the block when it stopped. I slid to the edge of the bench to look, turning down my music.

Carmen stepped off the curb and waved. "Helllooo," she called out, "we're down here." She placed her hand on her hip. "What are they doing?"

I got up from the bench and stepped into the street. The sun reflected off the bus's windshield so I couldn't see inside. I paused my music. The only sound was the idling of the engine. Suddenly, the bus started to rock. A thud, as if something hit the ceiling, echoed through the streets. All of us froze. The doors slid open and the bus driver stumbled out, rolling onto his back after he missed the last step. He struggled to his feet and ran toward us. Two of the students, I recognized them as seventh graders, got off the bus. They almost fell down the stairs, and I wondered if they hurt their knees because they didn't seem to want to bend them. As they stepped into the sunlight, they flinched and seemed slightly confused. They turned to their right, then to their left, and when they noticed me and the other students, they moved forward. As they drew closer, I noticed their eyes were bloodshot with dark circles underneath. They both walked slowly, and one of them dragged his foot.

I was convinced they injured themselves. I knew they were on the JV basketball team, so they could have fallen on the court, but I couldn't figure out why they were getting off the bus. It must have something to do with the sound I heard. The one who wasn't dragging his foot opened his mouth and let out a low moan. A shiver ran down my spine. The bus driver ran into the center of our group and grabbed Carmen by the shoulders.

"Run!" he yelled.

Carmen pushed him away, mumbling, "Eww, don't touch me."

Baa-Baa One stepped to her side and whispered something I couldn't hear. A look of disgust covered both their faces.

He turned to another boy. "You've got to get out of here."

All of the kids stared at him. Was this some kind of joke? A few of them grabbed their backpacks and headed away from the bus. Carmen watched the man, her hand still on her hip.

"We've got to get to school, you know!" she said.

The driver took off down the street, glancing only once over his shoulder.

I stared after him and then back at the seventh graders. There was something not right about how they were moving, something bizarre about their stare. I moved a little to the right so the glare was off the bus's windshield and noticed what looked like blood on the window. I pulled my earbuds out and grabbed Carmen by the arm.

"We've got to go," I said.

Carmen jerked out of my grasp. "What's your problem? We're supposed to go to school."

Baa-Baa One stepped closer to Carmen, her eyebrows furrowed as she cracked her knuckles. I think she thought she was being intimidating, but with her styled hair and manicured nails, I wasn't worried. I rolled my eyes.

"I think she's right," Baa-Baa Two said from the sidewalk. "I think we should go."

Carmen threw her a dirty look. "When I want your opinion, I'll give it to you."

The seventh graders were now within ten feet, and I decided I wasn't going to fight with Carmen. If she wanted to go to school, she was going to have to find her own way there. I ran a ways up the block before a scream caused me to turn back around. The seventh graders made it to Carmen and held her by her arms. They bit deep into her flesh, and blood pooled on the sidewalk. Baa-Baa One tried to pry one of the boys off, but she only succeeded in tearing more flesh off Carmen's arm. She lost her grip and fell backward. The boy dropped on top of her and gnawed on her throat. Baa-Baa One's scream turned into a gargle. Baa-Baa Two took off running.

I inhaled a sharp breath and ran for my house. When I got there, I slammed the door and locked the deadbolt. I looked quickly out the window, but the street was quiet. Running into the living room, I grabbed the phone and dialed 911. Oddly, I got a busy signal. I hung up and turned on the TV.

"Krista?" Mom's voice called from upstairs. "Is that you?"

I didn't answer. I flipped through the channels until I found the news.

"Krista?" Mom said right behind me. "What are you doing home? I thought you left for the bus ten minutes ago."

"Mom, something weird's going on. Two seventh graders just attacked Carmen and her friend."

Mom rolled her eyes. "Of course they did, sweetie. Carmen probably deserved it." She reached for the remote, but I jerked it out of her grasp. Mom huffed and placed her hands on her hips. "Krista, really. I don't know what this is about, but I can imagine it has something to do with those serial killer magazines you've been reading. I will take those away if this is how you're going to behave. I'll be ready to leave in five minutes." She turned and headed back upstairs.

The news droned on about how nice the weather was going to be for the rest of the week before switching to local sports. I changed the channel, but there was nothing. I turned the TV off and switched on the radio. I found the local country station. A George Straight song was just ending, and the DJ came on the air, preparing to take the next caller.

The woman's voice was frantic. "Something is going on!" she screamed over the air. "Haven't you guys had any reports? People…people are acting crazy."

"Whoa, lady, slow down." The DJ's voice was low and calm. "How are people acting crazy?"

"They're attacking!" The woman broke into sobs. "My husband…my husband."

"What about your husband?"

"He's dead."

There was silence over the radio.

"Do you hear me! He's dead and he's attacking pe-" Her voice cut off.

The radio crackled and the DJ came back on. "Sorry about that folks. We don't screen our callers before they are put on the air. We'll be back after these messages with some more good, ole country to get you through your morning commute."

As the radio switched to a commercial, Mom came back downstairs and grabbed it out of my hand. "It's time to go to school, my dear."

I stared at her. "I don't think we should leave the house."

"Nonsense. Everything is fine. Now, get your butt in the car."

I stepped back and shook my head.

"Young lady, I am not going through this again. Get your butt in the car right now." Mom moved to grab my arm but a pounding at the door interrupted her. "Who could that be?"

Mom glanced out the window before unlocking the deadbolt and opening the door. Dad came flying into the house and slammed the door behind him. He bumped into his wife and she landed on her side.

"Charlie, watch it!"

He turned and noticed her on the floor.

"Laura, I'm sorry." He placed his hands under her arms and pulled her up. "Where's Krista?"

"I'm right here, Dad."

He breathed a sigh. "Get upstairs. Both of you."

Mom stared at him. "Charlie, what in the world is going on?" she asked.

"I don't know. Just get upstairs!"

The panic in Dad's voice caused me to take the stairs two at a time. Both of them were right behind me, and we went into the master bedroom. Dad locked the door behind us. He went to the closet and grabbed his 1911 pistol and two rifles, which he handed to Mom and me.

Mom stared at him, wild-eyed. "Will you please tell me what is going on?"

I cradled the weapon against my chest and stared at him.

"I don't know," he said. "I was on my way to work and stopped at a red light. I noticed some people on the sidewalk, walking really slowly, as if they were drunk, and they attacked the people in the car in front of me. They reached through the open window and started biting them. There was blood everywhere. I would have helped, but a group of them converged on my car. I got out of there and hurried home as fast as I could."

"That's what happened to Carmen," I whispered.

Mom pursed her lips and stared from Dad to me before shoving the gun into her husband's arms. "Do you two really think I'm an idiot? I hate it when you get together and try to prank me."

"Laura, I'm serious."

"Mom, really, something is going on."

She rolled her eyes and headed for the door. "Fine. You two play your little game, but I have to go to work. Charlie, make sure Krista gets to school." She flipped the lock and flung open the door.

Normally, Mom would have been correct in her assumption. Dad and I loved to play tricks.

They were usually harmless—ice cubes with flies in them, replacing the regular coffee with decaff, or putting colored Vaseline in the jelly jar. There was one time we pulled a really bad one. Dad and I were goofing around in the front yard, whacking rocks with a stick, pretending to be golfing, and one of them broke the window next to the door. Dad thought it would be fun if we made it look like someone broke in and killed us, so we poured some fake blood on the floor. We hid in the closet and waited for Mom to get home. She freaked when she walked in. We stopped her before she called 911, but she didn't talk to us for two days.

As we cowered in the room, I wished I had never pulled *any* pranks on Mom. She never really trusted us after we pretended to be dead. Dad lunged after her, but she was already half way down the stairs. I watched from the top of the stairs as he intercepted her before she made it into the garage.

"Laura, please, this is not a joke." He grabbed her arm and tried to get her to stay in the house.

She wiggled out of his grasp. "Charlie, seriously. This has gone on long enough."

Dad stuffed the pistol into his belt and grabbed Mom around the waist, flinging her over his shoulder. She started kicking and screaming, but he wrestled her up the stairs and back into the bedroom. I locked the door behind them and watched as Dad tossed Mom onto the bed.

Mom's face was red and her jaw clenched. "I swear to God, Charlie."

A scream from outside interrupted her threat.

The three of us went to the window and looked out. A neighbor, who lived three houses down, ran down the street in her robe. She had on one slipper and half her hair was curled. Blood dripped from her arm and the back of her leg. Three others behind her walked in the same slow, jerky manner the seventh graders had. She screamed again.

Dad grabbed the pistol from his waistband. "We've got to help her." He turned and made his way to the door.

"There's no reason to, Dad. They surrounded her," I said.

He came back to the window just in time to see the group converge on the woman, who tripped on her remaining slipper. One of the people grabbed the neighbor's bottom lip between his teeth and ripped it clean off her face. Another took a sizable chunk out of her arm, and the third tore off an ear. I shuddered and turned from the window. Dad sank heavily onto the floor.

I turned to Mom. She swayed back and forth. Her face was white. I grabbed her before she fell and eased her to the floor. In the bathroom, I wet a washcloth and gently dabbed Mom's forehead while Dad held her up.

"What's going on?" Mom whispered. "Why did they attack that woman? Please tell me she's part of the prank. Please."

Dad shook his head. "This is not a prank. I don't know why they killed her. But we can't let them get in here."

The sound of shattering glass echoed up the stairs. I ran to the window and peered out but couldn't see anything. Dad ran to the door and opened it a crack before slamming it shut a second later.

"They're in the house," he whispered loudly.

Mom's eyes grew wide and she scrambled to her feet. "They're in the house? They're in the HOUSE?"

Dad clamped a hand over her mouth and moved her toward the closet. I followed them in, and he pulled the string for the attic stairs. I climbed as fast as I could, then turned to help Mom up. Dad followed behind and pulled the stairs up after him. We crouched in the dark and waited.

More glass broke and footsteps thudded up the stairs. Mom grabbed me and backed into the corner farthest from the door. The muffled sounds of things breaking drifted into the room. I placed my arms around Mom's waist and buried my head in her shoulder. Mom wrapped her arms around my head, and I felt her cheek on the top of my hair. It reminded me of when I was little girl, waking in the middle of the night from a nightmare. I used to have dreams about being chased by dinosaurs. They always caught me and ate me. I would wake up screaming, and Mom would come into my room with a glass of water. She would hold me and hum until I fell back asleep.

Every crash and thud made my entire body jerk, and Mom shook beneath me. This was almost like my dreams because the creatures would eat us if they caught us, but unlike my dreams, I knew there was no waking from this nightmare.

After a while, it was quiet. I assumed Dad remained by the door, his gun in his hand ready to fire. Mom and I slowly uncurled from the corner and made our way to him. We moved carefully so we wouldn't make a sound. When we were close, Dad gathered us into his arms and we sat hugging by the door.

"It's all right. I think they're gone." Dad's voice was almost inaudible.

"What are we going to do?" Mom whispered. "We can't stay up here forever. We're going to need food, water."

Dad pulled away and the attic light clicked on. I squinted at the brightness and held up my hands to block the light. Mom fumbled for the cord.

"What are you doing? They're going to find us," she said.

Dad grabbed her hands and calmed her down. "It's all right. They won't be able to see the light. Even if they got the closet door opened, they can't get in here. I locked the attack door. They'll need an axe to get us." He glanced around the room. "We've got to see if there is anything in here we can use."

My eyes adjusted and I took in our surroundings. Boxes full of Christmas decorations, old clothes, and stuffed animals were everywhere, and I doubted any of it would be useful. I watched Dad rip open a box and pull out some strings of tinsel and a few ornaments before stuffing them back inside. He moved to another, opened the top, and peered in. He knocked the box over. Glass ornaments skittered across the floor and a few shattered into red and silver shards.

"Isn't there anything up here besides Christmas crap?" he spoke almost to himself.

Mom approached him slowly and wrapped her arms around his shoulders. He buried his face in her neck and they hugged for several minutes. Eventually, he looked up and wiped his nose on the back of his hand.

"Okay. We need to figure out what we're dealing with. Any ideas?" He looked at his wife.

Mom shook her head and folded her arms across her chest. "Maybe it's gang related."

Dad grimaced. "What gangs do we have in Oregon?"

Mom slapped her hands on her thighs. "We have Neo-Nazis here. It's not that unheard of. Gangs attack and kill people all the time."

"I don't think it's Neo-Nazis."

"Then what is it?"

"Maybe they're escaped convicts. We probably wouldn't hear about a prison break," Dad suggested.

"Seventh graders were attacking other students, Dad," I interjected. "I don't think it's escaped convicts."

He glanced at me. His look told me he wanted to know what I thought it was.

"What if it's zombies?" I said.

Mom cocked her head to the right. "Zombies? Yeah, that's more believable than a gang or escaped convicts. You really watch too many horror movies. As soon as we get out of here, I'm taking all of your books and movies away."

"Think about it. They don't move very fast or very well. They're attacking the living and eating their flesh. What else could they be?"

"Maybe they're crazy," Mom said.

Dad huffed. "How many crazy people do you know who eat people?"

"Jeffrey Dahmer."

Dad shook his head. "He cooked them first. He didn't eat them raw. Besides, he never attacked them on the street. Or in a group."

Mom unfolded her hands and threw them up in the air. "You can't expect me to believe that the dead have returned to life and are killing people. That kind of stuff only happens in the movies. It's *insane*."

"What if the movies were right?" I whispered. "What if the movies were made to make us believe it can only happen in the movies?"

Mom chuckled, a small nervous sound. "And why would anyone release zombies onto the world?"

"What if it's a biological weapon?" I asked.

Mom's breath caught in her throat and her skin paled. Dad stared at me.

"It would be the greatest weapon because no one would believe zombies were actually attacking."

Dad and Mom stared at each other for a moment.

"We've got to get out of here," Mom whispered.

"And go where?" asked Dad. "If Krista is right, then this thing might be spreading across the entire country. If no one believes that zombies are attacking, how are they going to defend against it?"

"I don't care where we go, but we can't stay here." Mom folded her hands across her chest. "We have no food and no water. We have to try and find help."

Dad sighed. "All right. But we're not going to run out there without a plan. We need to figure out where we're going and how we're going to get there. What do we know about zombies?"

CHAPTER 2

By the time my parents and I made a plan, it was night. We agreed that whatever we learned from the movies probably wouldn't translate into real life. We talked about all the movies we had seen and decided the creatures were more like George Romero zombies than *28 Days Later* zombies. They didn't move very fast and craved human flesh. Although, we were pretty sure they weren't turned into the undead by a meteor. Other than that, we couldn't make any comparisons. None of us had a chance to study the undead. Like we'd want to. We hoped zombies could be killed by a shot to the brain or by beheading, but the only way to test our theory was on a zombie. We were all still too scared to poke our heads out the window and start firing.

We figured our best hope would be to get to the nearest military base. On a good day, the closest one was forty-five minutes away, but we had no idea what the roads would be like or how many zombies we would encounter along the way. We had a 1911 and four rifles but not that much ammunition. We knew we couldn't stay and wait for help; we had to go find it. We would stay in the house for the night and start out in the morning.

Dad lowered the attic stairs cautiously and listened. I strained my ears also to make sure he didn't miss anything. Nothing. He slowly made his way down into the closet and opened the door. I peered over the edge of the attic and watched him shine a flashlight into the darkness. I assumed he didn't find anything because he signaled for us to follow him, and Mom and I crept down the stairs. Dad's task was to go to the kitchen to grab as many cans of food and bottles of water he could carry. Mom was in charge of grabbing bedding and extra clothes, and I gathered ammunition and a bucket to use as a bathroom in the attic. We worked fast. We figured we would get enough supplies to see us through the night, and we would gather more before leaving.

It didn't take me long to get my stuff and, after taking them up to the attic, I waited for my parents at the closet door. I had the rifle in hand and waited anxiously, switching my weight from one foot to the other. I heard them rummaging through the house, along with another sound I couldn't place. It was so distant, it could have been the wind howling through the trees, but as it drew closer, it was unmistakably human, yet somewhat primal. It sent shivers down my back, and I whispered under my breath for my parents to hurry.

At first, there was only one constant moaning, but soon enough, it was joined by a few more, then a lot more. I didn't know exactly where the sound came from, but I knew it was somewhere in the neighborhood. My parents made it back into the attic when the moaning sounded like it was at the front door.

As Dad pulled up the attic stairs, the sound muffled but never went away. I popped in my earbuds and cranked the music so the sound was drowned out. I was listening to "Needles" by System of a Down when I felt a hand on my shoulder. I turned and Mom handed me a bowl. I pulled out one earbud and listened. The moaning was still prominent, so I put the bud back in.

We ate a dinner of cold Spaghetti Os, then Mom and I attempted to fall asleep. It was impossible to get comfortable on my blankets and pillows, and my music was so loud I got a headache. The few times I did fall asleep, I saw Carmen and my neighbor being eaten alive.

At close to three in the morning, my batteries died. Groggily, I pulled the buds out of my ears and braced for the moaning. I was surprised when I didn't hear anything and sat up on my makeshift bed. Mom's soft breathing and Dad's low snores sounded on the other side of the attic. I crawled toward them. They were both curled up on the blankets I had brought for them, and I wiggled my way between them. They both wrapped their arms around me, and we slept for the rest of the night.

We awoke late the next morning, around ten, and had a quick breakfast of granola bars and water. Dad opened the attic door and surveyed the area before we climbed downstairs. Equipped with duffel bags and backpacks, we loaded up with as much food, water, clothes, and blankets as we could carry. I glanced out the window into the empty streets. The sun shone and it seemed like a normal day, but everything was quiet. Not even a dog barked. My stomach knotted. I knew we couldn't stay in the house, it was a death sentence. So much could happen. The greatest worry was what we would do if we ran out of food and water. But other things could happen, too. Like the house could catch fire or fill up with zombies. We'd be trapped in the attic and have to endure a slow, painful death. But even those thoughts didn't make me feel any better about venturing out into the open.

When all of the supplies were collected, we met at the garage. As quietly as possible, Dad strapped our belongings and extra gas tanks to the two four-wheelers.

"Are you sure we can't take the car?" Mom whispered. "I would feel so much safer with sides and a roof."

Dad handed Mom her helmet. "I know. But if people abandoned their vehicles on the road, we won't be able to make it in the car." He placed his hands on her shoulders and his forehead against hers. "We discussed this last night. The fastest way to get to the base is by four-wheeler. It might not be the safest, but we don't have any other option."

Mom nodded. Dad kissed her gently on the mouth and patted her shoulder. Mom pulled the helmet onto her head. I took a deep breath and did the same. Dad made sure both of our chinstraps were secure before pulling on his own helmet and climbing onto his ATV. Mom climbed onto hers, and I climbed on behind Dad. We all took a collective breath, then started the engines. The garage door rose.

I held my breath and waited for a horde of undead to swarm the garage. I released it when Dad gunned the engine and the ATV shot out into the street. I glanced over my shoulder to make sure Mom was behind us.

We zigzagged our way through the deserted streets. Dad had been right about the main streets in town—they were blocked with abandoned cars. The going was slow at first, but not as slow as the zombies that followed us. At first, there were only a couple, but after ten minutes of threading through the streets, the number grew. I gripped the back of Dad's jacket until my knuckles were white and my fingers ached. I kept turning around to make sure Mom was behind us and didn't relax until we made it to the highway, where the cars thinned out and the zombies were left behind.

Dad threaded through the trees near the highway to stay away from any cars that had been left on the road and any zombies that might inhabit those vehicles. We stopped after a while to refuel and get something to drink. My throat was dry, but my stomach was in knots, so it was difficult to swallow the water. Every little sound made me jump. A bird tweeted and I almost peed my pants. I had to force myself to take deep breaths and calm down. Mom and Dad wouldn't let anything happen to me.

"The base should be right over that ridge." Dad pointed to the hill on his right. "We should approach it slowly in case it's been taken over by zombies."

Mom and I nodded our agreement. Dad gave me a rifle, and I laid it across my lap. When the four-wheelers were refueled and we had our fill of water, we climbed back on and headed toward the hill. We made our way to the top of the ridge and stopped. The base was right below us. Hundreds of people were lined up to get into the gate. Soldiers with automatic weapons kept the masses in order and shouted instructions for them to follow. As I surveyed the area, I noticed ambulances at the far end. I tightened my grip on the stock of the gun.

"Dad, I'm not sure going in there is such a good idea."

He turned to look at me. "Why?"

I pointed at the ambulances. "What if they're bringing in infected people? If they get loose in there, all these people are sitting ducks."

Dad sighed. "What do you want us to do? We can't camp out in the open—we're the sitting ducks then. We can't go back to the house, it's too risky."

"I have a bad feeling about going in there."

Dad stared at Mom.

"What can we do?" Mom said and shrugged. "We'll stay one night, formulate a new plan, then head out."

Dad let the clutch out and was about to head down the hill when I grabbed his shoulder and made him stop. "What about the cabins?" I suggested. "We could stay in there. We have enough food to last a couple of days. We can figure out what to do after that."

Dad glanced at Mom again, then focused his gaze on me. "Are you really that afraid of staying at the base? They have guns. They might have medicine to treat whatever this is. I mean, we don't know if we're actually dealing with zombies."

I shook my head. "Even if it's not zombies, look at the amount of people. Mass hysteria is bound to set in and something bad will happen. People are scared and don't know what's going on. They will easily fall prey to ideas and suggestions from others and start rioting." My psychology lesson had no effect. "What if they take our four-wheelers away?"

"She has a good point, Charlie," said Mom. "We can't afford to lose our things. When we planned on coming here, we didn't expect there to be this many people. We can stash our stuff at the cabins then come back and find out what's going on."

Dad sighed and stared down at the base. He was silent for a long time. "Fine."

The cabins were a cluster of six buildings owned by the Forest Service where my family and I stayed during the past three summers. I didn't want to stay in the cabins but in the lookout tower nearby. It was used to spot forest fires, and the only way in or out was to climb a rope. I hoped no one else had thought about the tower as a hiding place, but if they did, I prayed they would be nice enough to share.

As we approached the cabins, Dad slowed down and stayed within the tree line. The ground was extremely uneven, and several times I almost dropped the gun and careened off the back of the four-wheeler. When we were within ten yards, Dad cut his engine and signaled Mom to do the same. He told us to wait while he checked out the situation.

Dad was gone for five minutes, but to me, it felt like five hours. Mom and I stood together next to the four-wheelers, each with a rifle. Do you have any idea how many sounds there are in the forest? Twigs snap and fall off trees and sound just like someone or something stepped on them. Plus, with the echo, you're never really sure which direction the sound came from. It's very nerve wracking. It's understandable why people accidentally get shot in the woods.

When Dad approached, both of us raised our weapons in his direction. When we realized it was him, we lowered the guns with a sigh of relief.

"It's clear," he told us and unloaded the four-wheeler. "We'll stay tonight and figure out what we're going to do."

The three of us loaded our supplies in the basket, and Mom and I climbed the rope into the tower. Dad made sure we were safe and the supplies had been pulled up before following after us.

We stared out the windows onto the tops of the trees until it got dark. I could see the top of the military complex on the horizon and shivered. The floodlights from the roof of the barracks clicked on, and I hoped everyone was safe.

A snap resounded through the room, and the acrid smell of sulphur tickled my nose. I turned to see Dad lighting a fire in the fireplace.

"Do you think that's a good idea?" Mom asked.

Dad shrugged. "What's it going to hurt? Even if someone sees it, they can't get to us. I pulled the rope up so no one can climb in here."

"Yeah, but they might destroy the four-wheelers."

Dad grimaced. "No one is going to mess with the four-wheelers. Without tools, it's going to be pretty hard for them to take those babies apart. Even if they pop the tires, we'll still be able to get back to the base. If there are other people out there, they deserve to be saved."

I stared at Mom. I didn't think a fire was the best thing either, but Dad knew best. Mom's jaw muscles tighten.

"It seems really reckless," Mom snapped. "We don't know what or who we're dealing with and you set a beacon that gives away our position."

"We're going to be fine," said Dad, but something in his eyes made me wonder if he believed it himself. "Now, c'mon, cook up some of that canned stuff for dinner."

Mom shook her head before picking out some food. I took one last look at the lights on the complex, then joined Dad on the floor in front of the fire. He placed his arm around my shoulders, and I laid my head on his chest.

"Thanks for letting us come here, Dad. I had a bad feeling about the base."

Dad shrugged. "I want my family to feel safe."

"Did you see how many people were at the base?" Mom set a pan of chili on the screen above the fire. "There had to be three, four hundred people."

"Yeah, but if you consider that over a hundred thousand live within an hour of the base, that percentage isn't very high."

Mom sat next to Dad.

"Do you think there are more survivors out there?" I pulled my knees up to my chest and stared at Dad.

"I don't know. I hope so," Dad answered.

"Do you think any of them will come here?"

Dad sighed. "I don't know."

The chili sputtered, and tiny dots of red jumped out of the pot. Mom stood and stirred the food slowly. She looked at me and Dad. "What are we going to do?"

"Tomorrow I am going to go to the base and find out what they know. You two will wait here until I return. After that, I don't know. We'll have to play it by ear."

"Why do we have to wait here?" Mom complained. "Wouldn't it be safer if we stuck together?"

"Yeah, Dad, it's not a good idea for us to split up. That's when bad things happen."

"It'll be faster if I go by myself. No offense. Plus, what if Krista is right? What if they take the four-wheeler? If that happens, I'll need you to pick me up. We at least have to try. We have to see if there are answers out there."

Mom and I nodded. I still didn't think it was a good idea, but arguing wasn't going to get us anywhere. Mom took the chili off the fire, and we ate in silence.

Darkness enclosed the observation tower, and I snuggled into my sleeping bag. The fire crackled in the hearth, but I didn't feel at peace. My stomach fluttered with unease, and I couldn't fall asleep. I wanted to tell Dad not to go, but I knew he had to. We needed to know what was going on and if there was a way to combat the threat. I stared at my parents as they held each other in front of the fire. Any other time it would have been romantic, and I would have gagged, but I only felt sadness as I looked at them. I rolled over and drifted into a restless sleep.

I awoke the next morning to the salty, meaty aroma of canned hash, and for a brief second, I felt the joy I always felt when I camped, but then I remembered why we were there. I climbed out of my sleeping bag and approached the fire. The warmth radiated through my body, and Mom smiled wanly at me.

"Did you sleep well?"

I shook my head. "I didn't really sleep at all."

The door to the bathroom opened, and Dad stepped into the living space. He had his coat on and his pistol in its holster at his side. He was ready to head out. He glanced at his watch.

"It's six right now. Hopefully, I will be back by noon. If I'm not, wait until tomorrow then head to the base."

My throat tightened. "Why tomorrow? Why not tonight?"

"I'll need some time to talk to people, get some answers, figure out the lay of the base. If I get the answers quickly, I'll be back by noon. If not…"

"You'll be back," I said.

Dad smiled. "Of course I will." He wrapped his arms around Mom and I and held us for a long time. The only thing that made him let go was the smell of burnt meat that was filling the room.

Mom pulled the pan from the fire and approached Dad. They kissed, then Dad headed down the rope. Mom and I stood on the observation deck until Dad was out of sight and we could no longer hear the four-wheeler. We came back inside and filled our plates with burnt hash and scrambled eggs.

I scowled at the food. "He could've at least eaten before he left."

"You know your father. When he has his mind set on something, nothing distracts him. Not even food."

I set my plate down and stared out the window. I wasn't hungry. I watched Mom nibble on her eggs, then she set her plate next to mine. I don't know why we thought we were going to be able to eat. I suppose we were trying to make things normal. Even though we both knew there was nothing normal left.

Noon came and went. Both Mom and I stood at the window, waiting for a sign of Dad. The horizon darkened and a chill filled the room before I turned away to start a fire.

"I'm sure he's okay, Mom." My voice was small. "He's gathering information. Helping with the wounded."

Mom stared out the window. I wished she would say something. Confirm my hypothesis in some way. After all, she knew Dad better than I did. She had to have some idea of what he was doing.

I grabbed a can of Spaghetti Os and dumped them into a pot. I knew we needed to eat, but I still wasn't hungry. Again, it was that normalcy thing—the idea if one small thing was right, maybe everything else would follow. As I placed the meal above the fire, a series of small pops followed by a loud bang resounded in the distance. I made it to the window in time to see the horizon engulfed in an orange hue.

"I'm sure Dad wasn't in there." I tried to convince myself of it more than anything.

Mom grabbed me and held tight.

"I'm sure he'll be back any minute," I said.

I waited for my mom to agree with me, I needed her to, but she didn't say a word.

We stared out the window, watching the orange light flicker until the Spaghetti Os stared to boil. It gave me an excuse to pull away from Mom. It was weird, but as she held me, it felt like something was missing. There was no comfort in her arms. I stared at her from across the room; she looked out the window. I wondered what she was thinking.

The fire died a while later. Mom and I had moved to the floor in front of the door and wrapped in a blanket. I didn't want to be alone, and I knew she needed comfort. Neither one of us slept, and we kept waiting for Dad to walk through the door. He never did.

CHAPTER 3

Mom and I spent the morning holding one another in silence. Clouds from the fire darkened the sky, and a gray ash fluttered on the wind.

Mid-day, Mom rose. "Get packed. We're not staying here anymore."

"Where are we going to go?"

Mom stuffed the sleeping bag into its sack and threw cans into a box. "He told us to get him the next day."

"Mom—"

"He might not be dead," she snapped. "He might still be at the compound."

I didn't argue. I didn't want to imagine the unthinkable had happened. Like Mom, I was optimistic we would find Dad alive. We didn't know the extent of damage or exactly what happened at the complex, so anything was possible. I helped Mom finish packing, then we headed onto the deck. Mom peeked over the rail and lowered the rope before placing our belongings into the basket. She was about to lower it when a man burst through the trees. His hair stuck out, and his face and clothes were covered in soot. He ran to the rope and started to climb toward us, but he lost his grip and slipped. He tried again and had more luck.

My heart leapt into my throat when I met the man's gaze; his eyes were red and flared with intensity. I couldn't tell if he was a zombie or if he was human. He moved quickly, so it was safe to assume that he wasn't the undead, but the intensity in his eyes didn't make me believe he was there to protect us. Maybe he was infected. We didn't know what the victims looked like before they turned into zombies.

"Hey!" Mom yelled down to the man. "What do you think you're doing?"

The man didn't answer but kept climbing frantically toward us.

Mom aimed the shotgun over the rail. "Hey! I asked you a question!"

The man glanced up and noticed the gun but didn't slow his climbing.

"I'm giving you one more chance! If you don't answer me by the count of three, I'm going to blow you away." She cocked the gun. "One…two…three."

I gritted my teeth and waited for the explosion of the gun, but it never came. I turned. Mom held the gun over the railing, her finger flexed on the trigger. I turned back to the man. He was a few feet from the top of the rope.

"This is your last chance," Mom yelled.

The man glanced up at us. His lip curled into a snarl.

There was a deafening crack, and the man's head split in a spray of blood and bone. His body lingered on the rope for a few seconds before flopping onto the ground. My throat tightened. I couldn't catch my breath, so I sat on the deck.

Mom knelt next to me and placed a hand on my shoulder. "We have to get to the base." She pulled me up and toward the rope.

I grabbed the rope and slowly lowered myself down while Mom kept watch. Bile rose in the back of my throat as I slid through the blood and brain matter that stuck to the fibers. When I made it to the bottom, I pulled out my own weapon and kept an eye on the forest, listening for anything out of place. Mom joined me on the ground and we jumped onto the four-wheeler. I sat uneasily on the back. What possessed Mom to kill that man? Yeah, it was possible he was going to kill us, or worse, but I never knew she had it in her. Something was wrong with her, and I desperately wanted to know what it was.

It took us an hour to reach the base. We stopped on top of the same hill we had been on several days earlier and stared down at the complex. The buildings that were still standing were charred black, wisps of dark smoke curled into the sky. The chain link fence that surrounded the place had been toppled in several areas and laid on the ground. The blackened corpses of people lay strewn about the yard, and the smell of burnt flesh permeated the air. Any hope I had of finding Dad disappeared when I saw the destruction. I knew there was no way he survived.

Mom gunned the ATV and headed into the complex. Just inside the gate, she stopped and took off her helmet. She swung her leg over the ATV and placed the helmet on the handlebars. She glanced at the bodies closest to her before calling loudly.

"Charlie!" she yelled. She stepped deeper into the complex and examined a few more bodies. "Charlie!" Desperation entered her voice and she spun around, calling his name.

I remained at the four-wheeler and removed my helmet. I stood on the seat and scanned the area, the rifle ready to fire. My stomach was in knots and my palms were sweating. I heard Mom, who ventured even further into the complex, still calling Dad's name. I wanted to call her back, make her leave, but a voice at the back of my brain told me it was pointless. She had to see for herself, figure it out on her own, that Dad wasn't coming back. Movement caught the corner of my eye, and I turned to the building on my right. I stared into the blackness and strained my ears. Nothing. But I couldn't shake the feeling that something was there, that something watched me. I was about to turn away when a pinpoint of light caught my attention. My breath caught. I brought the rifle up to my shoulder and lined up the sights. The light moved, first to the right, then straight for me. A soft hissing sound that turned into a low moan echoed from the blackness. My breathing came in rasps and all the muscles in my body stiffened.

When the zombie stepped into the sun, I almost fell off the four-wheeler. I squeezed the trigger on the rifle, but the shot sailed into the air. I jumped down and steadied myself on the ground, raising my weapon. The bullet caught the zombie in the midsection, but it didn't fall. I climbed onto the four-wheeler and turned it on. I scanned the area for Mom and found her a hundred yards to my left. How did she get so far so fast? She gazed into a burned out building, still calling Dad's name. I was about to accelerate toward her when she staggered away from the building. She tried to raise her rifle, but she didn't make it in time. She fell to the ground as three half-charred zombies limped out of the doorway.

"Mom!" I pushed the throttle.

Mom scuttled away from the undead and got to her feet. She turned to meet me, but five more zombies stepped out from another building and encircled her, slowly closing the ranks. Mom fired a few shots at the menace, and a couple went down, but now close to twenty were closing on her position. One of them grabbed her hair from behind, and Mom was lucky enough to duck out of the way before getting bitten, but the creature was too close to shoot. She swung the butt of the gun around and knocked off the man's lower jaw. Blood and teeth sprayed into her face, temporarily blinding her and allowing the undead to get closer. Mom blinked and wiped her eyes. Several others were now within an arm's length. She couldn't get away. The creature closest to her sunk its top teeth into her forearm. She yelped and pushed him away.

"Go!" she yelled. "Get out of here!"

"Mom! I won't leave you." I was close, very close, and several zombies knew it. They turned and headed toward me.

A zombie grabbed the back of Mom's hair and chomped down on her shoulder. She screamed in pain and tried to wiggle out of the creature's grasp. Another grabbed her leg and took a bite out of her thigh. I stopped the four-wheeler and raised my gun. I fired several shots, but they all missed their targets. A creature with missing legs that pulled itself along the ground grabbed my shoe. I screamed and aimed the gun. The thing's head exploded, covering my face in brain matter. I glanced up and noticed another one directly in front of me, its arms extended and mouth snapping open and shut. I aimed and pulled the trigger. The gun clicked empty. I threw the rifle onto the ground and glanced back at Mom. Five zombies had a hold of her and pulled her down. She struggled and fought against them, but it was a losing battle.

"GO!" Mom yelled.

I hesitated. Part of my brain screamed to get away, telling me there was nothing I could do, but the other part said there was still a chance I could save her. When I felt the cold fingers of a zombie on my forearm, the survival part of my brain took over and I drove out of the compound as fast as I could.

I had every intention of heading back to the lookout tower, but tears clouded my eyes and I couldn't see through the trees. I wiped at my face and tried to keep the four-wheeler on level ground. When I felt I had put enough distance between me and the zombies, I pulled over to get my bearings. I turned off the four-wheeler and glanced at the surroundings. Pine trees encircled me in all directions, and each one looked exactly the same. I glanced in the direction I came from, but I didn't know where I was. *You idiot!* I thought. Why didn't you pay more attention to where you were going? I turned to look where I was heading. And why didn't you ever learn how to shoot? I burst into tears.

A moan resounded somewhere in the forest, and I drew in a sharp breath. I didn't even glance around before starting the four-wheeler and heading deeper into the woods. I ran the vehicle for another thirty minutes before stopping to figure out where I was, this time on top of a hill. I took in my surroundings and sighed. The tower was a long way off to my left. The highway was over two hills to my right. I wondered if it was worth going back to the tower. What if someone else tried to climb the rope like that guy did? Would I be able to shoot him? What if they came in the middle of the night while I slept? I shuddered at the thought.

I was pretty sure that the man my mom killed was human. I hadn't seen a zombie that could move like that. Maybe that meant there were other survivors from the complex. Maybe Dad was one of them. I glanced from the lookout tower to the highway. There had to be survivors. Human life always found a way to survive the most dire of situations. It was the only glimmer of hope I had. If they lived, they would probably follow the road. The terrain in the trees was almost too rough and uneven for the four-wheeler, so it would be difficult for any other vehicle. Assuming the survivors were in a vehicle. If they were on foot, the forest was the best place because they could outrun the zombies. I didn't know where or if there were survivors, but I knew I didn't want to be without my supplies. I decided to take a chance. I refueled the four-wheeler and headed for the highway. When I reached the pavement, I stared for a few minutes in each direction. There was no way for me to tell which way they had gone, so I would have to take another chance. If I went to my right, it would lead me to the road that led to the military base, but there was a good-sized city beyond. To my left was a long stretch of road that eventually led to a small town. I turned the handlebars to the left. If the complex was just attacked, more than likely the city was going to be overrun with zombies, too. If the survivors were thinking like I was, they would want to get as far away as possible from concentrated hordes of the undead. I revved the engine and headed toward the horizon.

* * *

I caught up to a group of survivors before sunset. I actually burst into laughter when I saw them. I couldn't believe my good fortune. The few that survived, about twenty, had piled onto a troop transport truck and headed east. They huddled under a bridge and used tarps and blankets to make a tent, with men I assumed were soldiers standing lookout on either side. They wore camo and carried automatic weapons. If they weren't soldiers, they were doing a great job of acting like they were. They were a motley group, covered in ashes and blood with puffy red eyes. A few of them jumped when I came toward them and cowered in a group. Those with guns surrounded them and pointed their weapons at me. I turned off the ATV and held up my hands.

"It's okay," I called. "I won't hurt you."

"Did any of them follow you?" A soldier asked. He was a young man, probably no older than twenty, with dark brown eyes. The skin that wasn't smeared with black soot was tanned, and his light brown hair was shaved close to his head.

I glanced over my shoulder. "I don't think so."

"You bit?"

I shook my head.

He jerked his head toward the four-wheeler. "What do you got in those boxes?"

"Some canned goods and water." I pulled out a bottle. "Would you like some?"

The soldier stepped forward and helped me take the supplies off the back of the vehicle. As we handed out the food, I examined the group. The oldest couldn't have been more than forty-five, and the youngest was six. It made my stomach churn to see that there were only three kids. When everyone had a can, I sat down and started to spoon out the cold contents. I wasn't really hungry, but it had been almost a day since I last ate, so I figured I needed some food. We were too afraid to start a fire, so we huddled together for warmth. When the sun went down, we climbed into the back of the truck and crawled under our blankets. The soldiers were relieved by the civilians, and they lay down on the benches to sleep.

"What happened at the complex?" I asked quietly.

The soldier who had helped me earlier stirred. "We were attacked by zombies."

"How did they get into the base?"

"They were already in there. They came in with the ambulances." He took a deep breath, and I was sure I heard a shudder in his voice, as if he was trying to hold back tears. "I shouldn't be telling you this, I was sworn to secrecy, but who's going to reprimand me? All the commanders are dead. We had scientists at the base, people who were studying the zombies. There was never supposed to be any civilians, just infected. But when they showed up at the gate, we couldn't turn them away. Somehow the secret got out that we were experimenting on the undead, and a rumor started that we actually created them. The people threatened to riot, so we locked the complex. No one in, no one out, until order was restored.

"They attacked in the middle of the night. I don't know if it was one of the subjects or a civilian who got bit and turned. I don't even know how many there were. I was on patrol in the building closest to the gate, and we heard the screams from the far end of the complex. We were given orders that if anything happened, we were supposed to gather up the people in our bunker and head out. There were protocols to make sure the zombies didn't get out. I followed orders. I tried to get everyone to leave, but most of them wanted to stay and help the others." He leaned forward so his face was inches from mine. "They set up a fail safe. Bombs had been planted in the sickbay and lab just in case anything like this happened. That's why everyone was supposed to be evacuated. But those things wouldn't die. They kept running around the yard, trying to eat people, and catching everything on fire. The only way to put 'em down is to put one right between the eyes." He emphasized his point by placing his finger on his forehead. He leaned back on the bench.

"Did the military create them?"

The man took a breath, moments passing before he answered. "No," he said flatly. "We were looking for a way to destroy them."

"There was a man, with short black hair about forty years old who would have showed up the other morning on a four-wheeler like mine. Did you see him?"

"I saw a lot of people come into that place. And a lot that didn't come back out."

"So you don't know what happened to him?"

The soldier shook his head. "If he was in any other bunker but mine, he'd be dead."

"Does anyone know how this all started?" I waited for the soldier to answer, and when he didn't, I glanced around at the faces of the others.

They stared at me with blank expressions.

"No one? No one knows what's going on?" I turned back to the soldier.

He shrugged his right shoulder and turned so his back was to me.

I pulled my sleeping bag up to my chin. Someone had to know something. There was no way zombies could be walking the earth and everyone was oblivious to how they got there. I averted my gaze to the sky and stared at the stars. I thought about my parents, and tears welled up in my eyes. I buried my head in my sleeping bag and sobbed softly until I fell asleep.

I was jerked out of a dreamless sleep by the sounds of moaning. I poked my head out of the bag and stared at the person sleeping next to me. I nudged their shoulder, hoping they would roll over and be quiet. Then, the sound came again, closer, and I shot straight up. The soldier who slept on the bench next to me was already up and searching for his weapon. The moan sounded again, echoed by several other grunts and sighs from the trees. I jumped out of my sleeping bag and scrambled to the side of the truck. Clicking on the flashlight, I shone the light out as far as it would go. More moans filled the air, and I caught a zombie in the flashlight beam. I pointed it out to the soldier and he nodded.

"If they get any closer, I'll fire. We don't have a lot of ammo, so I don't want to waste it if I don't have to."

Another soldier moved to the truck's cab and started the engine. The others woke and wondered what was going on. A moan sounded at the back of the truck, followed by a woman's scream, and the group turned to see what happened. I flashed the light toward the woman just as she moved out of the way. The zombie grabbed for her hair. The soldier raised his weapon and fired. The shot caught the creature right between the eyes and it fell over backward. Both the soldier and I almost fell over as the truck lurched forward and took off down the highway. We sat down on the bench and took a collective sigh.

"Is everyone all right?" He grabbed the flashlight out of my hand and shone it on the people.

They nodded as the beam passed their face.

"Good." He handed the light back.

"What are we going to do?" I whispered.

The soldier sniffed. "We need to find other survivors. If there are any. Then we need to form an army and destroy this menace."

"I say we head to Florida," a voice spoke in the darkness.

I squinted to find the speaker, but it was too dark. "Why?"

"It's the most easily defendable place. We put some mines in the water so nothing can get us from the sea, and we place a fence on the border. There's only one way in and one way out."

The soldier turned and looked at me. "Sounds like a logical option to me."

I shrugged. "It's not like I have any ideas."

He stood and pounded on the roof of the cab. "We're going to Florida."

CHAPTER 4

It took us three days to get to the Florida border, and most of that was accomplished by driving night and day. The farther east we went, the more hordes of zombies we ran into. We decided it was best just to stop for fuel and food. We were lucky not to lose any members of our group.

When we made it to the border, we were not the first to think it was the safest place. A group had already set up a perimeter fence and funneled all the traffic through a central location. I thought it was strange that something had been built so fast. How long does it take to erect a fence on 160 miles? How long had it been since my family and I were first attacked? I couldn't remember. The days mushed together in a blur. There were guards with guns everywhere, and I was pretty sure they weren't all military, even though they were dressed in camouflage. We followed a short chain of cars to Orlando, where the command station had been set up around Disney World. There, we were expected to register and would be reunited with any surviving family.

I had been to Disney World once before, and it had been one of the greatest times in my life. It was for my ninth birthday. We came down in July, which was a mistake. It was so very hot and the lines were so long. I don't remember much of the rides, but I do remember what a relief it was to be out of the heat. I thought air conditioning was the greatest invention ever. Mom, Dad, and I all got mouse ears with our names stitched on the back. This trip was nothing like that. Although, it was still hot. Small camps had been set up around Epcot. No one smiled at the happiest place on earth, and I wondered how many loved ones had been lost.

The transport truck stopped at the end of a long line of cars, and the others and I followed the crowd to the golf ball. Spaceship Earth had been transformed from a ride into a receiving center for refugees. The lines moved quickly through the various checkpoints, and I gave my name to the person sitting at the terminal, who typed it into the computer.

"Do you have any surviving family members?" The woman stared at me with soft brown eyes and waited for an answer.

I shook my head.

"How old are you?"

"Fifteen."

"And you don't have any grandparents or aunts or uncles around?"

I shrugged. "I don't know."

"What are their names?"

I told her the names of my relatives.

The woman typed them into the computer.

I tried to lean around and see the screen. "Are any of them still alive?"

The woman grimaced. "I'm not seeing anything, but that doesn't necessarily mean they're dead. It's possible they're not in the system yet. If they do register with us, they'll pop up. Do you know the names of any relatives that have recently been killed by the zombie horde?"

I nodded.

"What were their names?"

I told her, and she typed in the information.

"Okay, if anyone from your family registers with us, we will let you know."

"What am I supposed to do now?"

The woman grabbed a piece of paper off her printer, handed it to me, and pointed toward another line. I took the information and stood at the back of the line. When it was my turn, I handed the paper to the man behind the desk. He looked at it briefly and stamped it before telling me to get on the monorail and head to the Disney Contemporary Resort. I was given a room and a schedule of classes I was required to attend. I stared at it in disbelief. This was way too weird. Zombies just attacked, were actually still roaming the country, and I was supposed to go to school? These people were taking the normal thing to a whole new level. Of course, I was only 15, so I didn't really expect to get drafted into a zombie-killing army. I supposed they needed to do something with me and the other orphans, and this was their best solution. I went to my room, threw my sparse belongings onto the floor, and with a sigh, collapsed onto the soft bed. I was able to relax for a couple of minutes before there was a knock on the door.

The girl standing in the hall was about my age and had long sandy blonde hair and green eyes. Freckles danced across her thin nose, and a smile was on her thin lips.

"Hi," she held her hand out, "I'm Tanya. We heard there was a new girl on the floor."

I glanced over Tanya's shoulder. Two girls stood behind her, one with black hair cut in a spike and the other with brown hair curled in ringlets. The first thing that popped into my mind was Carmen and the Baa-Baa Twins. I tried to hold back my contempt, to give them a chance, but I was tired from being on the road. I did my best, though.

"This is Nancy," she pointed to the one with brown hair, "and this is Pearl," she pointed to the other girl, who both nodded in my direction. "If you want, we'll give you a tour of the place."

I nodded and closed the door. What I really wanted was a shower, but I figured these girls might have some answers as to what was going on.

"There's not too much to show," Tanya said. "Most of the hotel houses the refugees, except the conference rooms have been converted into classrooms. They think we need to continue our education and life like zombies haven't taken it over." Tanya snorted a laugh. "Like we're ever going to have real jobs after this!"

We stepped into the elevator and headed into the lobby.

"Who's they?" I asked.

"The Families. There are five of them who set up shop down here in Florida. There are the Johnsons, the Lees, the Scorvids, the Youngs, and the Sanchez's. They put up the fence along the border and bought the weapons for the army." Tanya held up two fingers on each hand and bent them like quotes when she said the last word.

I furrowed my brow. "But the attack has only been going on for about a week. How could they have set something up so fast?"

The three girls stared at me.

"Where are you from?" asked Pearl.

"Oregon."

"Well, the attack might have just reached you, but it's been happening on the East Coast for about three weeks now."

The elevator dinged and the doors opened, the girls filed out, and I stared after them in confusion.

"Three weeks? But that's impossible. Nobody ever said anything. Or warned us."

It couldn't be true. Three weeks? That would have made it two weeks before it reached us. Assuming my math was correct, but that was impossible. We never heard a thing. The news surely would have picked up on it. Someone would have said something.

Nancy chuckled. "What were they going to say? The dead have risen from the grave and are attacking the living? From what I've heard, they wanted to keep it quiet. They thought they could take care of it before it got out of hand. They tried to keep it contained, but it spread too quickly."

"Who are they?"

Nancy shrugged one shoulder and folded her arms across her chest. "I don't know. The government."

The three girls turned and headed toward the front doors. When we were out on the lawn, they turned back to the hotel and Tanya pointed at the building.

"The third floor is where all the guys are staying." She looked at me. "Well, the good ones anyway." She snorted again and headed farther into the grass.

Guys? Who the hell cared about guys at this point in time?

"Wait a second, I'm not done asking about the zombies."

Tanya didn't slow her pace. "What else do you want to know?"

"Uh, lots of things actually, but I'll start simple. Why more wasn't done? Why wasn't there some warning?"

Tanya stopped and clicked her tongue. "I don't know. I'm not in charge of that kind of thing."

My face flushed and I balled my hands into fists. Yep, I was right, Carmen. Tanya obviously didn't care about anyone or anything except herself. I figured I had better keep my questions simple. If she didn't know details, maybe she had information on the bigger picture.

"What about the President? Where is he?"

"If he's not dead, he's probably holed up in that secret mountain of his."

"What about the people from other countries? Why haven't we asked them for help?

Tanya stared at me. I was getting nowhere. I needed to find someone who knew what was going on. We stared at each other for a moment, our eyes narrowed to slits. Eventually, she turned away.

"C'mon girls, let's go find someone cooler."

The three of them headed toward the lake. Pearl paused for a moment and stared back at me. I threw my hands into the air before stomping to my room and slamming the door shut. Flinging myself on the bed, I buried my face in my pillow and screamed. How could they be so stupid? The world was slowly spiraling into chaos, and they were pretending like nothing was wrong. It was frustrating and maddening and ridiculous. I sat up on the bed. But it was also something I couldn't spend my time worrying about. If they wanted to pretend nothing was going on, fine. That was their problem, not mine.

I went to the bathroom and stepped into the shower. It was human nature to try and pretend bad things didn't happen. It helped ease the stress. The brain was actually very sophisticated when it came to burying bad things. In some cases, it even created alternative personalities to deal with the hardship. Of course, those suppressed memories never actually went away, they manifested in other ways. Some people drank, others became killers.

I doubted that what Tanya and the rest of Florida experienced was that serious. I guessed they were probably afflicted with acute stress reaction, which arose from a traumatic or terrifying event. I tried to remember exactly what the symptoms were, but without my psychology book in front of me, it was a little difficult. The initial stage was the subject going into a type of daze, and then they could either withdraw further or become highly agitated.

I washed my hair as I thought about it, and I stopped abruptly. Of course! Why hadn't I seen it before? My parents showed classic symptoms. I probably didn't see it because I was more than likely experiencing a little bit of it myself. It almost gave them a good excuse to justify their actions, but it wasn't enough. They should have been able to pull themselves out of their daze and focus on the important things. Like making sure their only daughter was safe.

I rinsed out the shampoo and slammed the water off. I dried off before heading back into my room and pulled on a clean pair of shorts and a T-shirt. I ran a comb through my hair, then lay down. I stared at the ceiling. It was unfair for me to be mad at my parents. After all, it was their brain forcing them to react, but I couldn't help it. They should have been stronger. They should still be here. I rolled onto my side and stared at the wall. I had to stop thinking about it. I was going to drive myself crazy. I couldn't change the past. I took a deep breath and closed my eyes.

A while later, I heard a soft knocking on my door. I rolled over and looked at the clock. 6:30 pm. I rolled off the bed with a groan and opened the door. Pearl stood before me, and I set my jaw.

"I thought you would like some company for dinner." Pearl lowered her head and grabbed her left arm with her right. "I'm sorry for the way Tanya acted earlier."

"You don't have to apologize for her."

I eyed her suspiciously. Pearl seemed different from Tanya, like she actually had a brain, but they were still friends, so I didn't know what to think.

"I know. But she really is a nice girl. She's trying to get on with her life."

I closed the door, and we headed toward the elevator.

"Everybody has lost someone to the zombies, you know. And Tanya thinks that the sooner we quit talking about it, the sooner they'll go away."

The doors slid open and we stepped inside.

"I don't think the zombies are going anywhere anytime soon." I punched the button and the doors slid shut.

"I don't know. They might. They've all left Florida."

I furrowed my brow. That was news to me. "Where did they go?"

Pearl shrugged. "I don't know. Oregon I guess."

The doors opened and we made our way into the dining room, which was filled with mainly teenagers and a few adults. They were all talking loudly, and no one looked up as we entered the room. I was reminded of my school cafeteria as we grabbed trays and loaded them with food. We headed to a table at the back of the room, and Tanya and Nancy gave us dirty looks as we walked by. I glanced over my shoulder as we passed. Tanya leaned into the table and whispered to the other girls. We found two empty seats and sat down.

I looked at the food on my plate—pizza with a salad and chocolate cake for dessert. It might not have been much better than school food, but it was better than cold slop from a can. I bit into the pizza greedily and relished the cheese that ran down my chin.

"How long have you been out there?" Pearl stared at me in amazement.

I slurped up the mozzarella and spoke with my mouth full. "I don't know. I kind of lost track of time." I wiped the grease on the back of my hand and swallowed. "You said that all the zombies left Florida, do you know why?"

Pearl nibbled at her slice of pizza. "I heard some of the teachers say that it was because of the humidity."

I stuffed another bite into my mouth and pushed my eyebrows together. "What would humidity have to do with it?"

"Something about speeding up the decaying process. They are dead, you know, and they decompose right before your eyes. Humidity would speed up the process of decomposition."

"But that would mean the zombies would have to be conscious of their condition. Are they really that smart?"

Pearl shrugged. "I don't know. How else would you explain why they left?"

I finished my pizza. There was no way to explain it. I was still having a hard time *believing* it. I was beginning to like Pearl, and I believed she was different from the others. I decided it was time to get to know her.

"Did you lose your family to the zombies?"

Pearl set down her pizza and folded her arms on the table. "We all did. That's why we're here. If you have family, you get to live with them in the cities."

"Are there a lot of people in the cities?"

"I don't know. I don't think so."

"Where are you from?"

"North Carolina."

"How long have you been in Florida?"

"About ten days."

"What do you think is going to happen to us?"

Ten days was enough time to figure out what was going on. She probably knew something, had some idea what people were planning.

Pearl picked up her slice of pizza. "Who knows? What we need to worry about now is surviving. We have it pretty good here. The zombies won't bother us, and we get to live our lives."

"Yeah, but to what end?"

Pearl stared at me. "Why does there have to be an end? Can't you be content to be alive?"

I found her question a little odd, but true. I should be happy to be alive, but we also had to face the fact that everything we knew changed. Life wasn't the same, which meant survival was a whole new game. I could've pointed that out to her and probably started an argument, but I decided to keep my mouth shut.

When we finished, we went into the lobby with several of the other kids and watched "Sleeping Beauty." I found it difficult to focus on the film because my mind wandered elsewhere. Florida was a large state, but it surely couldn't house that many people. And what was the business of the East Coast dealing with zombies for three weeks? That was really troublesome to me. Why hadn't there been any warnings? Was someone trying to cover something up? It didn't make any sense. Even if they played it up as a biological attack, someone would or should have done something. How many survived? How many were still out there?

My mind drifted to the guy on the transport. Was it coincidence that he suggested we come to Florida, or did he know something? There were so many questions and no answers. It gave me a headache.

At ten we were all sent to our rooms. I said goodnight to Pearl and took my shorts off before scooting under the covers. The sheets were stiff and a little scratchy, but they were much more comfortable than my dirty sleeping bag. I clicked off the light and stared at the ceiling. Taking a deep breath, I closed my eyes and saw Mom's face, her mouth twisted open in a silent scream, blood smeared on her cheeks, and the fleshless hands of zombies clawed at her skull. I gasped and jerked my eyes open. I rolled onto my side and folded my hands under my head. I hadn't had any trouble sleeping before because I had been so exhausted. When I actually had the chance to relax, I also had time to think. If only we hadn't gone to the complex. What was Mom thinking? She knew as well as I did that Dad was dead. Did she really expect to find him alive? My hands curled into fists and I clenched my jaw. She would still be alive if she hadn't been so stupid. She shouldn't have left me all alone. What was I supposed to do?

I sat up in bed and stared at the floor. I wanted to cry, to mourn the loss of my parents, but I was too angry to muster any tears. I felt abandoned and neglected. But worst of all, I felt like I wasn't important. Of all the things they were concerned about, why wasn't I their first priority? We should have never separated. I snatched the remote off the nightstand and turned on the TV. Static flickered through the room. I turned the TV off in disgust and threw the remote.

If they cared about me at all, I wouldn't be in this mess. We would all be in Florida together, happy. Well, as happy as we could be with zombies roaming the Earth. I stood from the bed and paced the room. Maybe Tanya was right. Maybe we shouldn't dwell on it anymore. We can't bring them back, and if we could, I would tell my parents to go straight to hell. How dare they leave me alone!

I threw myself back on the bed. Eventually, I drifted into a restless sleep. Visions of my mother's demise projected themselves onto my mind's eye, but they no longer made me sad. She got what she deserved.

The next morning, Pearl came by my room and took me to our first class. Since we had so little space at the hotel, each grade was crammed into a separate conference room with the same teacher teaching us all the different subjects. There were about two hundred total teenagers ranging in age from thirteen to eighteen. We learned the same things we would have learned at any other high school, but there was a sense of pointlessness to the whole process. There weren't any colleges to go to. Even if there were, where would we find jobs afterward?

I found out the majority of the population on the East Coast had either been devoured by or turned into zombies. It was pretty safe to assume the same thing was happening on the West Coast. The most conservative estimates anyone could come up with was that eighty percent of the population would be obliterated by the zombie horde. Where they were getting those numbers, I had no idea. I wasn't exactly sure who "they" were, but it was the talk of the students during breaks. It was tragic and devastating and pretty much the end of life as we knew it. Those of us who survived were extremely lucky.

Besides being taught reading, writing, and math, all of the teens were expected to help around the complex. Some were taught farming skills, others were trained as electricians, there were construction workers, and others were placed in the service industry. I wanted to go into the electrical field, but I was placed in housekeeping. My main duty was to make sure the suites where one of the five families lived was always clean, but I was also expected to serve meals and cleanup afterward. I was assigned to the Johnson family. The news did little to brighten my already sour mood. I was a glorified maid. The one good thing about the job was that I got to do it with Pearl, who was highly liked by the Johnsons. Since money was obsolete, they showed their appreciation for a job well done by giving her things. Pearl had her own personal computer, which I used to charge my iPod. I would often stick in my earbuds and block out the entire world. It wasn't much, but it was better than being dead, or even worse, undead.

CHAPTER 5

I woke up every morning for the next two years and went to classes. After that, I went to my job. I didn't have any other choice. What was I going to do? This was my new life. The new normal. Then, on the day of my seventeenth birthday, I couldn't do it anymore. I woke up and felt a pressure on my chest, and every time I thought about going to class, I broke out into a sweat. The thought of scrubbing another toilet made me nauseous. I was tired of pretending everything was fine. I wanted out. I made it a point to leave my room before Pearl arrived and went to sit by the lake.

The sun peeked over the horizon, and I inhaled a humid breath. By that point, the zombies had all migrated to the West, and there was an invisible line, starting at the panhandle of Nebraska, extending north to Canada and south to the Gulf of Mexico, that the zombies refused to cross. There had been plans in the works for several months to build a wall to keep the zombies on one side, and the humans would repopulate the nation on the other. It was assumed that if given enough time, the zombies would decay away to nothing.

I put in my earbuds and turned up the volume. White Zombie's "More Human than Human" thumped in my ears. I sat down on the beach and threw some sand into the water.

I watched the ripples for a second, then leaned back on my elbows. What was I going to do? I may have been tired of my "life" and ready to escape, but it wasn't like there were that many options available to me. I leaned my head back and sighed. A shadow crossed my face, and I turned to see an entourage of soldiers heading into the hotel. The man at the front was bald with a pock-marked face and had tattoos of pin-up girls on his forearms. His sleeves were rolled up to his elbows, making them prominent. He glanced down at me and smiled. I stared at him and the group until they disappeared inside, then I jumped up and followed after them. The hotel buzzed with rumors for days that an elite group of solders was going to be visiting. They had supposedly been hand picked by Mrs. Johnson to oversee the construction of the wall. I didn't believe it, of course, because rumors like that floated around for weeks and nothing ever happened. But, my interest was piqued with the new group and I could only hope the rumors were true.

    I lagged behind and stayed out of sight until the elevator doors closed. I watched the lights to see what floor they were heading to. They stopped in the penthouse. I was curious but not stupid. If I went upstairs, I would have to wait on them. If they turned out to be plain soldiers who weren't tasked to build the wall, I would be pissed. I decided to play it safe. My plan was to head back outside when someone grabbed my arm.

"There you are," Pearl pulled out my earbud and hissed in my ear. "They have been looking for you all morning."

"No," I groaned. "I don't want to go up there."

Pearl directed me toward the elevators. "They said they have something important to tell you."

Another new development. My curiosity went up another level. "What?"

"I don't know."

The elevator doors closed, and I turned off my iPod. "Who are those people who just came up here?"

"They're the soldiers in charge of the wall."

I raised my eyebrows. I was right to hope. "So they are going to build one. Who's the guy with the tattoos?"

Pearl stared at me for a moment. "That's Liet. He's been promoted to general. You don't want anything to do with him."

I shrugged and turned my music back on. Normally, Pearl would have been right. Most of the soldiers in Florida weren't very nice to be around. They had attitudes that they were untouchable and could do anything they wanted. Some even stole things from the local markets because they knew no one would do anything. Not all of them were bad, but the vast majority of them were. I had a different feeling about Liet and his soldiers, though. I mean, they were going to build the wall. They were going to make it possible for life to go on.

They thought of the greater good. I'm sure that meant they were the good guys.

The elevator doors opened, and Pearl and I made our way to the kitchen. Olivia Johnson, the head of the Johnson family and our employer, grabbed my arms and pulled me to the corner.

"Krista, darling, where have you been? The genealogy department called. They found some of your family."

My eyes grew wide and my heart fluttered. "Really? Who is it?"

"Your second cousin."

My excitement faltered a little, but I was still curious. "Where are they?"

Mrs. Johnson smiled. "Well, my dear, it so happens your family is the new general." She patted me on the shoulder and left the kitchen.

I stared after her, mouth agape. This was too good to be true. I willed myself to fly, just to make sure it wasn't a dream. I didn't pinch myself like you're supposed to, mainly because I still feel pain in my dreams. For some reason, no matter what I'm dreaming, I can make myself fly, so that was the test I used. I couldn't, so I was awake. This was turning out to be the best birthday ever. I opened the kitchen door and stared at Liet. I could see him clearly, but I didn't recognize him. I wracked my brain, but had no memory of him.

I put my iPod in my pocket and carried the tray of food into the dining room. It was crap that I still had to do my job and Mrs. Johnson didn't introduce me to my family, but business was more important. As usual, my happiness would have to wait. Mrs. Johnson sat at the head of the table, and Liet sat to her right. They were talking softly about their plans for the wall. All I heard was that they needed more workers, and that the ones they had at the moment needed more motivation. I set the plate in front of Liet, who looked up and smiled. I hesitated for a moment and smiled back. I felt Mrs. Johnson's eyes upon me, so I hurried out of the room. I stood by the door, hoping to hear more about their plans and waiting to see if Mrs. Johnson would introduce us, but they switched their conversation to construction supplies, and that was boring. I turned my music back on and waited until it was time to clear their dishes.

I was in the kitchen, scraping uneaten food into the garbage can, when it felt like my earbud fell out. I went to grab it and was surprised to feel a hand. I turned abruptly and looked up at Liet.

He smiled and folded his hands across his chest. "Sorry. I didn't mean to scare you."

I turned my music off. "It's all right."

"I'm General Liet." He held out his hand.

I shook it briefly. "Krista."

"I suppose they told you we are related."

"Mrs. Johnson mentioned something. But, I have to say, I don't remember you."

Liet smiled. "The last time we would have seen each other was at the family reunion twelve years ago." He reached in his pocket and pulled out a folded piece of paper. He handed it to me. "That photo was taken at the picnic in the park."

I unfolded the paper and stared at the smiling faces of my family. I instantly found my five-year old self and my parents. I also recognized several aunts and uncles and my grandparents, but there were also several people I didn't know. Liet moved so he stood next to me.

"That's my mom right there," he pointed to a woman with frosted blonde hair holding a beer and smoking a cigarette. "She would have been your mom's first cousin. And that's me. I was fifteen at the time." He pointed to a skinny kid wearing short blue basketball shorts and a Led Zepplin T-shirt. "It was our last family reunion because we moved to Louisiana shortly after."

I squinted at the picture, then glanced at the man before me. There was definitely a resemblance, but Liet had come a long way from being the thin kid in the picture. I folded it and tried to hand it back. Liet held up his hand and shook his head.

"How long have you been here, Krista?"

"Two years."

"Pchoo. That's a long time. Do you like it here?"

I shrugged. "I don't know." I wanted to tell him I thought I was in the ninth level of hell, but

I just met him, I needed to play it cool, figure out his intentions.

"What do you do here?"

"Go to class, then come up here and wait on the Johnsons."

"When I saw you by the lake, weren't you supposed to be in school?"

I nodded.

"Why weren't you in class today?"

I shrugged again. "I didn't see the point in it anymore."

"What do you mean?"

"I mean, why do we have to go to school and learn math and all that other stuff if we can't use it in the real world. I mean, there is no real world anymore." I threw the plate I was holding into the trash. "And I'll be damned if I'm going to be someone's servant for the rest of my life."

Liet's smile grew wider. "What you really want is a little adventure."

I nodded. "Yeah. That would be nice."

"You ever been outside of Florida?"

"Not in two years."

"Well, Krista, since you and I are the only family we have left, we need to stick together. Would you like to go with me to Nebraska?"

I straightened up. "Yeah."

"How much skill do you have in fighting zombies?"

I hunched my shoulders. "None. They don't teach us anything of value here."

Liet waved. "Not to worry. I can make sure you have all the skills you need. Be ready early tomorrow. I'll take care of everything." He turned and left.

I found it hard to suppress a smile. I looked at the rest of the dirty dishes and threw them all into the trash. I walked out of the penthouse and went to my room to pack my belongings. When I finished, I went to find Pearl. I didn't think it would be right to leave without saying goodbye to my only friend.

Pearl was still in the penthouse cleaning up, so I waited outside until she was done. We made our way to the lake, and Pearl sat on the beach while I threw pebbles into the water.

"I'm leaving tomorrow."

Pearl stared at me in disbelief. "Where are you going?"

"Liet said I could go with him."

Pearl stood from the sand and grabbed me by the arm. "I don't think that is a very good idea. I've heard bad things about him, Krista."

I pulled away from Pearl's grasp. "Yeah? Like what?"

"I heard he's an ex-con."

"So? Lots of people get reformed in prison."

"I don't think he's very nice. What do you know about him?"

I sighed and pulled the picture out of my pocket. I handed it to Pearl. "He's my family."

Pearl unfolded the photo and stared at it in disgust. "How is he your family?"

"He's my second cousin."

Pearl huffed. "How do you know that for sure?"

"Look at the picture. That's me. There are my parents. This is Liet's mom. And this is Liet."

Pearl shook her head. "I don't think it's a good idea."

"But staying here is? What are we even doing here? We go to school to learn stuff that we are *never* going to use in life. Then, we have to wait on jerks. I don't know about you, but I am *not* going to be their servant for the rest of my life."

"What are you gonna do out there? Huh? Fight zombies? Build a wall? Yeah, that sounds like such a better deal. At least here you have a roof over your head and food on your plate. Did Liet guarantee that you'd have that?"

"At least I'd be doing something. At least I have family."

We turned our backs on each other and stared off in opposite directions for a long time. Why did Pearl want to stay? There's nothing. At least out there there was a chance for adventure. To do something with our lives. I didn't want to be a slave. I might not know Liet very well or remember his family, but he was all I had left. I threw a rock into the water.

"Look, Krista," Pearl's voice was soft, "I understand not wanting to stay here. I've thought about it a lot, too. But I've seen what's out there. I've seen what the zombies can do, and I'd much rather stay here where I know I'm safe."

I sighed. "I've seen what the zombies can do, too. But pretending they don't exist is not going to make them go away. Something has to be done."

"Well, I hope you're successful in what you do." Pearl attempted to walk away, but I grabbed her arm.

"I don't want you to be mad at me. You're my only friend, and I want you to stay that way."

Pearl forced a smile. "I'm not mad. I'm sad you want to leave. But I do understand that you should be with your family."

"Then come with me."

Pearl shook her head. "I'm not that brave."

I wrapped my arms around Pearl's shoulders, and we held each other for a while. Eventually, we let go and headed into the hotel to spend our last few hours together.

* * *

Liet showed up at my door at six. I grabbed my duffel bag of clothes and headed into the morning sun. Liet opened the door to a transport truck, and I climbed into the passenger side. I glanced out the window behind me and noticed three more trucks were making the trip, two of them were filled with kids from my class and other civilians from the town. The third was full of the soldiers who came with Liet. He smiled as he climbed behind the steering wheel and turned the key.

"You ready?"

I smiled and nodded.

"You better be because we ain't ever coming back here." He put the truck into gear, and we headed down the road.

My stomach fluttered, but I didn't look back. I thought about Pearl, wished briefly that she had decided to come, then focused on what lay ahead. It had been two years since I'd been outside of Florida, and I was anxious to see what happened in that time. From what I had been told, most of the country had been abandoned. Cities lay in ruin, and bodies were left to rot in the streets. The power on the East Coast had been redirected to Florida so the survivors could live in comfort. There were some stories that pockets of survivors stayed in the West, eking out a living on the sparse reserves that were left. I wasn't sure if I believed it all. The country had been populated by millions of people, it was hard to believe only thousands of them were left. All I knew was I was leaving Florida. I was going to be free.

Liet stared at me out of the corner of his eye, so I pulled myself out of my thoughts and turned toward him.

"So you're a general, huh?"

He nodded.

"How did you get that position?"

"No one else wanted it."

"Really? Why not?"

"They're scared." He glanced at me. "You haven't been out for a while, but the world is a much different place than what you remember." He focused his gaze back on the road. "Life won't be easy in North Platte. In fact, it will be hell." He smiled and looked at me sideways. "But you're lucky, I'll be there to take care of you."

"I don't want you to take care of me. I want you to teach me to fight."

"Oh, you'll learn to fight. You'll have to. Or you won't survive."

"I hear you're an ex-con. Is that true?"

Liet snorted a laugh. "Yeah. It's true."

"What did you do?"

He shrugged one shoulder. "Does it really matter?"

I stared at him for a second. "Probably not. Did you escape from prison or did they let you go?"

His knuckles turned white as he gripped the steering wheel and his jaw muscles tighten. "What kind of question is that?"

"I didn't mean anything by it. I was just curious."

"I did my time. I paid my debt to society."

"Okay. I'm sorry. I didn't mean to offend you."

His grip loosened, and his face relaxed. "It's okay."

I decided it was best to change the subject. I didn't know what that was about, but I was pretty sure I didn't want to see it again. "Tell me about North Platte."

"What do you want to know?"

"What does it look like?"

"Nothing much. The town still exists, and we've set up camp in the most viable buildings and houses, but most of the buildings are in ruins. When the threat got out of hand, the people tried to burn the undead down. But you can't kill a zombie like that, you have to destroy their brain. All you do when you light them on fire is make them a walking torch. They light everything in their path until they can't walk anymore."

"Have you killed a lot of zombies?"

The right side of his mouth pulled into a smile, and he looked at me. "More than any man you'll ever meet."

"Are they hard to kill?"

"Nah, not if you know what you're doing. Like I said, you have to destroy the brain or behead them. After that, there's nothing to 'em."

"If there's nothing to them, and they're so easy to destroy, how did they get out of hand?"

"Because they have numbers on their side. You see, your average zombie isn't very smart. They have one thing on their mind, and that is to eat. And you don't want to get bit. If you get bit, you have about twenty-four hours before you turn into the walking dead. They don't move very fast because they're dead and their bodies are falling apart. So we have that as an advantage. But where there's one, you can bet in a few minutes there will be more. If you can remain undetected, you'll be fine. If you see one, make sure you kill it before it can summon its friends."

"How do they summon their friends?"

"With the most god-awful moaning you have ever heard in your life."

I thought back to the night my family and I hid in the attic and shivered. "How do they track you?"

"I don't know. No one knows. We're not here to study the darn things."

"How many are there?"

"Too many." He looked at me. "We've got a long time to talk about zombies. Let's talk about something else." He turned back to the road. "Tell me about yourself."

"There's not really that much to tell."

"Tell me about your parents. I don't really remember them."

I averted my gaze to my lap. "They're dead."

"They weren't always dead, were they? You did have a childhood, right?" He pushed on my knee. "Or were you the first kid in the history of the world to be raised by zombie parents? Was it your family that started the plague? Tell me what it was like to grow up in Oregon."

I looked at him, and he smiled. I smiled back and told him about my childhood. He listened intently and asked a lot of questions. Occasionally, he told stories of family members he remembered, who I saw frequently, and we laughed. It was the first time in years I focused on happy memories of my parents. I was sure I made the right decision to leave Florida.

CHAPTER 6

It took us two days to make it to North Platte. I spent most of that time contemplating life and the apocalypse. Like I said before, I never understood people's interest in it. I suppose thinking about it is a luxury when you don't *really* think it's going to happen. If you're lucky enough to survive it when it does occur, all you feel is helpless and depressed. All the planning and foresight doesn't make coping any easier and it doesn't change anything. The world ends and you realize how insignificant you are. But there is a vague glimmer of hope. With every end, there is a beginning, and people start focusing on how they are going to make things better. We survived the freaking apocalypse, although fleeting, we were entitled to a little optimism.

In reality, not everyone was ready to start a new life. In fact, most people wanted to pretend that zombies never rose from the grave and have life go on as usual. Those were the people who stayed in Florida. For the rest of us, we were ready to make a difference and rebuild what we lost.

I had fallen asleep in the passenger seat, and when I woke up and looked out, I was sorely disappointed. There were a few buildings still standing in the middle of town— the courthouse, the jail, and a few stores. Houses with peeling paint and broken windows surrounded the perimeter. Tents were set up everywhere else. The town was overcrowded with workers who were in poor health, desperately needed a bath, and were malnourished. I wasn't expecting Paris, but I thought North Platte would have been slightly more habitable. I took it back. Florida was the third level of hell, Nebraska was the ninth. Maybe I was spoiled. I mean, life in Florida was pretty cush. It would be fine, though. I could make the best of it. What other option did I have?

The wall was on the west side of town. It wasn't much to look at, just the beginnings of a trench and a row of razor wire. Guard towers were set up at varying intervals down the length of the fence, and guards stood in each with guns trained on the field outside of the city. Others patrolled the grounds with dogs, and the rotting corpses of dead zombies filled the field on the opposite side of the fence. I choked down the urge to vomit.

I opened the door to the truck and hopped into the mud. The stench of rotting flesh permeated my nostrils, and my stomach clenched. I placed my hand over my mouth to keep the vomit in. Liet stepped around the truck.

"You'll get used to that eventually." He placed his hands on his hips and arched his back.

I swallowed down the bile. "Isn't there something you can do with them?"

Liet popped his neck by placing his hands on his cheeks and twisting. "Yeah, we're actually planning on burning them. We haven't had a chance to build the pyre yet." He stepped forward and placed his arm around my shoulders. "Let me give you a tour of the place."

It took five minutes for Liet to show me the grounds. My stomach unclenched a little, but I was sure I would never get used to the smell. He took me to a house and explained that it was the women's dormitory. It had been blue at one time, but the color faded to gray. The windows were covered with particleboard that had been warped by rain, and the door practically fell off its hinges when Liet pushed it open. As we stepped inside, the smell of mildew drifted into my nose, and, sadly, it was a welcome relief from outside. There wasn't much furniture, a couch and a couple of chairs. Dishes were stacked in the sink, and clothes hung around the room. Cots had been set up in the empty spaces, and a few women soldiers eyed me as I walked in.

"Ladies, this is Krista. Please make her feel at home."

I furrowed my brow. "Aren't I staying with you?"

Liet nodded. "Eventually. They're finishing the remodeling on my apartment. As soon as it's done, you can move in." He grabbed the door handle. "I'll see you at dinner." He winked, then turned on his heel and left the house.

I tightened the grip on my bag and looked around the room. "Um, should I set my stuff anywhere?"

One of the women stepped forward. I tried not to flinch, but the soldier was almost a head taller than I was and twice as wide. Her hair was pulled back in cornrows, and lines etched her face. She placed her hands on her hips and looked me up and down.

"How old are you?"

"Seventeen." The word caught in my throat and I choked it out.

The woman laughed. "Seventeen? What in God's green earth are you doing out here?"

"I couldn't stay in Florida."

The woman laughed again. "I bet you're rethinking that right about now." She stepped forward and gently grabbed my bicep and pulled me into the room. "You can sleep on the cot next to the kitchen. What did you do in Florida?"

"I was a housekeeper."

The woman turned to the others in the room. "Well I'll be! We were just talking about how we needed someone to help us clean this mess up. Look girls, God does answer prayers."

The others chuckled.

"Here, set your stuff down. Where are my manners? I'm Pam." She stuck out her hand.

I grabbed it, and my hand was engulfed in calluses and sandpaper skin. "Krista."

"It's nice to meet you, Krista. I assume that since Liet didn't put you out in a tent that you are somethin' special. What kind of combat training do you have?"

I set my bag on the bed and shook my head. "None."

I thought about telling her Liet was my cousin, but since she didn't specifically ask, I didn't say a word. It wasn't that I didn't trust her; on the contrary, she was nothing like the others. I didn't get any Carmen vibes at all. But I didn't want to be treated differently. I wanted her to treat me like a soldier.

"None? What the…?" She turned to the other girls, who had come forward and surrounded us. "We'll have to remedy that situation."

"Liet already told me he would teach me to fight."

Pam laughed. "That'll be the day. More than likely, he'd pawn you off on one of us. Since that's the case, let's make a deal. We'll teach you how to kill zombies, and you make this house livable. Deal?"

I looked around the house and frowned. The carpet was torn and frayed with an inch-thick layer of mud, and the walls were yellowed. "I guess."

Pam slapped me on the shoulder. "Good. We'll start tomorrow. But you do have a few hours before dinner, perhaps *you* could get started now."

I nodded and took a deep breath. I thought the easiest thing to start would be the dishes, so I headed into the kitchen. As I ran the water, I desperately wished I had my iPod. I didn't make the journey to be another maid. I scrubbed furiously at a plate. I probably could've gotten out of it, all I had to do was tell them I was related to Liet, but I made a deal. I didn't want to be treated special because the General was family. I wanted to make my own way. I hoped they were going to teach me something worthwhile, or I was going to be angry. I felt eyes on me and looked over my shoulder. A few of the girls stared, but they didn't say anything. I turned back to my work.

After I finished the dishes, I made my way to the courthouse. I stepped through the threshold and took a deep breath. The room had been converted from the courtroom into Liet's office. He'd kept the bench and jury box but had the other seats ripped out. He spoke quietly to a man I assumed was one of his officers because of his uniform, and he smiled at me as I entered.

"I'm glad you could make it. How are you settling into your new home?"

"It's almost like I never left Florida."

Liet chuckled. "Good. I'm glad to hear it." He snapped his fingers in the air, and some soldiers brought in a table and two chairs.

We sat down, and plates of roast with carrots and potatoes were set in front of us. I didn't realize how hungry I was until the smell drifted into my nostrils. My mouth watered, and I dug into my plate. I was halfway through my food when I looked up. Liet stared at me.

"After we eat, I'd like to show you where the new burning grounds are going to be."

I swallowed my bite of food. "Okay."

"I know it doesn't sound that thrilling, but I want you to know we're trying to make this place habitable. Besides, there's really nothing else to do here."

I smiled. "Wonderful. By the way, Pam seems to think she is going to be teaching me how to fight."

Liet stabbed at the meat on his plate. "Oh, good. So the two of you made some arrangements?"

"I thought you were going to teach me."

"Krista, you have to understand. I am a very busy man. I have an entire camp to run. I will certainly be there when I can, but if Pam has the time, I would recommend learning from her."

"Oh, okay." I finished the food on my plate and waited.

Six guards escorted us to the first guard tower as the sun set. Shades of orange, pink, purple, and red lined the sky. If it hadn't been for the stench, I would have enjoyed the moment. We climbed the stairs and looked over the area. A few workers were in the trench digging postholes, filling them with cement, then sticking in the metal poles for the chain link fence. The horizon was flat, and the ground was covered with thousands of corpses. In the distance, I saw a few mobile ones limping their way to the perimeter. I glanced at the guard tower to my right; they tracked the zombies with a pair of binoculars and spotting scopes. I squinted at the horizon to get a better view.

"Over there about five hundred yards will be the pyre."

I turned to where Liet indicated. A group of twenty men dug a hole in the soft earth. Ten soldiers surrounded them, but they still glanced over their shoulders nervously. I would've been freaked out, too. From the looks of it, zombies were a constant threat, but one that could be taken care of.

"They're not used to being on that side of the fence," Liet commented. "Even when they're on our side, they still fall prey to the zombies. The zombies may be slow, but they are crafty buggers. Sometimes when you think you've killed one, they pop right back up and bite you."

I glanced back down at the bodies and shivered. "How often do they attack?"

Liet placed his hands on the rail and leaned forward. "It's been getting more and more frequent since we moved the camp in. I'm sure they've used up the majority of their supplies on the west side, and the enticement of fresh meat is very alluring." He stared at me and smiled. "But you don't need to worry about them getting in. We have guards watching vigilantly night and day."

"What if one of the workers gets bit and doesn't tell anyone?"

Liet shook his head. "Won't happen. Every shift is inspected before they are allowed back into the city."

"Inspected?"

"Yeah. They strip down in the showers and the soldiers check them."

I cringed. That had to be humiliating. But I'm sure it was necessary. Without rules and precautions, the world would spiral into chaos. Plus, I knew if one of the worker's did get bit, they would never say anything. They would carry on with their work and head home like it didn't happen, telling themselves the entire time everything was going to be fine. It was a survival mechanism. The thought of turning into a zombie wasn't frightening because it hadn't been experienced. Yeah, it happened to others, but the person who got bit was immune. They were special.

"How long does it take to turn after they've been bit?"

"Twenty-four hours."

"What happens if they find someone who's been bit?"

"They're taken care of."

What a gentle euphemism. Like I didn't know what he meant. That would be another deterrent, too, for someone who was infected not to say anything. They knew what a bullet to the head meant, and since most of us are afraid of dying, they would rather take their chances with becoming the undead.

"You mean they're killed."

"To save hundreds sometimes you have to kill one. Besides, they're dead anyway. A bullet saves them from the torment that is being undead."

That was the truth, no argument here, but try to convince the person at the end of the barrel it's for their own good. I wasn't one to judge, but I was curious. "How many workers have been killed?"

Liet adjusted so his butt rested on the rail, and he folded his arms across his chest. "I don't have those figures on me."

"What if you were wrong? What if they weren't bitten by a zombie?"

Liet shrugged. "Better to be safe than dead. But it's pretty apparent when someone's been bit by a zombie."

"What do you do with the bodies?" I didn't remember seeing a graveyard on our short tour through town.

He nodded over the rail. I looked down at the bodies and noticed that some of them were naked and weren't as decomposed as others. I could understand needing to keep the humans safe. I mean, if you get bit, you're dead anyway. But to treat them like trash? They hadn't turned yet. There was still humanity left in them. It made me a angry to think they didn't give them a little dignity in death.

I buried my anger and changed the subject. "How are you going to destroy the zombies after the wall is built?"

Liet scoffed. "We don't need to worry about destroying the zombies. We'll keep guards on the wall to ensure that none of them get through, and we'll worry about populating the rest of the country."

"What about the people who live in the west?"

"They made their decision. If they want to live in a zombie-free nation, they need to come to our side of the wall."

Come to our side? Weren't we all part of the same nation? What if they were trapped? Or sick? They might need help and we were abandoning them. It didn't seem right. But what could I do? I wasn't exactly in a position to do anything. Plus, maybe Liet was right. Maybe they wanted to stay over there. I didn't know.

The sun fell below the horizon, and darkness crept in. The guards clicked on their floodlights and panned across the field. The workers digging the pyre were escorted to the inspection area, and those who were digging postholes continued to do so. I had seen enough, and Liet and his soldiers took me back to my house.

I lay awake on my cot and stared up at the mold-stained ceiling. What was I doing? This was no place for me. I should've stayed in Florida. At least there I had luxury. I rolled onto my side. But I wasn't happy. Was it possible for me to be happy in North Platte? I closed my eyes and saw the field of bodies. A shudder ran through my body. Maybe it would be all right once I learned how to fight. At least then I'd have some piece of mind. I closed my eyes again and tried not to think about the dead.

When I was unsuccessful, I got up from my bed and headed out the back door. The back yard was fenced, but several boards were missing, and one side was ready to fall over. The grass was brown and crunchy, and the clothesline had been knocked over. A tree in the northwest corner of the yard had a tire swing hanging from the branches. I tugged on the rope to make sure it was sturdy. It didn't seem like it was going anywhere, so I sat down. I folded my arms on the top of the tire and stared up at the stars. I couldn't remember the last time I had seen the stars. I never took the time to look in Florida. Even at that moment, the majority of them were blocked out from the light pollution caused by the floodlights. But it was quiet. I never got any peace in Florida. Kids yelled at each another or the sounds of construction resounded through the school. I smiled to myself.

"Enjoy the view," a voice echoed in the darkness, "because it will probably be the last time you see it."

Pam stood at the back door, lighting a cigarette. She stepped forward and offered me one, but I shook my head.

"Yep, by this time tomorrow, that funeral pyre should be burning pretty high. The smoke will probably block everything out for at least two miles." She took a drag. "But I guess that's the price we pay for civilization. Should improve the smell, though. Now instead of rotting flesh, we'll get to inhale burning flesh." She took another long drag off her cigarette and flicked the butt into the grass. "You might want to get some sleep, you have a long day ahead of you." She turned and headed into the house.

I stared at the sky for a while longer, then returned to bed. I closed my eyes and dreamt about zombies.

CHAPTER 7

Pam woke me before dawn. My back was sore and my eyes burned. It took every ounce of strength I had to pull myself out of bed. The sky was gray with the promise of light, the air cool. We walked to the fence and climbed into one of the guard towers. Workers planted metal poles into the postholes and poured cement, and a new group finished the pyre hole. Pam handed me a Zigana T.

"You ever shoot anything before?"

"Sort of. My dad took me to the range once."

Pam scoffed. "Your gun is your best friend. You'll learn how to use other weapons, but if you don't have to get that close, don't. There's more of a chance you could get bit. Now, hold it like this." She straightened her arms out in front of her. "This is your sight." She pointed to the back of the gun. "You want to line this knob up with whatever it is you're going to shoot."

I extended my arms in front of me and closed one eye. I lined the sight up with a body on the ground.

"When you have your sights lined up, you want to gently squeeze the trigger."

I put my finger on the trigger and fired. The gun jerked upward and the bullet sailed wide. I saw a puff of dirt far away from where I aimed. I lowered the weapon and sighed.

Pam smiled. "No one ever gets it on their first try. Shooting is not inherent. You have to practice. Try something a little closer."

"Shouldn't I be practicing on targets or something?"

"Why? You think you're going to be firing at targets out there?" She jerked her head toward the field. "Here, let's make this a bit more realistic."

We headed down the tower steps. Pam pulled one of the workers away from digging a posthole and ordered him to retrieve a body. Reluctantly, the man obeyed, and he set the corpse up on the fence. Pam motioned toward the body. It was a young man, probably college age, who wore tattered blue jeans and a green T-shirt, which had been ripped open in the middle. Blood and mud caked his blonde hair. I shivered.

"Go ahead, shoot it."

I frowned. "What if I miss?"

"Then the bullet sails harmlessly into the field. I'm sure you'll miss. Despite what the movies portray, the human body is actually a pretty small target. Especially the human head. You can hit a zombie in the chest and slow it down, but you won't kill it. You have to hit it in the brain." She stepped back.

I lined up my sights and squeezed the trigger. The bullet flew over the corpse. I couldn't see where it landed. Frustration crept into my chest. "Isn't there a trick to this?

Something to make it easier?" Why didn't I stay in bed?

Pam shook her head. "Nope." She set some boxes of ammunition on the ground. "You keep practicing till you hit it." She turned and headed to the top of the tower.

I spent the entire morning trying to hit the zombie's head. I could hit it in the torso fine, and wing it, but a dead-on shot was impossible. My hands were sweaty from holding the gun, my thumb throbbed from reloading bullets, and my jaw was sore from clenching. By the time I was on my fifth magazine, I was so frustrated I dropped to the ground and folded my legs in front of me. I set the gun down and buried my face in my hands. I heard someone approach and assumed it was Pam.

"This is impossible!" I yelled into my hands. "Besides, don't we have to conserve ammo?"

Pam laughed. "Are you kidding? We've raided every sporting good store, gun dealer, and pawn shop from here to New York. We've got ammo. And when that runs out, we've got supplies to reload our own. Ammo is not an issue."

I flopped my hands into my lap and sagged my shoulders. "I'm never going to get this."

Pam grabbed my arm and lifted me up. "Then maybe you'd better go back to Florida. If you don't learn to shoot and defend yourself, you're as good as dead. You wanna go back?"

I straightened my shoulders and took a shaky breath. "No."

"Maybe you should try this." She moved me within five feet of the corpse and placed the gun in my hand. "Line the sights up and fire. When you've hit it ten times, move back another foot. Keep doing that until you run out of bullets or you can hit it every single time."

I was getting to the point where I didn't think anything was going to work, and I still had some problems hitting the target, but after a while, I got the hang of it. I was only six feet away from the corpse, but I hit it every time. I felt pretty good. I figured out the nuances of the gun, and felt confident in my abilities. Pam came down from the tower about the same time, and we headed back to the house for lunch.

I made us a pot of chili and some grilled cheese, and all the girls ate greedily. When we finished, I cleaned up the dishes. Pam told me she had some things to do, so I lay down and took a nap. Every ache and pain became pronounced, but it was a great feeling. I was much more exhausted than I imagined, and the next thing I knew, Pam shook me awake. I glanced at the clock. I slept for three hours. Pam told me to follow her, and we headed back to the wall.

"Although we have a large cache of ammo, you cannot carry an infinite supply. If you get too deep into the West, you're going to run out. Once that happens, you still have to be able to defend yourself. Different people prefer different weapons. I personally like to keep a katana handy." She reached behind her back and drew out a sword. "They're light weight and have incredible slicing power. You can take the heads off a hundred zombies and the blade never gets dull. You don't have to be as accurate with one of these babies as you do with a gun. But you have to be close." She handed me the weapon . "There's really no right or wrong way to behead your opponent. I've never been trained in martial arts, but that doesn't make the weapon any less deadly. The most important thing is to be fast." She walked over to the corpse I riddled with bullet holes. "Go ahead, take its head off."

I gripped the handle in both hands and planted my feet. I had never handled a sword before, but I had seen movies. I knew it wasn't the same thing, but it was the only example I had. I swung the katana over my right shoulder and swung it at the corpse's neck. It sliced a quarter of the way through, then got stuck. I tried to pull it out, but my hands slipped and I fell backward. I caught myself before I hit the dirt. I stared at Pam. She tried to hold back her laughter.

"You can't expect to get everything right the first time. With a little practice, you'll be able to take a head off in one swipe. Let me show you some exercises to strengthen your upper body."

We worked together until the sun started to set, then we headed back to the house and I prepared dinner. After we ate, I dragged upstairs to take a shower. The water felt good on my sore muscles, and I stayed in long enough to fog the mirrors. When I finished, I headed back to my cot and lay down.

"You did a great job today," Pam said. "Tomorrow you can rest and get the house cleaned up a little more." She stepped out the door for her second shift on the watchtower.

I cringed. I didn't really want to spend the day cleaning, but I knew it was part of the deal. I had to hold up my end of the bargain. Plus, with as sore as my arms were, I wasn't sure I would be able to hold the gun. I rolled onto my side and thought about the lessons I learned. I drifted to sleep thinking about all the zombies I was going to destroy with my newfound skills.

I woke late the next morning. The soldiers already had breakfast and headed out to their jobs. I must have been extremely tired because I slept right next to the kitchen and didn't even hear them. I rolled out of bed slowly and sat on the edge. I looked around the house and sighed. The sink was full of dishes, the floor was still covered in mud, and clothes were still strewn around the living room. I was never going to get ahead in my cleaning. I stood slowly and made my way to the kitchen.

By mid-morning, the kitchen was spotless, and I had most of the clothes picked up. I searched for a vacuum in the closet when I came across a cache of weapons. Pam had been nice enough to let me keep the Zigana, but I couldn't keep the katana. I picked through the rifles and shotguns, wondering if it was all right if I took a few. There was an assortment of knives and broadswords, but the thing that caught my attention were the arm swords with the collapsible blades. I pulled them out of the closet and took them to my cot. I grabbed one and fitted the straps around my forearm, depressing the button on the handle. The blade snapped out. I pressed the button again, and the blade snapped back into place. I smiled. I took the arm sword off and placed it under my cot.

Pam returned at lunch, and we ate before heading back to the fence to train. I asked about the weapons, and Pam told me I could take anything I wanted. I brought the arm swords with me and started learning how to use them. The metal was light and sturdy, but after several hours of attempting to chop off a zombie's head, I was exhausted and sore. I did better with the arm swords than with the katana because I had more leverage and could use the weight of my entire body to swing the blade. I worked a little more with the gun and was actually getting the hang of it.

By late afternoon, I was tired and my arms were extremely sore, so I climbed the watchtower and leaned against the rail. Several workers hauled bodies to the pyre pit, while a guard prepared to light the flame. He doused the corpses in diesel and tossed in a torch. A whoosh resounded through the air, followed by the scent of burning flesh and a dark pillar of smoke. Surprisingly, it wasn't as bad as I thought it would be. It kind of smelled like a campfire. I closed my eyes and thought about the last time I went camping with my parents. It was the only way to keep from thinking about what was really happening. The zombies didn't bother me, but the humans who lost their lives doing their job made my stomach turn. Footsteps approached behind me, and I turned to see Liet.

"Should be a nice night," he smiled.

"If you say so." It was hard for me to imagine a night could be nice with smoke clouding the sky and bodies burning in the fire.

He stood next to me and placed his hands on the rail. "I hear your training is coming along pretty well."

I shrugged. "It's all right. I'm still not very good. I'm sure if it came down to it, a zombie would still get the better of me."

"Just keep practicing, you'll get it."

I nodded. "I will."

Liet averted his gaze so he stared at the horizon. "If you're not busy, I would really enjoy some company for dinner."

I smiled. "I would like that."

Liet turned and headed toward the stairs. "I'll see you at six."

Movement caught my eye on the horizon, and I squinted to get a better view. Workers still moved bodies to the fire, and several zombies closed in on their location. The guards noticed their approach and waited for them to get closer before firing. The workers noticed them, too, and they dropped their loads and headed onto the safe side of the fence. The guards fired, and several of the undead went down. I pulled my gun out. I hit one in the shoulder and the leg, but couldn't put one in its head before someone else did. Even though they were slow, it was still difficult to hit a moving target. I knew I needed a lot more practice.

* * *

Dinner that night was chicken with fresh vegetables and potatoes. After my workout, I was starving, so I ate quickly. Liet stared at me from across the table.

"Where does all this food come from?" I asked between bites.

"The workers tend a garden and raise a few animals. We tried to plunder the grocery stores, but all the frozen and refrigerated stuff had gone bad. Canned food is a bit more abundant, but we don't have an eternal supply."

I rolled my eyes. "I know. I cook for the girls, remember?"

Liet chuckled. "Of course." He leaned back in his chair and folded his arms across his chest. "You know, Krista, I was pretty convinced I would never see another member of our family. I accepted the fact that they were all dead. And for a few of them, that doesn't really hurt my feelings."

I lowered my gaze to the table. That last comment was a little creepy. I know you don't always like your family, but you don't wish them dead. I didn't really know what to say, so I tried to ignore it.

"I know what you mean." I referred to the seeing my family part, not the last part, but I don't think he caught that.

"Since we're all that's left, we have to take care of each other. Watch each other's backs."

I choked down my food, staring at Liet. For any other family member, I would have agreed, but to hear it from Liet, it was weird. I would have found it more convincing if he actually took the time to teach me to fight. Or was involved in my life. How many times had he come to visit me in the house?

He chuckled. "I know. It sounds like a line from a movie. All I'm saying is I'm glad I found you. When you're finished, why don't we go for a ride?"

He was trying too hard, trying to force the relationship instead of letting it happen. My first reaction was to fight against it, to resist his advances.

Liet took me to the river. Three soldiers escorted us, but they kept their distance and set up a perimeter around our location. Liet set a blanket down on the beach, and I sat on it with my legs crossed. The smoke from the fire billowed through the air, but the smell dissipated. A few insects buzzed around our heads, and the air was thick with humidity. Liet took a seat next to me and reclined on his elbow. I guessed this was his way of making up for his absence.

"I come here sometimes to get away from the stress. To be alone with my thoughts."

"You're not really alone with the soldiers around you." My hands started sweating, and I wiped them on my pants.

Liet smiled. "The soldiers don't bother me when I'm out here. Half the time I forget they're even there."

"Why do you bring them with you? I thought all the zombies left this part of the country."

"The majority of them have. But you'll still encounter some. I've seen a lot who have been locked in closets or houses, and when you go to get supplies, you let them out. Sometimes, the building falls down, and they get out. It's not completely clear."

I pulled my knees to my chest. "How long have you been out here?"

He shrugged. "I've always lived in the West, but I've been here for about six weeks." He looked at me. "I was the only one willing to supervise the building of the wall." He shrugged his right shoulder and picked at the weeds. "But let's not talk about that now. Let's enjoy the evening."

I stared at the river and watched the water flow. I took a deep breath and set my chin on my knees. We sat quietly until the sun set, and then headed back to the city. Liet walked me to the door of my house.

"I really enjoyed the time with you." He spoke softly. "I hope we can do it again sometime."

"I would like that." I really wouldn't, but I thought it better to be polite.

He wrapped his arms around my shoulders and pulled me into a tight hug. He released me and smiled. "I'll see you tomorrow."

I sucked in the breath he crushed out of me and mumbled something not even I could understand. Liet walked back to the vehicle and disappeared down the street. I went to my cot and pulled on my pajamas, my head swam with the events that just happened.

I didn't begrudge Liet for his absence the last few days. After all, he was busy. He was trying to organize workers and build a wall. But I did find his approach to our relationship a bit disconcerting. I wasn't really one for hugs, especially from a guy I didn't really know. Yeah, he was family, but I didn't know him. He was still a stranger with a creepy past.

I should have been fascinated by Liet. He was the guy I wanted to grow up and study.

But he scared me. Partly it was the ex-con thing and part of it was something I couldn't pin down. Something in his eyes and sneer. Bundy and Manson had the same look in their eyes. It would have been easy to say it was insanity or pure evil, but there was more to it than that. I didn't know. But despite all that, things were changing, and a lot of it was because of Liet's initiative. Even though he wasn't there to teach me to fight, I was still learning, and I would still be able to take care of myself. At least I had something to look forward to. I drifted to sleep for the first time in two years thinking that there might actually be some hope for the future.

CHAPTER 8

A month after coming to North Platte, I moved out of the women's house and into Liet's place. He remodeled the top floor of the courthouse to be his very own apartment. It was three times the size of the house, and he had maids, so I didn't have to clean anything if I didn't want to. I had my own room with a bathroom, and was able to set up a stereo system with CDs I got from a local store. I decorated my room the way I liked, and I finally felt like I had a space that was all my own. It had been a long time since I had anything I could call my own. The last thing I owned was my iPod, and I knew it would be worthless in North Platte, so I'd given it to Pearl. Even having CDs was frivolous, especially since electricity was spotty, at best. Rolling blackouts would have been a luxury, but we made do. My room became my place of normalcy, and I cherished it.

The town was going through several changes also. More workers were brought to the site from Florida, and the tents that housed the workers were being replaced with shanties. All of the lumber and houses in the town that couldn't be salvaged were re-used to build better protection against the elements. Liet was frustrated that building the houses took the focus away from the wall, but he didn't want a worker's riot on his hands, so he didn't say much.

The fence itself hadn't progressed far. A few yards of chain link fence had been erected, but not much else. The workers were so busy hauling bodies to the fire and building their houses that they didn't have time for anything else. Liet was sure that would change in the coming year. He vowed he would encourage the workers to get the wall finished within five years. But with all of his good intentions, it came down to a matter of supplies, and we were running out.

I sat in the jury box and watched as Liet looked over some reports. Pam and a few other soldiers stood in front of him and waited. I didn't really have any duties in North Platte, so I drifted wherever I wanted. Most of the time, I followed Pam around and helped her, but occasionally I watched Liet. That got boring pretty fast, so I practiced shooting. But when both Pam and Liet were in the room, I had to be present. I had nothing else to do.

"How did we go through this much food?" He glanced at the soldiers and waited for an answer.

Pam cleared her throat. "Um, I think we underestimated the amount of children. There were a lot more families in this last group."

"It looks like people are eating too much. Ration their food."

Pam's eyebrows furrowed. "Excuse me, sir?"

He slammed his fist into his desk. "You heard me! Ration their food. Anyone who protests will be shot on sight."

Liet's stress levels had been through the roof lately. I think the pressures of leadership were getting to him. I hoped he really didn't want soldiers to shoot innocent people, but I never knew with Liet.

"Yes, sir," Pam answered.

He glanced at another piece of paper. "You've got to be kidding me. How is this possible?" He turned the paper toward the soldiers. "They've gone through their concrete supply already? What are they doing?"

"They've been using it to create or repair the foundations for their houses, sir." Pam's voice was barely over a whisper.

Liet slammed the paper down. "They're more concerned about their comfort than they are in keeping the zombies out. If one more person uses *my* construction supplies for personal use, they will be *shot on sight*!"

"Yes, sir. In the meantime, what do you want us to do about the supplies?"

"Get an excursion team together. See what you can find in the abandoned cities."

The soldiers responded with a "Yes, sir," in unison, and headed out of the courtroom. Liet sat heavily in his chair and buried his face in his hands. I made my way to him and placed a hand on his shoulder. Things were getting a little better between us, and he didn't scare me as much anymore. I knew he didn't have anyone else, so I thought I would show him some empathy. He brushed it off violently.

"It'll be okay," I said, surprised. It became readily apparent I overstepped my bounds.

"How do you know that?"

I shrugged and sat on his desk. "I don't know. But it'll work out the way it's supposed to."

Liet jumped to his feet and shoved the papers onto the floor. "The way it's supposed to? Do you have any idea what is going on out there? Those people are using supplies that are supposed to keep the zombies at bay for their own personal gain." He stuck his face inches from mine. "Do you know what will happen if one zombie gets in here? Huh? Do you?"

I flinched. "We'll all be dead."

He grabbed me roughly by the upper arms. "That's right. We'll all be dead. It's not about *them* and their personal needs and wants, it about *us*, as a community. The sooner those people figure that out, the sooner we can get the wall built." He released me and turned away.

I rubbed my arms.

"Why don't you go with them on their supply mission? It might be a good idea for you to see what's really going on."

I left the room without saying anything. I wanted to run but thought it best to keep my composure.

I was about finished packing when Liet came into the room.

"I'm sorry for what happened downstairs. Sometimes I get so caught up in my job and stressed out with everything that's going on, I forget how to act. Do you forgive me?"

Liet was so unpredictable. One minute he was sweet as pie, and the next he was ready to gouge your eyes out. My fear of him renewed. I thought it best to keep the situation calm and not do anything to upset him.

"Of course. I understand how stressful your job is."

Liet smiled. "Thank you. You don't have to go on the supply run if you don't want to. In fact, I actually prefer it if you don't."

"No, I think you're right. I should get out there and see what's going on."

He placed his hands on my shoulders. "Be careful. You'll be in the East so there aren't a lot of zombies, but there are still some. Keep your eyes open and use your head. I'll be anxiously awaiting your return."

"I'll see you soon." I brushed past him and headed downstairs, never so thankful to be out of the house.

I climbed into the semi with Pam and we headed east on I-80. We traveled all the way through Nebraska and into Iowa. At Des Moines, we stopped for gas at the military checkpoint. I got out and stretched while Pam filled up and talked to the soldiers. The air was sticky with humidity, and the sky was gray and threatened to rain. I stared at the ruins of the city, wondering how many zombies hid in closets or locked cars. Pam called my name, so I headed back to the truck and climbed into the driver's seat. Pam pulled a map out of the glove compartment.

"We're going to have to head to International Falls. According to the soldiers, there's nothing left around here. Between our needs and the demands of Florida, they've been picked clean."

I leaned forward and stared at the map. "International Falls? Where is that?"

"In Minnesota. Near the Canadian border."

"Why International Falls?"

Pam sighed. "It was some kind of international port of entry. It's on the border near Canada, so he thinks it might have supplies."

"But we're not supposed to go to the border."

Liet told us that once at a meeting a few weeks ago when the possibility of supply trips became inevitable. I think everyone was curious as to why, but no one asked.

"I know."

I furrowed my brow. "Why aren't we supposed to go to the border?"

Pam shrugged.

"How far away is it?"

"Another six to seven hours. If you drive half way, then I'll drive the other half. They weren't too optimistic that we would find anything, though."

I frowned. "How could all of these places be picked clean? There aren't that many of us left."

Pam squinted and stared out the windshield. "I know. But nothing new is being made. There is a finite amount of usable material out here. We'll have to make do with what we can find." She folded the map and put it back. "Let's head out."

I turned the key, and we headed down the road. I was still a little rusty at driving a semi, and Pam had to coach me for the first few miles, but once I got into our cruising speed and didn't have to shift anymore, it was smooth sailing.

After four hours, I relinquished my driving rights, and Pam took over. We fueled up when we needed to and kept a vigilant eye out for zombies. We reached International Falls at two in the morning. Pam parked the vehicle on the outskirts of town and turned off the engine. The full moon illuminated the buildings. We both stared out the windshield. Nothing. Not even a stray cat or dog.

"Do you want to try it?" Pam's voice was barely over a whisper.

"I don't know. We can't be the only ones who know about this place. It might have been looted by both sides right after the outbreak."

"It might have. There's only one way to find out." Pam looked at me.

"True. But it might be better to wait until daylight. I'm not going into an unfamiliar town in the dark." I returned Pam's gaze.

"Good point. You take first shift." She climbed out of the driver's seat into the sleeping cab.

I placed my feet on the dashboard and stared out the window. Pam's rhythmic breathing resounded from the back. I rested my chin on my knees. Staring at the silhouettes of the buildings, I sighed. For a brief second, I thought I saw a flash of light, like a light switch being flipped on and off. I lowered my feet to the floor and leaned forward. I strained my eyes, and out of the corner, I was sure I saw it again. When I tried to look at it directly, I saw nothing. A knot developed in the pit of my stomach, and I was suddenly very uncomfortable. I pulled the gun out of its holster and set it on the dashboard. I rubbed my palms on my thighs. I waited for the flash. Nothing.

All I could think of when I stared out the window was the military base. The lights clicking on and illuminating the horizon were still fresh in my memory, along with the explosions and the zombies. I hoped we weren't walking into a zombie infestation, but the coincidences were too close to be ignored. A voice at the back of my brain told me we should find another place, but logic told me there weren't any other places. I pushed the fear deep into my gut, knowing we didn't have any other choice.

Pam woke a few hours later, and told me to try and get some sleep. The sun skimmed over the horizon, and I told her I would be all right. Pam climbed into the driver's seat and started the engine.

"You ready to chance it?"

"I don't know. Something weird is going on over there."

"Weird? What do you mean?"

"I saw flashes of lights last night while you were sleeping. I don't know what they were from, but I don't like it. I have a strange feeling about this place."

Pam grimaced. "Did you see any people or zombies?"

I shook my head.

"Then I'm sure it will be fine. You have your weapons?"

I fastened my arm swords onto my forearms and pulled the gun off the dashboard.

Pam put the truck in gear and crept forward. Both of us were surprised the streets had been cleared of abandoned vehicles. That either meant someone was still there and had cleared the roads, or they were all dead or zombies, or everyone was lucky and got out when they could. I told myself it was the latter. We drove toward the port, which was near the bridge, and stopped the truck. The bridge had been destroyed in the middle, more than likely by some sort of bomb. The debris was piled in the river. The banks of the river, on both the U.S. and Canadian side, were lined with coils of razor wire and pikes, with bodies tangled in the wire. Well, I told myself, that explains what happened to some of them, but where are the rest? I adjusted my grip on my gun.

"It looks like there are some warehouses over there." Pam pointed to her right. "The gate looks locked, but I can climb over and see if there is anything we can use."

"I don't like this. We should leave."

The voice at the back of my head talked again, telling me something was wrong. It wasn't screaming yet, but it was very insistent.

Pam clicked her tongue. "I'm sure it will be fine. We'll get in and get out. There's no one here. They would have attacked already." She put the truck in gear and got as close to the warehouses as she could. "You wait here and keep and eye out. I'll see what I can get."

I stepped cautiously down from the truck and surveyed the surroundings. The smell of rotting flesh permeated my nostrils. I shivered. I placed my finger on the trigger of my gun. It was quiet. There were no birds or insects, and that worried me. Something splashed in the water, and I spun to face it, my gun up and ready to fire. A small boat with a camera and motion controlled gun ran into the bank. I stepped forward to the razor wire to examine it. A light was affixed to the camera, and it flashed on and off at random intervals. The gun spun on its pivot and clicked as if firing. That explained the light from last night, but it didn't make me feel better. What was it still tracking? It hadn't zeroed in on me, so something else must have triggered its sensors. Maybe it malfunctioned. God, I hoped it malfunctioned.

I glanced back and noticed Pam opening and closing doors. I turned to head back to the truck when the wire in front of me shook violently. I glanced down the length. The bodies, which I had assumed were dead, writhed and tried to free themselves. Why had I assumed they were dead? Just because they weren't moving? Maybe it had been wishful thinking. Either way, it was obvious they weren't dead. I backed toward the truck. A moan echoed through the deserted streets. My heart stopped for a brief second and I closed my eyes. Please tell me I didn't hear that. I reopened them and swallowed hard.

Several creatures emerged from the water and made their way toward me. One of the zombies freed itself from the wire, leaving behind the skin from the top of its thigh to its ankle, and crawled toward me. I fired and the bullet hit it on the top of the head. Several other zombies were able to get loose from the wire. Mechanically, I lined up the sights and rhythmically pulled the trigger. Pow. Pow. Pow. The creatures were down, but close to twenty emerged from the water and approached the fence. I holstered my weapon and flipped out my swords. As much as I would have preferred to stay back and shoot them from a distance, I didn't have the ammo. Plus, with them tangled in the wire, using my swords would be faster.

The moans of the zombies reached a deafening level, and I was afraid it would attract creatures within a two-mile radius. I stepped forward and started swinging. It became a pattern. I used my right arm first, then the left. A small thudding sounded as my sword sliced through their necks, followed by a metal clink when my sword contacted the fence. It turned into a rhythm. Thud, clink. Thud, clink. The moans even took on a musical tone, and a gruesome orchestra echoed through the streets of Industrial Falls. At one point, I looked up and noticed Pam on the opposite end, her katana glistening with blood. We worked systematically, making our way down the length of the fence. We were both covered in blood and rotting flesh and panting before we took a moment to survey the situation. We both killed about forty zombies, but more still poured out of the river.

"Is there anything we can use?" I called over the melee.

Pam nodded. "Yeah. But I don't know how we're going to get it. I couldn't find the keys for the gate." She pulled out her gun and fired several rounds into the horde of zombies.

I glanced at the truck. "We should be able to knock it down, but then we'll have to load it quickly. I don't know how much longer the razor wire is going to hold."

I wasn't going to come this far and leave empty handed. It was a vendetta, and I wasn't going to let the zombies scare me.

Pam nodded and glanced at the truck before running to it. She gunned the engine and rammed it into the gate. The sound of clattering metal was barely audible over the moans, and Pam positioned the trailer of the truck so we could load it. I snapped my blades into place and joined Pam at the warehouses.

The zombies' moans grew louder, and they strained harder against the wire. I found a forklift and raised the gate so we had some protection if the zombies broke loose. I ran to Pam's side.

"What do you want me to do?"

"Grab that other loader and start loading those pallets." She pointed to one of the open storage sheds.

I nodded and ran to the loader. Before turning the engine on, I thought I heard some rattling from a nearby storage room, but I couldn't be sure. I strained my ears, but all I heard was moaning. I shrugged and turned on the machine. I grabbed a few of the pallets and made my way to the truck. Pam loaded another forklift with supplies and filled up the trailer. On my way back, the rattling on the shed door grew louder, and it resounded from some of the other units as well. I approached Pam.

"Do you hear that rattling?"

Pam nodded. "Yeah, there are some zombies trapped inside the buildings. One almost bit me when I threw open the door."

I stared at her wide-eyed.

"Don't worry, he missed me. Just be cautious if you open the doors."

I steered my forklift back to the pile and loaded it as full as I could. There was no way I was going to open any of the doors. I was about finished loading my pallets when a loud scraping sound reached my ears. The zombies succeeded in loosening the razor wire and drug it across the concrete. I couldn't count how many creatures there were. The majority of them were so tangled in the wire, they were being cut to shreds. They all pulled at different speeds, so we had some time before the horde made it to the gate, but then hell was going to break loose. I grabbed one more pallet and headed to the truck. Pam saw the oncoming trouble and loaded her last load. She jumped from her forklift and ran to the one holding up the gate. I abandoned my machine and climbed into the cab of the truck.

Both of us underestimated the time it took for the zombies to reach our location. I threw the truck into gear and was about to stomp on the gas when the group reached the passenger side. Pam jumped into her seat and was closing the door when a half-rotted hand grabbed her leg. She squealed and kicked furiously. I grabbed my gun and aimed. I would have fired, but Pam moved so much, I didn't have a clear shot. Another set of hands grabbed her calves and a mouth latched onto her boot. I started to drive. A few of the creatures lost their grip, giving Pam time to unholster her weapon and use her handgun bayonet to saw off an arm. She kicked at the undead biting her boot, but he wouldn't let go. She stabbed him in the eye with the bayonet and pulled the trigger. Brain and bone splattered the inside of the cab. My ears rang from the bang Pam finally closed the door.

The zombies surrounded the truck, so I floored it and plowed through the onslaught. The razor wire caught the tires and shredded half of them before we were out of the city. I fought to keep the truck under control and sped down the road. I drove for twenty miles before Pam stopped me and told me we were safe. I put the truck in park and stared at her.

What had I been thinking? A vendetta against the zombies? I shook and felt nauseous. We were lucky to make it out alive.

Pam took a deep breath. "Well, I guess that explains why we're not supposed to go to the border."

CHAPTER 9

I actually threw up when I stepped out of the semi and examined the tires. Part of it was from the smell and fluids that covered me from head to toe, but part of it was from fear. I glanced over my shoulder to make sure the zombies hadn't followed us. I knew they were probably on our trail, and even though they were slow, the less time we lingered, the happier I'd be. Pam walked up beside me.

"Good thing we altered these things so they could drive on flats. Otherwise, we'd be stuck out here." She smiled and slapped me on the shoulder. "It's okay. We're clear. There's nothing to worry about."

I tried to smile. It was one thing to stand on a tower and shoot down at the zombies. If you missed, someone was always there to back you up. It was completely different to be right in the middle of a horde. I couldn't believe I kept my cool the way I did. All I could think about at the time was how much I hated the zombies. I hated what they did to my family and friends and the world. I wanted them to pay. Every bullet or slice of my sword was justice. Then, when I was away from them, all I could think about was that I could have been killed. It freaked me out.

"We'll need to get a vehicle up here to tow us back. There are a couple of four-wheelers in the back we can take to the next station."

"Can't we drive it the way it is?"

Pam shook her head. "No, there's too many tires damaged. If we had blown one or two, we'd be fine. It's all right. We'll get the stuff back." She walked to the trailer and opened the door.

We jumped on the four-wheelers and headed down the road.

It took two days to get the truck towed to the nearest station. I spent the time replaying the scenario in my head and becoming more comfortable with my decisions. Yeah, I could've died, but I didn't. That said a lot about my luck and skill. Plus, I couldn't change it, so why worry about it?

The soldiers weren't too optimistic the truck could be repaired since only a few people had the equipment and know-how to change a semi tire. While we waited, it gave Pam and I a chance to take inventory of the goods. We only had time to fill up half the truck, but we loaded several crates of building supplies (boards, bags of concrete mix, wire), some canned goods, and Pam found a crate of exotic nuts. In the end, it turned out they couldn't fix the vehicle, so we transferred the goods to a smaller truck.

"We'll have to send some guys back," Pam said, her hands on her hips as she stared at the semi. "We have the ability to do it in North Platte." She turned to me. "But we should get the supplies back now."

I nodded my agreement and we headed for home.

The trip went well until we crossed the Nebraska border, then I became nervous. Liet had been nice when I left, but I wasn't sure how he would react when we pulled up without the semi. I mean, supplies were already short, and we lost an entire truck. He told us not to go to the border, and even though he didn't tell us specifically why, I still had a feeling he wasn't going to be happy.

We pulled into North Platte and took the truck to the storage yard. A few soldiers milled around, and I noticed one of them run off. I assumed he went to tell Liet we were back. The blood and ooze from the undead dried into my clothes and hair, and they were crunchy. I wanted desperately to take a shower, and I thought about sneaking back to the courthouse, but if Liet was going to be mad, I didn't want Pam to have to face him alone. I paced the grounds until he showed up.

He stared at the truck, his hands on his hips. His jaw muscles tighten. "Where's the truck I sent you out with?"

"We ran into trouble," I explained.

He scowled. "What kind of trouble?"

"Well, zombies. Is there any other kind of trouble out there?"

He took a deep breath and folded his hands over his chest. "Where in the world did you go to run into *that* kind of trouble with zombies?"

I lowered my head. "The Canadian border."

"The border?" Liet tried to keep his voice calm. "I told you not to go to the border!" It was a lost battle.

"We know," Pam interjected. "But we didn't have a choice. Everything has been picked clean."

He pointed a finger at her. "In my office now."

They turned and headed off.

I felt sorry for Pam, but I knew I didn't want to be in the courtroom. I went to my room and climbed into the shower, wondering how bad Liet was chewing out Pam.

When I climbed out of the shower and got dressed, I headed into the kitchen to find something to eat. Liet sat on the couch in the living room. I opened the fridge and stared at him out of the corner of my eye.

"Is everything all right?" I asked cautiously.

"No, everything is not all right." His voice was soft with a menacing tone to it.

My heart skipped a beat. "Is there anything I can do to make it all right?"

He glanced at me and anger flashed through his eyes. "No, there's not." He stood and went into my room.

I followed behind him and watched as he took a stack of CDs off my shelf.

"What are you doing?" I squealed.

"Punishing you. You disobeyed me. You could have been killed. I'm taking something important to you so you'll know how it would feel if I lost you."

I didn't really understand his logic, I mean, they were just CDs, but if it made him feel better, fine. I moved so he could get by. I went back to the kitchen and grabbed some food. I took it to my room and ate, then went to bed.

The next day, while practicing my marksmanship and beheading techniques, Pam found me in the field.

"How did it go last night?" she said, interrupting my workout.

"Fine. He took some CDs. How did it go with you?"

"Not bad. I've been yelled at worse. He wasn't so much worried about the truck as he was about you. Once he knew you were all right, he calmed down a little and listened to the supply problem. Took CDs, huh? That's kind of weird."

I folded up my swords and took a seat on the ground. "Yeah, it was. I was expecting a lot worse. He said something about wanting me to feel what its like to loose something important. I don't know. Whatever."

Pam laughed. "Yeah, I don't think he really knows how to handle a teenager. But you should feel lucky. If you had been a worker, you'd be dead. The only reason he's different with you is because you're family."

Her comment shocked me a little, and I didn't know what to say. That couldn't have been true. He needed the workers. He couldn't haul off and shoot them because they angered him. Could he? Pam motioned for me to follow her, and we climbed the steps into the tower. We sat and stared out over the field. The wind shifted directions and blew the smoke from the funeral pyre into our faces. My eyes watered.

"Well, in a way, I did deserve it, I mean, we did disobey orders. As long as he doesn't start acting like he's my dad, we should be fine."

"Oh, you'd be lucky if he started acting like he was your father. Then, he might show some restraint. I mean, he's your second cousin, which really isn't a relation at all. In many ways, that might make things worse. He's older, and he thinks he's protecting you, so he'll go as far as he thinks he needs to in order to make sure you're safe." She adjusted in her seat. "I've seen it before. He was in the prison system, so the only thing he knows is power. He has power over everyone else in this camp, why wouldn't he have power over you? The more you question that power, the more angry he's going to get. You watch, he'll do strange things to punish you."

Pam was starting to worry me a little. I wasn't exactly sure what she talked about, and I wondered if it had something to do with what he said to her in his office. I decided to press a little further.

"What do you mean? What do you think he'll do to punish me?"

"I don't know, but you'll know when it happens."

I sat silently for a moment, wondering what he could possibly do to punish me. I shook my head. "No, I don't think he'll do anything. I'm not planning on disobeying any more orders."

"You might not have to, he might feel like he needs to exert his power over you."

"Well, there's not much I can do if he does. It's not like I have anywhere else to go."

"You can come back and live in the house with us."

I shook my head. "If he is a control freak and wants to keep me under his thumb, living at your house won't do me any good. He'll find me there. Besides," I smiled, "you just want me there to keep the place clean."

Pam smiled back. "Well, it hasn't been the same since you left." She squinted through the smoke and onto the field. "Looks like we've got about ten looking for a meal."

We stood from our seats and fired at the approaching zombies.

I got home right before dinner. I undid my holster and set it on the table near the door. I thought about what Pam said and didn't immediately notice the door to my bedroom was shut. I walked to the kitchen and pulled out the onion to chop when it hit me. I stepped into the hallway and stared at it for a few moments before approaching it cautiously. Grabbing the handle, I pushed the door open and noticed a girl standing in the middle of the room. She stared at herself in the mirror, holding up one of my shirts. She already had a pair of my jeans on, and one of my CDs played softly in the player.

"What do you think you're doing?" I asked and ran into the room.

The girl jumped and dropped the shirt onto the floor. "Liet told me it was okay," she said softly.

I turned off the stereo. "This isn't Liet's room. Take my clothes off right now."

"What's going on in here?" Liet asked from the door.

I turned to look at him. "Your friend here was going through my stuff."

"So?"

"So? So?" The heat rose into my face. "So this is my stuff. She has no right to touch it."

"Technically," Liet said calmly, "this is my stuff. This is my house. I'm just nice enough to let you use it."

I narrowed my eyes to slits. How dare he allow someone to invade my normal. Without my room, I had no sanctuary, no place safe to go to get away from everything.

"Oh, so that's how it's going to be. Fine, then I'll move out."

The girl took off my pants and feebly handed them to me. I grabbed them, found a bag in my closet, and stuffed them inside. Liet stepped into the room.

"And where do you think you're going to go?"

"Back to the soldier's house. Pam already said I could live there."

Liet took a deep breath. "Now, let's not be hasty. Megan, why don't you wait for me in my room?"

Megan left, and I folded my arms over my chest. I didn't care how much power Liet thought he had over me, this was my space and I was going to fight for it. I knew it would bother him if I left, I had him in a tough position. Like Pam said, he didn't know how to deal with a teenager, so I was going to use that to my advantage.

"There's no need for you to move out. It won't happen again."

"I hope it doesn't."

Liet turned to leave the room, and I slammed the door behind him. I turned back to my belongings and proceeded to put them away. I heard Liet and Megan through the wall, they were fighting, but I couldn't hear what they said. The front door slammed, and Liet came back to my room.

"You know, you weren't very nice to my friend."

I huffed. "Not very nice to your friend? What was I supposed to do? Let her have anything of mine she wanted?"

"She lives in the worker's camp, Krista, she doesn't have a lot of nice things."

"How is that my fault?"

"It's not, but like I said, this stuff is not yours. It's mine. Everything in this town belongs to me. I'm nice enough to let you have it."

I threw the clothes I had in my hands at him. "I don't want your charity," I shouted. "Take it. Take it all back." I grabbed my CDs and dumped them on the floor.

Liet grabbed my arms. "You're being ridiculous. If they make you that happy, then keep them. I won't let anyone else touch them." He released his grip. "I'm going to bed. Clean this mess up." He left the room.

As soon as he left, my knees shook and I collapsed onto the floor. I didn't know what possessed me to stand up to him like that. I didn't know what he was going to do to me. All I knew was I had to keep the one and only place I felt safe. I really didn't care about the things. He could've taken them if he wanted to, but I needed my room. I needed my own space. I took a deep breath and started cleaning up.

* * *

The next morning, I was summoned to a meeting in Liet's office. All of his colonels were there, and he looked particularly sullen. I took a seat in the jury box and waited.

"We have got to do something about our supplies," Liet spoke quietly. "We are running low, and there is nothing left on the East Coast."

I felt contentious, so I threw my arm over the back of the chair and placed my feet on the seat in front of me. "We couldn't have picked the *entire* East Coast clean. There has to be something left."

Liet set his jaw, and the other officers stared at me out of the corners of their eyes.

"There are still places in the east that have supplies, but getting them is not feasible. It would take a lot of time and gas to get to New York or Maine, and we don't even know if they'll have the supplies we need. Even getting gas is going to be an issue. The stations we used before have all dried up. Most of the guards who manned the posts along the way are now working for me and keeping their eyes on the work crews as we extend north and south."

"So then go west," I suggested.

Liet's eyes flashed with anger as he stared at me, then they brightened. "That's a good idea." He turned to his colonels. "There are people who live over there, they know the land. Send out a broadcast. Let them know that anyone willing to help with supplies will be amply rewarded."

The colonels saluted before leaving the building.

I stood to head upstairs.

"I'm glad you decided to stay," Liet said.

I snorted and walked out of the room. I wasn't exactly sure how to take the comment, and his Jekyll and Hyde routine was really getting old.

CHAPTER 10

I switched shifts so I worked nights in the guard tower. I thought that one of the easiest ways to stay on Liet's good side was to stay out of his way. Plus, I wanted to do something constructive to help the community. Since he was so busy during the day, I had plenty of quiet time to sleep. Then, when he came home angry at night or with a girl, I left so he could have his privacy. We attempted to keep things cordial and our family ties strong by having dinner together, talking about the mundane happenings that occurred earlier in the day, then I was off to work.

The schedule worked for weeks, then one day, I was summoned from sleep to meet Liet in his office. It was important. Liet knew I worked all night, and he usually let me sleep. My curiosity was piqued. What was going on? I went down and took my usual seat in the jury box. Three guys stood in front of Liet's desk. He stared down at them, his eyebrows pushed together in contemplation.

One of them looked to be the same age as me, with a round face and bright brown eyes, his face reddened from the sun. He wore a tight pair of Wranglers and a plaid shirt with cowboy boots. He carried a holster on his hip, but it was empty. The guards must have taken his gun when he entered the gate. No one but the soldiers were allowed to have weapons.

Pam explained that to me my second day in North Platte. She never told me why, but it wasn't hard to figure out. Guns were power. Those who possessed them had the power, those who didn't, didn't. It was your typical tyrannical setup.

One of the other two with him was older, probably in his late twenties. He was stick thin, and his jeans hung loosely around his legs. His boots were faded and worn, and the sun tanned his skin. The other guy was a younger version of the older, although not much older than I was, so I assumed they were brothers.

"So, now, tell me why I should trust you? You don't even look over eighteen."

"Age has nothing to do with experience. You need someone to get you supplies in the West, I can get you supplies." His voice was low, quiet. I noticed a faint accent, a subtle twang that wasn't quite Southern but close.

"And that is a guarantee?"

The guy shrugged. "I can't guarantee anything, but I know where your chances are the best."

Liet's eyes narrowed. "I suppose that will have to do." He straightened some folders on his desk. "Give me a few days. I need to find someone to send with you."

I slid forward in my chair. "I'll go."

Liet snorted. "I don't think so."

I stood from my seat. "Why not?"

"Because I need you here."

I stepped out of the jury box and up to his desk. I wanted to scream at him from across the room and stamp my feet, but I didn't want to embarrass myself in front our guests.

"For what? So I can shoot more zombies from the guard tower? Why did you call me down here if you weren't thinking about sending me?"

Liet leaned forward and lowered his voice to a whisper. "I wanted you to see that someone from the West answered our call. I have no intention of sending you into harm's way."

I lowered my voice to match his. "C'mon. All of your soldiers are busy watching the workers. You have no one to send and you know it. I'm the only one who can go. Pleeeease?" I folded my hands under my chin.

Liet sighed heavily and sat back in his chair. "Fine. But you had better be careful while you're out there." He turned to the guys. "This is Krista. She'll be going with you."

I nodded to the group and went upstairs to pack. This was the best news in weeks. Even though Liet and I were getting along better, I still dreaded every evening I had to see him for dinner. I never knew which Liet was going to show up, the nice one or the mean one. This way, I didn't have to worry about it.

Liet followed me up and stood in my doorway, his arms crossed over his chest. "I'm not very happy about this situation."

I rolled my eyes. "I know, but you have nothing to worry about. I can take care of myself."

"I realize that, Krista, but there are dangers in the West that you've never experienced. Dangers you can't even imagine."

"And I'm sure those guys will make sure I'm safe. Liet, this is the perfect opportunity for me to learn how to be on my own. I'm going to have to be eventually, you know."

"Not if I have anything to say about it," he mumbled under his breath. "How do you know those guys will make sure you're safe? You know nothing about them. They could be rapists."

"I have a gun. And swords. If any of them try anything, I'll cut them."

"I don't want you getting too close to them. Keep it professional. You don't need to share *anything* about your life. Hear me?"

"I hear ya." I grabbed my bag and headed downstairs to the waiting trucks.

I really hated when Liet tried to be the good guy. I think in some weird messed up way he really did care about me, but it was the same caring a serial killer showed their victims before they tortured and murdered them. What they thought was love, wasn't. Kindness and sympathy were *not* his strong suits, but both of us knew he had to try and make a show of it. Even serial killers know how to function in society.

Liet contracted with the guys to bring back a tanker of gas and a semi half full of food and half full of construction supplies. I rode in the semi, and the brothers were in the tanker. Liet showed up to say goodbye, and as I climbed into the cab, he grabbed me gently by the arm.

"Please be careful. I don't know what I would do if I lost you."

I smiled, it was probably more of a smirk, and he released his grasp.

We drove to the gate and stopped at the tower. The guard handed the guy's gun through the window.

"I hope you took good care of it."

The guard answered by turning and opening the gate. My heart rate increased. I was both excited and nervous about heading into the West. Memories of the trip to Industrial Falls entered my mind. There had been a fair amount of undead up there, but nothing compared to what was supposedly in the West. We were outnumbered at least a thousand to one, and that was a conservative estimate. No one really knew how many zombies there actually were. I envisioned all the zombies traveling in a massive pack, a writhing ball of rotting flesh and snapping jaws, millions of them clumped together looking for food. Even though I knew that vision wasn't true, it still made me shudder.

As soon as we were a few miles past the gate, the guy let out a sigh.

"Glad to finally be out of that place." He held his hand out. "We haven't been formally introduced. Quinn."

I took his hand. "Krista."

"Nice to meet you." He placed his hand back on the wheel. "How long have you lived in North Platte, Krista?"

"A few months. I'm not sure exactly how many. Time is weird out here."

He chuckled. "Yeah, it's hard to keep track of it when you don't have a calendar. Where did you live before?"

"Before North Platte or before the zompocalypse?"

"Both."

"Well, before North Platte, it was Florida. Before that, Oregon. You?"

"Wyoming born and raised."

"How old are you?"

"Eighteen. And you?"

"Seventeen."

The conversation drifted into silence, and I stared out the window. After a few hours, a sign on the road welcomed us into Wyoming. The landscape changed from flat burned out fields into rolling hills with an occasional zombie herd in the distance.

"How many zombies do you think there are?" I turned to look at Quinn.

He shrugged. "Hard to say. Where we live, they don't bother us much."

"Where is that?"

He flashed me a smile. "Now that is a secret."

Something in the pit of my stomach fluttered and my skin grew hot. Quinn's entire face beamed, and his eyes squinted a little. I could see the emotion in his smile, feel its warmth and sincerity. It had been a long time since I had seen a smile like that. My face flushed, and I turned away.

I suddenly became very self-conscious. I had always been on the thin side. Even at seventeen, I had very little curves. My hips were flat, and my chest only had a hint of breasts. It never really bothered me before. I was only fifteen when the first attacks happened, and then all I wanted in Florida was to be left alone. I liked boys, but I also read a lot of books about serial killers. In Junior High, I constantly scrutinized their actions and intentions. Like the girls, they started to think I was weird and avoided me. In Florida, I couldn't do it. I couldn't be "normal." The world was filled with zombies. Why would I care who was going with who to the dance? Why were we even having dances? Being out in a truck in zombie-infested land changed things. Was it the ideal place to find love? Of course not, but it was the new reality. If it was going to happen, I couldn't think of a better place.

I averted my gaze to my lap and cleared my throat. "I understand. You don't want us to find you."

He smiled again. "Sort of."

I stared. "How long have you lived out here?"

"All my life."

"Why didn't you leave when the attacks started?"

"Didn't have to. We weren't bothered by the zombies. Still aren't, really."

"How?"

Quinn shrugged. "I guess we're too far off their radar."

"Are there a lot of you out here?"

He shook his head. "Not really. Most of the population fled to where it was safe. Can't really blame them. It's not an easy existence out here."

My forehead wrinkled in confusion. "Then why do you do it?"

"Because it's better than the alternative."

Quinn slowed the truck down and turned off onto an exit. We pulled into a gas station, and Quinn scanned the area. A few zombies lurched on the horizon, but they wouldn't make it to our position for a while. The other truck pulled up to the pump next to us, and the younger of the two brothers climbed onto the roof of the cab. He signaled for me to open my door.

"If you get on top," he said, "you can see for miles. It gives them piece of mind and you the ability to watch their back."

I climbed on top of the truck.

Quinn got out and started fueling the truck without shutting it off. He and the other guy conversed with each other while they filled up, and I kept an eye on the approaching creatures. I found it odd that the guys could be so relaxed and talk like they weren't being hunted. What if there were undead in the gas station? What if they surprised them from the other direction? There was a lot to be on the lookout for. The zombies might be slow, but there were a lot of them, and they always seemed to pop out from the most unlikely place. I guess that was how comfortable they felt with us on the roof. That was a lot of trust to have in someone. I was slightly flattered.
    I didn't draw an easy breath until I was back in the truck and on the highway. Even though I was on the roof, well out of harm's way, I was still scared. I was very nervous for Quinn and his friend. What if one of us froze? Or missed the shot? I tried to put it out of my mind. It was part of life out here that I had to get used to. I volunteered to drive, but Quinn said he was fine. The landscape changed again from rolling hills into expansive valleys bordered by rocky mountains. The sky turned a deeper blue, and the air was crisp and cool. I cracked my window and sucked in a deep breath. I closed my eyes and focused on the breeze as it blew through my hair. I couldn't remember the last time I smelled air so clean. I was about to fall asleep when the truck bumped me awake. I opened my eyes and

looked at an expansive city before me. Quinn stopped the truck in front of a construction yard surrounded by a chain link fence.

"Where are we?"

"Casper." He jumped out and opened the gate.

I stared in amazement as we drove into the construction yard. The supplies were covered in a thick layer of dust, and there was enough to last North Platte a year. I jumped down from the cab, my mouth open. It was too good to be true. There was no way this stuff was still sitting there, untouched. No one needed this? That was hard to believe. But I wasn't one to question good fortune. I turned when the second truck squealed to a halt and Quinn closed the gate. He stood next to me, his hands on his hips. The two guys from the other truck joined them.

"Krista, this is Kyle and his brother, Bill," Quinn gestured toward them.

I nodded.

They shook my hand before heading off to look for zombies. I thought it was a little odd they didn't say anything, but we had a job to do. There was no reason to stall with the undead roaming around. I turned back to the equipment.

"I can't believe it," I stammered. "They haven't been touched in years."

Quinn nodded. "Yeah, a lot of places are like this."

"Why haven't you taken any of the supplies?"

"Don't need 'em." He stepped forward and climbed into a loader.

"How can you not need them?" I called after him.

His hand paused on the key. "'Cause we don't." He smiled, and the loader roared to life.

I shook my head in confusion, then turned away to see what I could load.

It took us a couple of hours to fill the truck with construction supplies. When we finished, we stopped at the first grocery store we found. We left the engines running as we stared through the glass windows at the front of the store. I hadn't actually seen a zombie since we arrived, and that worried me. Again, the trip to Industrial Falls crossed my mind.

"There should be a loading dock around back, but I want to make sure we're not walking into a nest." Quinn put the truck in park and grabbed a shotgun from behind the seat. "You and I will sweep the store, and Kyle and Bill will stay outside and watch our backs. Cool?"

My stomach knotted. I glanced from him to the store and back to him before nodding. I pulled my gun out of the holster and opened the door.

Quinn let the other two know what we were doing, then we stepped into the store. The air was humid and thick with the smell of rotten meat and moldy fruits and vegetables. Pam taught me the fastest and safest way to clear an area was together. You stood shoulder to shoulder and pointed your guns in opposite directions. That way, you always had a 360-degree view of what's around you. Clearing a building is not like what you see in the movies. You don't split up and meet in the middle. That's a good way to get shot.

Quinn and I held our weapons in front and made our way to the far end of the store. I told myself to take deep breaths and relax. We started with the furthest aisle, and while Quinn peeked around the corner, I watched his back. Empty. We hurried to the next aisle. Quinn peeked around the corner. Empty. We were about to move forward, when a glass jar shattered on the floor, followed by a low moan. My body tensed, and I physically willed myself not to pee my pants. Quinn fired a shot into the aisle. A thumping sound echoed through the store, and I risked a glance around the corner. A zombie lay crumpled on the tile.

"This one is the only one I've seen so far, but there might be more. I don't think his moan was loud enough to alert the others, but let's do a quick sweep of the storage area."

I followed him to the back, and we stepped through the swinging doors. The room was dark, and the smell of rotting food was overpowering. I gagged. Quinn grabbed some flashlights and batteries from the store. He handed one to me. By that point, adrenaline kicked in and I felt pretty good. If any zombies wanted to mess with me, they were going to get a face full of lead. I clicked the light on, and we stepped into the room. I flashed the beam into a corner and illuminated three zombies. With three shots, I dispatched them before they knew I was there.

"Nice shooting," Quinn whispered.

I couldn't help but smile and felt the confidence wash over me. We finished our sweep without running into any more creatures.

"It's clear," he said. "I saw the cargo door in this corner over here," he pointed to his right, "so if you want to bring the truck around, I'll get it open."

I nodded and headed outside. As I stepped into the sun, my gait had a little more snap to it and the knot in my stomach dissapeared. Not only had Quinn given me a compliment, but I just killed three zombies with only three shots using a flashlight. That was pretty freaking good. I realized at that moment I didn't need to worry about the creatures, they needed to worry about me. I cautioned myself about being cocky, but I thought I deserved to bask in my awesomeness for a few minutes.

We filled the rest of the truck with the nonperishable food items we found in the store. It took us another couple of hours, then we went to fill the tanker. Quinn led us to a station on the outskirts of town. The place was surrounded by a chain link fence, so we didn't have to worry about zombies. While Kyle and

Bill filled the truck, Quinn and I kept watch. The sun set as we finished loading the truck, and Quinn suggested we find a place to stay for the night. We drove to the center of town, and he parked in front of the jail. I stared at him.

"The jail? Why here?"

"It's the safest place in town. Everything is divided into sections, so even if there are zombies in there, they're trapped and can be taken down easily. Plus, there are beds and restroom facilities. Where else do you suggest we go?"

I thought Quinn's reasoning sounded logical, and I didn't know any place, so I trusted his judgment. "How are we going to get in? Aren't the doors locked?"

"Most of the locks are triggered by electricity. We hotwire the system, and the doors will pop right open."

"How are you going to do that?"

He smiled. "We have our ways."

The outside doors weren't an issue, they were unlocked, so we headed to the second floor where the holding cells were located. We opened the stairway door onto the admittance desk, and Bill walked around to the backside. He pulled what looked like a car battery out of his bag. He popped open a panel on the underside of the desk and attached the wires. With a flip of a switch, the doors buzzed and popped open. I looked at Quinn and smiled. I was impressed. We cleared the area, then picked a cell.

The holding cells were a combination of the new and the old. They had concrete walls with two bunk beds and a toilet and sink in the corner. The doors were black iron bars. There were no windows, and there were five cells on both sides of the hall.

"Now, the doors won't lock when you close them," Quinn explained. "So you'll have to tie them closed with this." He handed me a piece of wire.

"Isn't someone going to stay awake and keep guard?"

"What for? Zombies are terrible at climbing stairs, and we've secured the area. Even if they do get past the two doors and into this room, you're protected in your cell. You can still shoot the zombies, but they can't get you."

All of the confidence I felt earlier drained out of my body. Visions of being trapped in a tiny room, alone, with zombies reaching for me flashed through my mind.

"What if a hundred of them show up? None of us have the ammo to stave off that kind of attack."

Quinn shook his head. "There won't be that many. They don't even know we're here. You'll be fine."

I took a deep breath and glanced at the doors we just came through. The zombies would have to come up to the second floor, make it through the door at the top of the stairs, then get through the two doors that had been wired shut. It was secure enough. It had to be.

"Would you feel better if I stayed with you?"

"No," I answered quickly. Perhaps a bit too quickly because Quinn took a step back and held up his hands. "I'll be fine."

"Okay. I'm in the cell right next to you if you need anything."

I entered the cell and closed the door. I twisted the wire around the bars and made one last check of the hall. I climbed into bed, setting my gun on my chest. I stared at the door for a long time before eventually falling asleep.

CHAPTER 11

A soft thumping broke me from my dreamless sleep. I rolled over and placed the pillow over my head. For a brief second, I thought I was back home and Mom knocked on the door to wake me for school. Then, I remembered where I was and sat straight up in bed. As the effects of sleep wore off, I realized the thumping was a pounding and it came from the stair doors. I rushed to the cell door, my gun in my hand, and untwisted the wire. My heart felt like it beat in my ears, and I hoped I wouldn't run into anything rotting in the hall. I glanced around the corner and noticed the guys, so I joined them.

"Started a few minutes ago," Quinn said.

"How many are there?"

Bill shrugged. "Hard to say. Could be one, could be ten."

"What are we going to do?" It annoyed me that the guys looked so calm. There was nothing to be calm about. Yeah, the creatures couldn't get in, but we also couldn't get out. There was one door, and corpses blocked it.

"We're going to have some breakfast, then we're going to leave." Quinn turned to his bag and pulled out a propane-fueled burner. He grabbed some cans of hash and opened them into a pan.

I stared after them as they made themselves comfortable around the admissions desk. I wanted to scream, pull my hair, something, to get them to realize the danger we were in.

"They're not going to get in," Kyle reassured me. "C'mon. Have something to eat."

I fought back the urge to shake him. He hadn't spoken two words to me the day before, and now he was trying to reassure me? With who knows how many zombies at the door? How did they know the zombies weren't going to get in? If there were enough of them, and they pounded for long enough, they *might* get in. I didn't know a lot about them, but I began to think they were crazy. Either that or on drugs. Either way, they freaked me out.

The smell of salty meat and potatoes reached my nostrils, and my basic needs took over. I took a deep breath and stepped up to the desk. Quinn handed me a plate and fork, and I ate greedily. When we finished, we sat silently for a moment. The pounding still echoed through the room, but it lost some strength. Kyle leaned back in his seat and rubbed his stomach.

"Do we have anything else? I'm still hungry."

"Yeah," Bill said. "I could eat some more."

My stomach still growled, and I nodded my agreement.

Quinn pulled out two cans of beef stew and heated them. As it cooked, I took a seat. I figured if we were going to be trapped, might as well be comfortable. Quinn handed me my plate full of food. I burned my mouth as I shoveled in the contents. I cursed under my breath, and Kyle handed me a bottle of water. I took a quick drink and turned back to my food. After a few minutes, I realized the guys stared at me.

"What?"

They averted their gaze to their plates.

"What?"

Kyle chuckled. "I haven't seen anyone eat like that since I was fourteen."

I rolled my eyes. "You guys are eating just as much as I am."

"Yeah, but not as fast," exclaimed Bill. "Are you even chewing?"

I set down my empty plate. "How are we going to get out of here? They've blocked our only exit."

Quinn forked a hunk of meat into his mouth. "No they haven't. That's the beautiful thing about jails. There's always a hidden set of stairs that the guards can use in the case of an emergency."

I glanced at each of them, convinced they were messing with me. "Oh, yeah, then where is it?"

Quinn pointed to the floor by his feet. "Didn't you notice the brass ring?"

I looked where he indicated and sure enough, there was a brass ring and the faint outline of a door. I cursed myself in my mind. I should have been more observant. One of the first rules Pam taught me about going into any situation was to know where the escape routes were. I handed the plate to Quinn and waited for them to finish.

When we were done, we went back to our cells and packed our things. I kept my gun in my hand, despite the fact the guys told me I didn't need it. Bill pulled the brass handle on the floor, and the door swung open. He shined a flashlight into the hole. A ladder led down to the first floor, and I could see the light from outside.

"This should lead us to the alley, then to the street where we parked the trucks," Bill explained. "I'll head down and make sure the coast is clear." He grabbed a rifle from his belongings and stepped down the ladder.

A few minutes passed before his face reappeared at the bottom. "Coast's clear."

The rest of us followed him down, through the door, and into the trucks. Quinn started the engine, and I glanced out the window. A line of undead headed inside the building, each attempting to climb the stairs. There were quite a few of them, probably close to thirty. How did they knew we were in the building? A few of them turned when they heard the trucks, but they were too slow to catch us. The convoy pulled out of town and onto the highway. I took a deep breath and holstered my gun when we were a couple miles out of town. I sank down into the chair and placed a hand on my forehead. My head thumped, almost as if the zombies pounded on my brain. I was glad we got out of there safely and alive, and I thought maybe the guys weren't on drugs or crazy. Maybe they actually knew what they were doing.

"You don't encounter zombies very often, do you?" Quinn asked.

I shook my head. "We see our fair share. We like to take care of them from a distance."

"They're not as bad as you think."

I shot him a look. "Uh, yeah they are. They destroyed almost the entire population of the U.S."

He chuckled. "Well, they are that bad, but you don't have to worry about them quite as much as you do. Sure there are a lot of them, but they don't move very fast, and they are easy to take down. I've seen one person surrounded by fifty zombies come out unscathed. I've seen people walk right through a field of them, and they don't even know they're there."

"I've seen people get eaten alive," I spoke quietly.

Quinn frowned. "Yeah, I've seen that, too. But my point is, as long as you use your head and stay calm, you're going to survive."

"Have you ever seen anyone turn?"

Quinn was quiet for a moment. "Yeah."

"What's it like?"

He glanced at me. "It's nothing you ever want to experience for yourself."

I opened my mouth to ask another question when something bumped against the driver's side of the truck. I sat up and tried to look out Quinn's window.

"What was that?"

"Zombie." He pointed out the windshield.

I turned to where he indicated, and my mouth fell open. A horde of undead—close to two hundred strong—slowly made its way down the highway. Quinn accelerated and plowed through the group at 75 miles per hour. I leaned forward to get a better view of the destruction. Bodies clanged against the grill, and arms and legs were ripped from their torsos. A few sprays of blood and other fluids flew over the hood and spattered the windshield. Quinn turned on the wipers and smeared the goo across the glass. The smell of decay permeated the cab.

We were through the horde in a few moments. The stench of rotting flesh was overpowering. The bile rose into my throat. Quinn squirted cleaner onto the windshield and swiped as much of the gore off as he could.

"We'll have to stop and get this cleaned off," he said. "Just be careful when you get out. Sometimes those buggers grab onto the side."

I stared at him in disbelief. "You know, there is a way to avoid that." I raised my eyebrows as Quinn looked at me.

"Not really," he smiled. I could tell he enjoyed what he just did. "You ever go driving with your parents?"

"Of course."

"Well, you know how sometimes on the road you hit these clouds of bugs and they coat your car like rain?"

I nodded.

"Well, the zombies are kinda like those clouds. There's really no way to avoid them and they stick to your car like glue."

We stopped at the next gas station and took a quick glance around. As I climbed onto the cab roof to stand lookout, I slipped in some of the blood and guts and proceeded to throw up. I couldn't help it. Between the smell and the slick texture, it came up. Quinn told me to climb back into the truck. I crawled into the seat and pulled my knees up to my chest. Both Bill and Kyle stood guard for him while he cleaned off the gore. I felt lightheaded, and the blood on my clothes nauseated me even more. Without thinking, I pulled off my shirt and pants and threw them out the window. I wanted them off and as far away from me as possible. I dug through my bag, looking for new clothes, when Quinn climbed into his seat. His face instantly turned red. My face flushed, too, and I couldn't climb into the sleeper fast enough.

"Sorry," he muttered and put the truck into gear.

I pulled on my sweats and lay down. A hand reached through the curtain with a bottle of water.

"This will help you feel better."

I took it from him and sipped at the liquid.

"We should be in North Platte in about four hours."

I sat up and poked my head through the curtain. "How often do you run into hordes like that?"

Quinn shrugged. "Depends."

I grimaced. "God, that was awful."

"Just wait till we have to wash it off. You ain't seen nothin, yet."

I pictured the severed limbs, blood, and pus, and my stomach lurched. I kept the vomit down, but became lightheaded. I shrank behind the curtain and lay back on the bed. I closed my eyes and swore I heard Quinn chuckling.

We stopped in a town called Pine Bluffs, which was on the Wyoming/Nebraska border. We hooked a hose up to the first hydrant we could find and turned on the water. Bill and Kyle kept an eye out for zombies, and Quinn and I cleaned the truck. He handed me a shovel.

"What do you want me to do with that?"

"After I spray it with the hose, you'll use this to pry any parts loose the water didn't get."

I looked at him in disgust.

"Do you want to use the hose?"

"Yes."

"Fine." He handed me the hose and I aimed it at the truck.

I turned the stream on, and even though it wasn't full power, it was still enough to knock me back. I staggered but didn't go down. The hose went a little crazy in the process, and I accidentally sprayed Bill and Kyle. They didn't say anything, but their looks told me they weren't happy. I gained a foothold and aimed the water at the vehicle. Water and zombie fluid splashed back and hit me in the face. I instantly snapped my mouth shut and froze in shock. Quinn lost it. He laughed so hard he doubled over. My eyes narrowed to slits.

"You think that's funny?"

"You should...you should see the look on your face!" He opened his mouth to say something else, but laughter poured out.

My face flushed, and I set my jaw. I turned the hose off and ran to the truck. I grabbed a handful of blood and something clear and stringy and smeared it in Quinn's hair. He stopped laughing and stared at me.

"You think it's funny now?"

Quinn wiped the gunk out of his hair and flipped it onto the ground. As he stared at me, a smile crept onto his lips. He was planning something. I waited to see what it was.

When he moved for the hose, I had a good notion what ran through his mind. I went after him, but he grabbed the hose first and turned on the water. He positioned it so it ricocheted off the truck and hit me. I was soaked. I stood there, my arms out to my side with water dripping off me, and I stared at him. I went to retaliate, to throw a shovel full of zombie parts at him, but Bill told us we didn't have time for such nonsense. Quinn repositioned the stream and washed the truck off. I picked up the shovel and took care of the bits the water missed, making it a point to throw the goop in Quinn's direction.

Quinn had his back to me as I dislodged an arm, and something from under the truck grabbed my calf. I squealed and fell onto the ground. Nails black with decay and soot tore through my sweats and into my flesh. I jerked my leg back, hoping to get free of the thing, but all it did was slice deeper into my flesh and tear a bigger hole in my pants. I grabbed the fingers and pried them off my leg. The skin was cold and the bones snapped like dry twigs. When I was free, I jumped up and backed away. The creature pulled itself from underneath the truck. It was a head, torso, and arm. The zombie opened its mouth to moan, but before it could get it out, I swiped its head off with the shovel. Pain burned through my leg and dots danced in front of my eyes. I had to sit before I fell. Quinn raced to my side and knelt.

"Are you all right? Let me take a look at it."

Reluctantly, I lifted my pant leg. I didn't look, I was too afraid.

Quinn stood and placed a hand on his hip, staring at me. "We need to get that cleaned out. You don't want it to get infected."

The blood rushed out of my head, but I kept my face hard. I didn't want him to think I was a weenie. I lowered my pant leg.

"I assume you have a First Aid kit in the truck?"

He nodded.

"Let's finish this, then I'll worry about it on the road. It's going to get covered in more crap. No sense cleaning it out twice."

It took us another ten minutes to get the truck washed off. Blood dripped down my leg and I had to limp, but we finished. Even though my sweats covered the wound, they were still soaking wet and smeared with blood—mine and the zombies'. When we climbed into the truck, Quinn handed me the First Aid kit from under his seat. I pulled up my pant leg. I winced as the material stuck and narrowed my eyes. I didn't have a choice, I had to look at it. Four crescent-moon-shaped holes penetrated my leg right above the ankle. I took the plastic tweezers from the kit and pulled a black nail from one of the wounds. I reminded myself to breath as I threw it out the window. I poured the entire bottle of alcohol onto the wound and held my breath as it stung the area clean. The thought that in twenty-four hours I was going to be a slow-moving craver of flesh crossed my mind, but I told myself that I had to get bit. I coated the punctures with some ointment then wrapped gauze around my leg. I crawled into the back and found a pair of dirty jeans to put on, throwing my sweat pants out the window. Quinn stared at me from the corner of his eye.

"From what I could see, it looks like you'll be all right."

I tried to find that reassuring, but it was difficult. I rested my head on the back of the seat and closed my eyes. Taking deep breaths, I tried to calm my shaking and force the bad thoughts out of my head.

By the time we reached the gate at North Platte, I felt better. My leg didn't hurt quite as much, and I didn't crave human flesh. The guard stopped us, and Quinn rolled down his window.

"What business do you have in North Platte?"

"We're delivering supplies."

The guard looked at me. He smiled when he recognized me. "Found some stuff, did ya?"

I nodded.

"Good. Things were getting a bit slim. I'll need you to step out of the truck and head to the inspection area."

Again, the color drained out of my face and my stomach fluttered. "What? Why?" When Pam and I went out, we didn't have to be inspected. I guess they assumed nothing was going to attack us in the east.

"You know the rules, Krista. No one gets into the city without being inspected."

Quinn and I stared at each other for a minute before pushing open our doors. Kyle and Bill joined us, and we made our way to the inspection area. I glanced over my shoulder and watched the guards pull the trucks through the gate and head toward the storage yard.

The inspection area was between two guard towers next to the trench. There were two lines, one for men and one for women, and they were separated by solid green plastic fencing. It was pretty difficult to see through when you were in there, but if the sun hit it just right, you could see the silhouettes of the men behind you. Not that I looked, I happened to notice. The fences were about 25 feet long, and the workers were lined against the wall and hosed down while another guard inspected every inch of them. Right before the fence were outfitters tents, where we were expected to strip down. A shift just finished, so we took our places at the backs of our respected lines. As I got closer to the tent, my skin felt hot and prickly and the voice at the back of my head told me to run. I knew, of course, that if I did, they would shoot me on sight. I told myself that it was going to be all right. When I stepped under the tarp, I followed the lead of all the other women and took my shoes off, then stripped down to my underwear. I visibly shook at this point, both from the cold and fear, and I folded my arms across my chest to keep my appendages under control. The group in front of me was sprayed with the hose.

Reflexively, they tried to block it. The guard then made her rounds. After a few minutes, they came back into the tent and pulled their clothes on. Another set went in. Two more and it would be my turn. I glanced down at the bandage on my leg. It was like a flashing beacon.

Finally, it was my turn to step in front of the wall. I was about to take my place when the inspecting guard stopped me.

"Whoa," she said and placed a hand on my shoulder. "What's up with your calf?" She pointed at my leg.

"Nothing," I squeaked. "Just a little scratch."

She pursed her lips and bent down. With one quick motion, she ripped the gauze off.

I sucked in a deep breath and almost fell over backward.

"You get grabbed by something?"

Tears stung my eyes. This was the end. I knew it. I was going to be led from the hose line to the firing line. I nodded slowly.

"Did it bite you?"

I shook my head.

"Okay," the guard said, surprisingly compassionate. "After I check the rest of you, this girl here will take you to the hospital."

It wasn't until the cold water hit my body that her words registered in my brain. She said hospital, not firing line. As I stood there, dripping wet and shivering, I couldn't help but feel a sense of relief. When we got the okay, we went back to the tent and pulled on our clothes. A different soldier escorted me to the hospital.

We went directly to the Emergency Room and immediately saw a doctor. He told me to sit on the gurney while he examined my leg. Without saying a word, he pulled out a needle and jammed it into my shoulder. The actual needle didn't hurt, but when he pumped the liquid in, I thought my arm would catch fire.

"What is that?" I yelped.

"Tetanus and an antibiotic." He pulled out the needle and patted me. "You're good to go."

"That's it?"

He smiled. "Yep. That's it. Try to be more careful next time."

I hopped off the gurney and walked to the courthouse where Quinn and the guys waited for me. They smiled as I approached.

"Did they say anything?" Quinn asked.

I shook my head. "Nope. Just gave me a shot and sent me on my way."

We headed up the stairs. I wasn't even nervous about seeing Liet. After what I went through, talking to him was going to be a breeze.

He sat behind his desk, conversing with a soldier I recognized from the gate. I assumed he informed the General of what we brought back.

Liet glanced at us as we approached. "Sounds like you had a fruitful trip."

"Everything went as we promised," Quinn said.

"Fabulous. I assume you'll want to freshen up before you head out on your next adventure. Krista, show them upstairs."

I turned to face them and pointed to the door near the back of the room. They headed toward it and I followed behind them. We got upstairs and I showed them into the apartment. The first thing we all wanted to do was shower. I was lucky, I had my own, and I left Quinn, Bill, and Kyle in the living room arguing over which one was going to go first.

CHAPTER 12

I was called into Liet's office seconds after getting out of the shower. I stood before his desk with my arms folded over my chest. I still felt dirty and violated. Even though I knew the process was for everyone's safety, it was still humiliating. I wondered if there was a better way.

"I see you were quite successful in the West."

"Yeah. You'd be amazed how much stuff is out there."

He smiled. "Would I?" He swung his feet onto his desk. "Well, it seems to me since there is such a plethora of goods to be had, we might as well stock our shelves. Besides, it's only a matter of time before Florida comes to us begging for supplies."

I tried to keep my excitement to a minimum. "You want me to go out again?"

"I'm still very short handed."

"How much do you want me to get?"

Liet shrugged one shoulder. "As much as you can. I'll send two more trucks. One for fuel and one for anything else you think we need. When you fill those, I'll send more." He pulled his feet from the desk and leaned on his elbows. "You'll leave in two days."

I nodded, trying to suppress a smile. Despite the danger and the vast hordes of zombies, I was excited I could go back out to the West. Life was so much simpler out there. All I had to worry about was zombies. I didn't have to worry about random girls in my room or Liet being overprotective; I just had to keep an eye on the horizon.

Quinn was incentive to go out, too. He was caring and kind and really cute. He knew his way around the West. I felt safe with him. The other two weren't bad, either. They were quiet but knew what they were doing. Unlike Liet, I didn't have to worry about what I said or if the evil twin would show up. Quinn and the guys were always nice.

The guys were seated at the kitchen table and smiled as I entered the apartment. I walked up to them, barely able to contain my excitement.

"Liet would like us to leave in two days and fill up two more trucks," my voice was slightly higher pitched than normal. I hoped it didn't annoy them, it kind of annoyed me. My face went red.

Quinn nodded. "Sure. What do we do until then?"

I shrugged. "There's not much to do. I usually bide my time by taking a shift in the guard towers or sitting in my room listening to music. I've found both are very relaxing."

Quinn smiled. "Well, I'm pretty sure Liet wouldn't want me hanging out in your room, so if you go to the guard tower, I'll join you. If you don't mind."

My face turned even redder, and I let out a nervous chuckle. I glanced at the other two.

Bill held up his hands. "Not me. I'm going to see what I can find in town. Kyle, you comin' with me?"

"Yep. Beats sittin' around here!"

I nodded and headed to my room to get boxes of ammunition for my gun. I wasn't surprised Bill and Kyle didn't want to come with us. They seemed to like to do their own thing. I hoped they didn't get bored.

Quinn and I took the late shift since that was my normal schedule. We had dinner with Liet, which was very uncomfortable. Liet asked Quinn about the West and supplies, but there was something about the way he looked at him that made my skin crawl. It was kind of a sideways glance, and his lips would curl up into a snarl when Quinn wasn't looking. When Quinn looked up, though, a smile was always on Liet's face. I ushered him out the door as quickly as I could.

We climbed to the top of the tower and took a seat. I placed my hands on the rail and stared at the horizon. The funeral fire had been stoked since I'd been gone, and greasy black smoke billowed through the sky. Quinn coughed and rubbed his eyes.

"You get used to it after a while," I explained.

Quinn spit over the side of the tower. "Why would you want to?"

"It's better than it was when I first got here. They were letting the bodies rot in the field."

Quinn wrinkled his nose. "Still, nothing beats the fresh air of where I live."

I sighed. He was right; there wasn't anything better than the fresh air of the West. I could actually breathe out there, my clothes weren't covered in a thin layer of ash, and I didn't reek of smoke. Everything seemed clean.

I heard shuffling to my left, so I grabbed the searchlight and swung it in that direction. The beam landed on a zombie, and I raised the rifle to my shoulder. I fired one shot, and the creature fell. I panned the light around to make sure there weren't any others. Quinn stood next to me, his gun cradled in his arms.

"Did you ever, in your wildest imagination, believe you would be here?"

I huffed. "Sometimes I *still* don't believe it. It started two years ago. Just two years." I angled the light into the field and sat down. "It all seems so long ago. Like it was a different life."

Quinn turned to face me and leaned against the rail. "Yeah."

I stared at him for a moment, then turned in my seat so my back was to him. The heat rose in my face. I don't know why, but he made me blush and my stomach flutter. It wasn't like we talked about anything embarrassing. I hoped he didn't notice. It really bothered me that he affected me like that. I wondered if Mom went through the same thing when she met Dad. My mind drifted to the day when Mom was killed. I would have assumed that after so long, I could forgive them, or at least understand why they did what they did. But as I stared out into the black field, I hated them more. If they were still alive, I wouldn't be in this mess. I would be someplace safe without a crazy second cousin trying to control my life. I lowered my head. A tear dropped onto my cheek, but I wiped it away quickly.

I thought about Pearl and wondered how she was doing. Then, I thought about Tanya. I was actually surprised that Tanya even entered my musings. I hadn't given her a second thought since she quit talking to me in Florida. I remembered how much it angered me that Tanya didn't want to talk about the zombies. How could someone ignore the apocalyptic nature of the situation? Life could get better, it could change, but *we* had to change it. If they wanted to live in their bubble, what did I care? I was doing what I wanted. I didn't need to concern myself with them.

Quinn shifted behind me and pulled me out of my thoughts. He shone the spotlight on a few more zombie intruders. I watched as he dispatched the menace, then turned back to stare into darkness. I would've liked to talk to him, to get to know him better, but I didn't know what to say. I was curious about his family, but I learned in Florida you don't ask about anyone's parents. If they didn't bring them up, they were probably dead, and they more than likely didn't want to relive that day. I knew I didn't want to talk about mine. We occasionally glanced at each other and smiled, but otherwise it was a quiet night.

The next morning, we met back up with Bill and Kyle. After a quick breakfast and shower, I headed to bed. I wasn't sure how long I slept, but when I awoke, I heard the guys talking softly in the living room.

"It's tragic," I heard Bill saying. "There is no reason for people to live like this."

"It's like a concentration camp," Kyle chimed in.

"Oh, I doubt it's that bad," Quinn said.

"Okay, that's exaggerating, but it's not good. A lot of these people are starving. Last night alone we saw three people beaten in the street by the soldiers for God knows what reason."

"The wall has barely extended outside the city limits," Bill exclaimed. "And I know all those bodies on the fire are not zombies."

"What are they even doing about the zombies?" Kyle asked.

There was a long period of silence.

"We knew it was going to be bad when we came here," Quinn spoke, but then his voice trailed off, and I couldn't hear what he was saying.

I climbed out of bed and walked to the door. Cautiously, I opened it and peered out.

"We need a contact. Someone on the inside who will distribute the guns. Was there anyone in the town who could possibly fit that profile?"

Bill shook his head. "They're all so afraid of the soldiers, they barely wipe their noses without getting permission first."

"What about Krista?" Kyle asked.

"I wouldn't count on her, she's related to Liet," Quinn explained.

"So? How exactly are they related? Not everyone enjoys their relatives."

"Keep looking. Someone has to turn up."

I closed the door and leaned against the wall. What were they planning on doing? Surely they weren't going to destroy the wall. That was the only thing protecting us from the undead. Just because they were suited to living in the West, that didn't mean everyone was. And why did they need to distribute guns? The soldiers had them and they protected the workers, wasn't that enough?

I knew life in North Platte wasn't ideal, but it was necessary. If they wanted to repopulate the East, they had to wall off the West. Things were bad, yeah, but they didn't have the supplies. Liet was doing the best he could. I shivered. Did I just defend him? Good thing no one could read my thoughts. I didn't agree with everything Liet did, but we all had to make sacrifices. I believed that when all was said and done, the people who built the wall would be honored as heroes. After all, it was their hard work and dedication that would make life in the East possible.

I took a deep breath and changed into some clothes. I headed into the living room. The guys smiled at me, and I nodded in their direction. I went into the kitchen and poured a cup of coffee. The guys went back to what they were doing: Kyle read a magazine, Bill cleaned his gun, and Quinn patched a hole in his shirt. I leaned against the counter and watched. They looked so normal. For a brief moment, I wondered if I had dreamed the whole conversation.

I finished my cup of coffee. "I have some things I need to do to get ready to leave."

"Okay," Quinn smiled.

I paused with my hand on the doorknob and stared at him for a second. The corners of my mouth twitched into a small smile, and I headed out the door.

It was late afternoon as I made my way through the streets of North Platte. The morning shift finished and headed to their homes. Their clothes were covered in mud or soot from the fire, but their skin was clean. I knew they just endured the showers, and I pitied them. They looked utterly exhausted. They dragged their feet over the broken asphalt. Soldiers lined the streets and watched the procession go by. One of the men from the crowd stopped to ask a question, and the soldier told him to keep moving. When he refused, the soldier drove the butt of his gun into the worker's stomach. He doubled over, but before he could hit the ground, two more soldiers grabbed him by the arms and ushered him to the courthouse. I watched for a few seconds before stepping into the female soldier's house.

Pam sat at the table eating an apple and reading a newspaper. She smiled as I walked in.

"Hey, check this out. Just got it from Florida this morning." Pam handed me the newspaper.

I glanced at the headline, "Zombie Threat Gets Worse," briefly before sitting across from Pam. I folded my arms on the table.

"What do you know about Quinn and his group?"

Pam took a bite and shrugged. "Not much. They live somewhere in the West and were the only ones to answer our request for help."

"What are they working for?"

"I don't know. Why?"

I glanced down and picked at an imaginary dot on the tabletop. "Just curious. Liet expects me to work with them and resupply the country. I wanted some information about them before we went out again."

Pam set her apple down and leaned forward. "Are you afraid they'll try to harm you?"

"Pfft, no! I can take care of myself."

"I know you can. I wanted to make sure." She leaned back in her seat and took another bite.

I picked at the spot again. "Do you like being here?" I glanced at Pam out of the corner of my eye.

Pam snorted. "If you're asking whether I'd rather be here or back home with my family, *without* the threat of zombies, I think you know the answer to that."

I pulled my hands into my lap and hunched my shoulders. "Of course we'd all rather live in a world without zombies. But we can't change the circumstances. Since you're stuck here, do you like it?"

Pam frowned. "I wouldn't call it a matter of like or dislike, it's just how it is. Like you said, you can't change the circumstances."

"Yeah, but if you had a choice, where would you go?"

"I don't know. What are you getting at? Why are you asking me this?"

I leaned forward and lowered my voice. "What about the workers? Did they choose to be here?"

Pam narrowed her eyes and leaned forward. "Some of them."

"What does that mean?"

"Just what I said. Some of them volunteered and others, well, they didn't have a choice."

A million more questions raced through my mind, and I wondered if I really wanted to know the answers. I hadn't really thought about the workers and their lives, but I decided I needed to pay more attention.

We stared at each other for a moment. Pam waited for me to ask more questions, I could tell by the look on her face. I finally sat back and folded my hands across my chest.

"I'm leaving tomorrow. I have to fill up two more trucks." I stood and headed out the door.

"Hey, Krista."

I turned around.

Pam hesitated. The look on her face told me she wanted to tell me something. It was a look of pain and sadness. Her forehead wrinkled and her eyes glistened with tears, but all she said was, "Good luck."

I smiled and headed back to the apartment.

* * *

The guys and I left early the next morning. My stomach fluttered with excitement. We were going back to Casper, but Quinn said he would take me a different way, let me see the countryside. I packed a few more weapons, just in case we ran into trouble, and stocked up on ammunition. I climbed into the passenger seat of the truck and glanced out the window. Liet stood in front of the courthouse with his hands on his hips. I stared at him, and he waved as we pulled away.

The trucks drove through the gates and onto the highway. When we were a few miles down the road, I cracked my window and sucked in a deep breath of air.

"Smell that?" I asked.

Quinn wrinkled his nose. "No. What am I supposed to smell?"

"Nothing."

He smiled. "Yeah. I do. Smells great."

I took another breath. "Yes it does." I sat quietly for a moment. "You know, it's weird, how you get used to something and don't even realize it until you're away from it." I turned to Quinn. "Take for example the smell of the fire. It never bothered me in all the months that I've lived in North Platte. Then you come along and point out how putrid it really is. Now, I can barely stand it. Why do you think that is?"

Quinn glanced at me out of the corner of his eye. "I think people get comfortable. Complacent. It's hard to imagine anything else exists if you haven't experienced it."

"Is that why you came to North Platte? To experience something different?"

"Sort of."

"Why did you come?"

"I wanted to see what it was like."

"And what do you think about it?"

"I think it's got to be the worst place on Earth."

"So why did you agree to go back?"

Quinn shrugged his right shoulder. "If I have a means to make someone's life a little easier, I'm going to do it." He smiled at me. "Besides, I wasn't doing anything else at the moment."

"What do you expect to gain out of it?"

"What?"

"Well, you can't be doing something for nothing. What do you expect for payment?"

"I don't expect anything."

"Something has to tempt you. Money? Power?"

Quinn chuckled. "Really, I don't want anything. Money has lost its value, and power is overrated. Too much stress. I'm doing it to help my fellow man. What about you? Why are you out here risking life and limb? What's your temptation?"

I opened my mouth to answer, but then closed it. Why was I out there? Mainly, it was because I wanted to get out and experience something new. Part of it was also so I could get away from Liet. But in reality, I could move back in with Pam. I turned and looked out the window. Why was I doing it?

CHAPTER 13

It took us two days to fill up the trucks and take them back to North Platte. I dropped in briefly to let Liet know I was all right, but he was busy so I didn't stay for long. I stopped in to say hello to Pam, but we left again within hours of returning the loaded vehicles. On our next trip out, we were instructed to get clothes and more food for the masses. Again, we headed toward Casper.

"How many more times do you think we can come here before it runs dry?" My foot was on the dash, and my fingers held onto the open window.

Quinn shrugged. "Depends on how much more stuff Liet needs us to get."

"You know, eventually, all the supplies are going to run out. They need to start making new ones."

"Maybe they'll start doing that once the wall is built."

I snorted. "Yeah, like that's ever going to happen. Do you know how long it took them to get where they are? Months. And the only thing they have to show is a chain link fence and the trench where they are going to put the stone wall." I shook my head. "No, I'm pretty sure that wall will never be finished."

"What about the people in Florida? Won't they make sure it gets done?"

I laughed. "You're kidding, right? What do they care if the wall is done? They live as far away as they can, they're not affected."

"What was Florida like?"

I turned my gaze out the window for a moment, remembering my time in the Sunshine State. I turned back to Quinn. "It wasn't anything spectacular. All of the orphans were put in one hotel where they were given an education and career. I was a servant in the Johnson family's suite. I hated every moment of it, so the first chance I got, I left."

"Who are the Johnsons?"

"Only one of the most important families in Florida. Without them, the world would have collapsed into chaos."

Quinn stared at me.

"Not enough sarcasm? I'll try harder next time."

He smiled. "You have any friends that are still there?"

I nodded. "One. Her name is Pearl. At least I think she's still there."

"When's the last time you talked to her?"

"I don't know. A while ago. She didn't want me to leave, but I didn't listen to her. I was so desperate to get out."

"You should write her."

I furrowed my brow. "Why? It's been months. I doubt she wants to hear from me."

Quinn shrugged. "If she's a good friend, she'll love to hear from you no matter how much time has passed. It doesn't hurt to try."

I stared out the windshield. I always wondered what Pearl was up to—if she had found any family, if she was still in school—but I didn't have the courage to write her. I was sure Pearl was mad at me for leaving. I would be mad if Pearl left. I thought about what I would say. Maybe if I opened the letter with a "You were right, life is pretty bad here..." it would smooth the way. Pearl was never one for gloating, but she might think I deserved whatever I got. After all, I did abandon her in Florida.

But then again, Pearl had every opportunity to leave, too. She didn't have to stay there. I shouldn't have to apologize for anything. I only did what I thought was best for me. If Pearl couldn't understand that, then she could go to hell. I didn't have to answer to anyone. Still, it would be nice to know what she was doing. Maybe I would write Pearl a letter.

The trucks pulled into the mall parking lot. A few cars still sat in the parking spaces, but otherwise the place looked empty.

I stared at the building. "How do you want to do this? The place is much too big for a detailed search."

"Why don't we secure Sears. If I remember correctly, each store has a gate that closes it off from the main hall. We could do a quick scan, close the gate if it's still open, and load up with what we need. If we think we need more, we can make our way through the mall." Quinn put his hand on the door handle.

"Okay. I'll follow you." I took a deep breath and opened my door.

As usual, Bill and Kyle waited in the parking lot, making sure the coast stayed clear. We walked to the doors, and both of us were surprised to see that particleboards had been placed over the glass. We glanced at each other, brows furrowed.

"Should we try and find another way in?" I whispered.

Quinn shook his head. "I think we can pry one of these off. We should be fine." He placed his gun in the holster at the small of his back and jerked on the boards. The wood creaked and snapped, and the corner lifted up. Quinn went down on his knees and stared in.

"Looks clear."

He pulled the gun back out of his holster and crawled into the building. I followed after him.

The store was dark and humid. The faint smell of mildew wafted into my nostrils, along with the scent of leather and old perfume. Clothes hung on the racks, and mannequins were still posed in the windows. The store was warm, but I shivered.

"We have a lot of ground to cover, we should get started."

I nodded, and we made our way around the room. As we proceeded deeper, it grew to almost pitch black. I clicked on my flashlight and shone the beam precariously around. Quinn clicked his on, too. Clothes no longer hung neatly on the racks, but were dumped on the floor, as if someone had gone through them and threw the ones they didn't want down. Empty hangars were everywhere, and shoes were piled haphazardly in the middle of the floor. We proceeded to the dressing rooms.

"I'll stay at the door," Quinn whispered, "you head in."

As I entered, something in the far dressing room clicked. I froze. At first, I thought it was my mind playing tricks on me, but then a soft scraping sound resounded through the room. That wasn't in my mind. I brought my gun up and slowly stepped down the hall. I hoped it was a cat or some other animal that moved into the store. I knew I could hit a zombie in the head with a flashlight and my gun, but that had been in a much larger area. The dressing rooms were pretty crowded. What if there was more than one? What if it lunged at me? I hated being in such a confined space.

When I made it to the door of the last dressing room, I kicked it open and prepared to fire. Much to my surprise, nothing was there but a bed made out of linens from the store's inventory. That didn't make me feel better. Who or what would have made a bed? I was sure the zombies didn't do it, so it had to be a person. I hoped they were friendly. I lowered my weapon and took a deep breath.

I was about to make my way back into the main store, when the sound of shuffling sounded off to my right. I readied my weapon again and headed toward the noise. The beam of the flashlight caught movement, and my heart skipped a beat. I paused at the door. Quinn wasn't there. I peered around the corner.

"Quinn," I whispered.

"What?"

"Did you see that?"

Before he could answer, a shadow ducked under one of the clothes racks. I spun out of the door and used my gun to move the clothes. Nothing. I glanced around the room again.

"Quinn? Where are you?"

I shone my light around the room, looking for him, when something kicked my hands. My gun and flashlight skidded across the floor, and I turned toward my attacker. A fist caught me in the left cheekbone. Stars danced in front of my eyes, and the pain spread through my entire skull, giving me an instant headache. I whipped around to face my assailant, but they scurried off to my right. I flipped out my arm swords and turned to follow. So much for them being friendly.

Since I lost my flashlight, my eyes slowly adjusted to the dark. Whoever attacked me was still in front of me, poised to strike again. The shape dipped down, and my legs were swept out from underneath me. I landed on my back, the wind knocked out of me. The shadow moved so it stood directly over me. I could barely make out its arms as it swung something over its head. I brought my swords up to defend myself. I crossed them over my face, stopping a metal rack as it was about to smash my head in. I pushed it out of the way and jumped to my feet. I swung my right arm over my left shoulder and was about to strike when the lights flicked on and temporarily blinded me. Thankfully, it affected the person attacking me, too. I shielded my eyes and kicked the man standing in front of me. He fell to the ground, and I raised the sword above my head. I hesitated. I had never killed a human, and I wasn't sure I wanted to start at that moment. The man took the opportunity to kick at my legs, but I jumped out of the way. He stood and ran away from me. I went to follow but was stopped by Quinn's voice.

"Are you okay? I heard you fighting with someone."

I folded my sword blades and placed my hands on my hips. "You mean you didn't run into anyone?"

He shook his head. "No."

"Where did you go?"

"I checked out the cashier stand. When I saw you lost your flashlight, I went to find the lights. Was it a zombie?"

I rolled my eyes. "How many zombies do you know are smart enough to knock a gun out of your hand? And did you hear a moan? It wasn't a zombie."

Quinn pursed his lips. "Where did he go?"

I threw up my hands. "I don't know. You distracted me."

"We should probably see if we can find him."

We were about to head off when a voice stopped us in our tracks.

"That won't be necessary."

We looked up to find a group of twenty armed people standing in front of us. The man who spoke was young, probably not much older than twenty-five, but his face was lined with stress and his black hair was turning gray. He was on the thin side, but an intensity burned in his eyes. I flicked arm swords back out, and a few of the individuals raised their weapons.

"We don't want any trouble," Quinn spoke, his hands raised in a surrender position.

"What *do* you want?" the man asked.

"We want to get some supplies and head out."

"Well, you can get them someplace else. This is our sanctuary."

"Please, it's just a few things."

The man shook his head curtly. "I've seen you in town before. You think you're the only ones here and can take anything you want. Well, you can't. We fortified this mall, and we stocked it with supplies. It was an awful risk for us to come here, and we're not about to give up our safety."

"I understand. We'll be on our way."

One of the men in the group stepped forward with my flashlight and gun. I folded my swords up and took them back. We backed toward the door, and right as Quinn was ready to crawl into the light, a skeletal hand grabbed at his face. He pulled back, but not before the tip of one of the fingers scraped against his cheek. Two men followed us, and when they saw the arm, they helped me push against the board to keep the creature out. A moan resounded. We succeeded in nailing the board back over the door, and the four of us ran back into the store. The man who confronted us earlier stared in disgust.

"I thought you were leaving."

"So did we." Quinn sucked in a deep breath. "But the zombies seem to have followed us."

The man scowled and stomped to the storeroom. We weren't exactly sure what we were supposed to do, so we followed him. He climbed the ladder that led to the roof and proceeded to the edge. I glanced into the parking lot. A horde of close to a hundred zombies closed in on the mall, moaning to attract others. I watched Bill and Kyle fire into the crowd. Several creatures fell, but they didn't have the ammo to fend them all off. They must have figured that out, too, because they climbed back into the cab. I glanced at the horizon and noticed several hundred more on their way. I glanced at the man.

"Sorry."

It was pathetic and I knew it probably meant nothing to him, but I didn't know what else to say. We really didn't mean to endanger anyone's lives. We didn't even know there were people there.

He stared at the undead. "It's not the first time it's happened. We'll be fine. They can't get in. But we've got to clear you a path to your truck."

My eyes widened. "What? Why can't we wait it out?"

The man turned to me, his eyes narrowed to slits. "And how long do you plan on waiting it out? And what about your friends in the truck?" He pointed to the parking lot. "Do you expect them to wait it out?"

I rolled my eyes and released the magazine. "I have nine bullets."

Quinn checked his gun. "Seven."

The man shook his head and glanced over his shoulder. The two men who escorted Quinn and I to the door hefted a mini-gun onto the roof.

"I suggest you get downstairs. We'll hold them off for as long as we can."

Quinn and I glanced at one another for a moment, then headed down the ladder.

The hum of the gun was deafening, even with my hands over my ears. After a few minutes, it stopped. Quinn threw open the doors, and we ran over a path of blood and body parts to the truck. Moans filled the air, and more creatures continued to limp and lurch to the mall. The asphalt was pocked with holes where the bullets hit. The zombies that weren't completely obliterated by the spray of ammunition reached for us, desperately clawing for our legs. At one point, Quinn glanced over his shoulder, probably to make sure I was still behind him, and tripped over an arm. He went down to his hands and knees and came face to face with an undead. The thing was a chest, neck, and head, its bottom jaw was missing, but it still tried to wiggle its way to Quinn. It looked like a grotesque slug sliding over its own ooze. I grabbed Quinn's arm and pulled him up. We climbed into the cab. Quinn slammed the truck into gear and headed down the road. I stared out the window and thought about how I hated malls. I always loathed shopping, trying clothes on, the hours and hours it took to find the right fit. After that, I pretty much vowed I would never go to another mall.

We were a ways down the road before I spoke. "Do you encounter that often? Groups of survivors, I mean."

Quinn shook his head. "Not really. We try to stick to ourselves, just like they do."

"Why haven't you all banded together? Formed one super group of survivors and taken out the zombie threat?"

Quinn smiled. "Oh, that would be nice. All of us working together to defeat one common enemy. Unfortunately, it doesn't work that way. First of all, there really aren't that many of us. Secondly, no one knows who they can trust. Why don't Liet and the families in Florida send out soldiers to take care of the zombie threat? They have the numbers and the weapons."

I shrugged. "I don't know. Most of the people in Florida are so far removed from any of the action, they don't really know what's going on out here. They live in their own bubble."

"Liet knows. Why doesn't he do anything about it?"

I chuckled. "Why? He's happy where he's at. He's got everything he needs."

"What about you? What makes you happy?"

I shrugged. "I used to think it would be living in North Platte. Now, it's being out here. In the West. There may be zombies, but at least I'm free."

Quinn's smile widened. "That's why I'm here. If you don't mind me asking, do you have a boyfriend or anything in North Platte?"

I chuckled. My cheeks felt hot. "No. It's not exactly a hot bed of boys my age. Besides, most of them are afraid of Liet. I'm sure if they came to the apartment, Liet would twitch and they'd pee their pants and run. What about you? Do you have a girlfriend?"

Quinn shook his head.

"Really? There's nobody special in your life?"

"Not really."

"Any particular reason for that?"

"No. I haven't found the right person yet."

"What are you looking for?"

Quinn's face turned red. "I don't really know what I look for in a woman. Looks aren't all that important, but they do matter. She has to be kind, intelligent, and love me for who I am. In this day and age, it doesn't pay to be picky, or you'll get left all alone. What about you? What's your ideal boyfriend?"

I took a deep breath. "I don't know. I agree with a lot of the things you said. Kind, intelligent, love me for who I am. But he'd have to be able to kill zombies, too." I smiled at him. "Wouldn't be a very long relationship if he couldn't protect himself."

Quinn smiled back. "Yeah. I want to add that to my list, too." He pulled the truck into the parking lot of a Walmart. "You know, I think Kyle might be available."

I stuck out my tongue and giggled. "I know I shouldn't be picky, but he's a bit too skinny for me."

Quinn chuckled. He put the truck into park and folded his hands on the steering wheel. "Looks pretty clear here. You ready to do a sweep?"

I did a brief scan of the area before nodding. We stepped out of the truck and into the store. The place was a disaster. Clothes racks had been knocked on their sides, and garments littered the floor. The smell of rotting food filled the air. I tried to ignore it as we did our sweep, but it was overpowering. When we were done, I was never more thankful to be back in the fresh air.

A few zombies closed in on our position, but we quickly eliminated them and headed to our next stop. After we loaded the trucks, we drove back to the jail. The zombies had long since dissipated, leaving only bits of clothing and a few body parts behind to show they had been there. We settled in and met at the admissions desk for supper.

Dinner was quiet until we were about finished. I thought about what Quinn said in the truck about Kyle being available, and was kind of saddened by it. I hoped that maybe Quinn liked me, too, but I was wrong. I wasn't really good at reading boys. In fact, I was terrible at it, but I thought Quinn and I were getting along great. Not that it meant we would become boyfriend and girlfriend, but I did have my dreams. At one point, I glanced over at Kyle and he smiled at me. I quickly averted my gaze to my plate. I poked at my Vienna sausages and green beans, and after a few minutes, looked up from my plate.

"So, what are you guys planning?"

They stopped and stared at me with eyes wide.

"What do you mean?" Bill asked.

"I heard you guys talking the other day in my apartment. You said you needed a contact. What for?"

Bill forced a chuckle. "Oh, that, we were, uh, talking about getting to know some people on the inside so we didn't have to impose on you when we're in town."

I set my plate down and stared at him. "Really? Then why do you need to distribute guns?"

Quinn took a deep breath and leaned forward. "We're working on a plan to liberate the people on the east side."

"Quinn!" Bill spoke sharply

"It's okay."

"She's related to the enemy," he hissed. "And you were the one to point that out in the first place."

"Yeah, if you consider second cousins related," I murmured. "You don't have to worry about me telling Liet. I'm not a spy. I want to know what you're doing."

Bill glared at me for a moment. "Whether *you* do or not, you're still related. And Liet is the worst human being I've ever seen. He'd as soon kill someone as look at 'em. And the more stressed out he gets, the worse it's going to get."

"Why do you need to liberate the East? They're happy with their situation."

"Are they?" Kyle asked.

I shrugged. "Well, yeah, the last time I was there, they seemed to be content."

"Only because they don't really know what's going on," Bill snarled.

I glared at him. "And what's really going on?"

He chuckled, a low maniacal sound, like one you hear from cartoon villains. "They're being brainwashed, Krista." He glanced at Quinn. "She's too close to the situation; she can't even see what's going on."

Quinn held up a hand to silence him and turned to me. "What Bill's trying to say is that the people in the East really have no idea what is going on in North Platte because they are being told lies and stories to keep them under control."

I blinked in disbelief. "No. They know about the zombies. They know what's going on."

"Krista, think about it. If they really wanted to build a wall, why would they only send two thousand people? Why wouldn't they send as many as they could? If they really wanted that wall built, they would try to get it done as fast as possible."

"Well, maybe, but—"

"There is no maybe about it!" Bill yelled. "They send criminals and undesirables to Nebraska so they can live in the utopia of Florida. And to keep those people under control, they tell them lies, make them live in fear that if they ever leave Florida, they will die!"

I opened my mouth to speak, but Bill interrupted me again.

"I don't even know why we're trying to tell her," he said to Quinn. "She doesn't get it. She's special. She's never had to endure any hardships in her life."

Anger flared in my chest that was quickly replaced with sadness. Tears stung my eyes, but I refused to let them fall in front of him. I got up from my seat and headed into my room.

The guys spent a few minutes arguing quietly among themselves before Quinn entered my cell.

"Bill wasn't trying to be a jerk."

I sniffed and wiped at my eyes. "Really? Because he's pretty good at it."

Quinn sat next to me on the bed. "Bill's suspicious because however Liet acts toward the workers, he seems to be pretty nice to you."

I stared at him, my lip curled in disgust. "Of course he's nice to me. We're family. But at the same time, he sends me out into the West to gather supplies. It's like he wants me around, but he doesn't. Plus, he has these really weird mood swings." I snapped my mouth shut. I doubted Quinn wanted to hear about my troubles. "I've had my share of hardships."

"I'm sure you have. I would never question what you've been through in your life."

A soft knocking sounded on the bars, and we looked up to see Bill standing at the door.

"Sorry to interrupt," he said, almost sheepishly. "But I wanted to apologize for what

I said. Quinn's right. None of us know what you've endured. I shouldn't have said that. If you want to help, you can. But, if I find out you are a spy, I will personally serve you to the zombies. Even if I have to do it with my dying breath."

I shook my head. "I'm not. I swear. What do you need me to do?"

CHAPTER 14

We returned the next morning with the filled trucks. After enduring another inspection, Quinn and I went to the courthouse to let Liet know we were back. As we stepped through the doors, Liet presided over a group of soldiers; one was shackled and kneeling on the floor. Quinn and I waited at the back of the room.

"They needed food. You can't let kids go hungry."

Liet slammed his fist onto the desktop. "*I* make the decisions of who gets what and how much." He pointed a finger at the soldier. "*You* follow orders." He flipped his hand in the air. "Take him to the pyre."

"What?" The soldier on the floor squealed and tried to get to his feet, but the two on either side pushed him back down. "It won't happen again. Please, please give me another chance."

Liet eyed the soldiers, his face pinched with irritation. "What is he still doing in my presence? I said, *take him to the pyre.*"

The soldiers grabbed the prisoner by the arms and dragged him out of the room. His pleas for mercy echoed for a long time after he left. I felt sick to my stomach, and Quinn went white. Things were getting worse. Liet was mean before, but now he was being down right cruel. Quinn and the guys were right.

Something had to be done. Liet glanced up and noticed us at the back of the room.

"Ah, I see you have returned. Another successful excursion I trust?"

I nodded mechanically.

"Wonderful." He smiled.

I swallowed the lump in my throat. "I assume you'll want us to head out again and fill up some more trucks."

Liet shrugged. "If you'd like. But we have enough supplies right now to last us a while."

"What about Florida?"

"What about it?" Liet leaned back in his chair and folded his hands on his stomach.

I couldn't believe how nonchalant he acted after sentencing someone to death. I tried to gather my thoughts.

"I thought you wanted to get supplies to take to them."

"I thought about it. But what have they done for us lately?"

It was baffling. Was he really that callous? "They sent you workers a few months ago."

"So? The workers they sent me aren't worth anything. Do you know what I have to put them through to get them to do the simplest task?"

I took a deep breath and struggled to keep my voice under control. "So, if you send them a gift of supplies, perhaps they will be more receptive to sending workers who actually work. Right now they send you those they don't want out there."

Liet stroked his chin as he thought. "What do you care if I have good workers or not? Eventually, I can motivate anyone to do anything I want."

"Maybe if you had better workers, you wouldn't be so stressed out. With better workers, you could relax. Spend an evening at the river. I think that sending a truck will be a gesture of good will. They will eventually run out of supplies and come here looking for them. Do you really want The Families subverting your authority? If you take the initiative, they'll stay put."

Liet stared at me intently. "Perhaps. What do you suggest I send?"

"Food. Maybe some clothes."

"I'll think about it." He sat forward in his chair and buried his face in his paperwork.

"So, do you want us to get some stuff?" I asked.

He waved his hand. "Sure. Just leave me alone."

Quinn and I headed out to the empty trucks and climbed into the cab. Bill and Kyle waited in their semi, and we headed down the road. A few miles outside of North Platte, I noticed a horde of zombies on the road.

"That's odd." I pointed out the window.

Quinn leaned forward and slowed the truck down. "Yeah, that is weird. Why are they heading away from North Platte?"

I shook my head.

As we got closer to the horde, we noticed someone running from the zombies. He was a good distance in front of the creatures, but more approached from the sides. Eventually, they were going to surround him. I recognized the man as the soldier from Liet's office. Quinn sped up and took out as many zombies as he could.

"Don't hit him!" I screamed.

The man was practically running down the middle of the road.

"I won't!" He merged into the other lane, and the soldier jumped into the ditch.

Quinn slammed on the brakes, and we waited until the man caught up to us. We had overshot him by quite a ways. Not that we meant to, it's difficult to stop a semi on a dime. Bill pulled his truck next to Quinn's.

"What are you doing, man?"

"We can't leave him out here alone."

"Where are you going to take him?"

"Back to the ranch."

Bill shook his head. "I don't think that's a very good idea. What if it's a trap?"

Quinn set his arm on the door and leaned forward. "We can't leave him out here to die."

"He could have a tracking device on him. Or a walkie talkie to tell them where he's at," Bill hissed.

Quinn pursed his lips. "You know as well as I do that short range radios don't work at the ranch. And I'm sure someone will notice if he tries to make it to higher grounds. But I don't think that's going to happen. I'm pretty sure this isn't a trap."

Bill spit onto the ground. "I sure hope you're right."

Quinn turned to me and signaled toward Bill with his eyes. "Paranoid," he said quietly.

I smiled, then covered my mouth with my hand, trying to suppress a giggle.

The man caught up to the truck and doubled over, panting. I opened my door.

"Thank you, thank you so much," he wheezed.

I moved so he could climb into the cab, and he took a seat in the sleeper cabin. Quinn put the truck in gear, and we headed down the road.

"There's some water in the bag back there." I pointed to the duffel on the man's left.

He unzipped the bag and downed the water before speaking again. "You guys saved my life. I really appreciate it. Lucky for me, Pam was my executioner. She gave me the chance to run, and I did."

I frowned. "Sending you out onto this side of the wall is just as bad as shooting you in the head. It's a death sentence either way."

"Yeah, but maybe she knew you were coming down the road. Maybe she knew I would be safe."

I turned so I faced the man. "What did you do?"

"I gave some children an extra ration of food. Their parents were stuck working overtime at the wall, and they were hungry. One of the other soldiers saw me do it, and he turned me in to General Liet. Really, I didn't do anything wrong."

I glanced at Quinn.

"You'll be safe where we're going," Quinn said.

"Where are we going?" I wondered.

"To my house in the hills. Unfortunately, Bill still isn't convinced that you are trustworthy, so I'm going to have to blindfold you so you don't know the way to our sanctuary."

I scowled. "You're kidding, right?"

Quinn smiled.

After traveling on the interstate for two hours, he turned the tanker truck onto a secondary highway, which we followed for another hour, then turned down a dirt road. The landscape changed from the flat desert into rolling hills covered with juniper trees, then into steep cliffs with pines and red rocks. We bumped and wound our way across the road until we came to a canyon. Large, wooden doors covered the entrance, and men with rifles were perched on top of the cliff. The gates to the ranch opened, and Quinn pulled the truck inside.

"We have about twenty-five thousand acres and a few hundred head of cattle and a couple of horses. After the zombie attack, the neighbors abandoned their open ranches to live on this secluded one." He pulled the truck into the circular driveway in front of the house and pointed to the side. "We planted a garden, although not too much grows. We have a pretty good supply of carrots, lettuce, tomatoes, beans, and peas."

I stared at the surroundings wide-eyed with mouth agape. The house was a two-story log home built directly into the wall of the canyon. The barn was a few yards away, as well as a storage shed. I counted about twenty adults and seven children running around. I opened the door and stepped onto the ground.

Quinn came around the front of the truck. "You okay?"

I closed my mouth. "I...I can't believe this. It's beautiful."

Quinn placed his hands on his hips and squinted at the house. "It's not much, but it's home. The house was originally built in the mid-eighteen hundreds as a hideaway for outlaws. There are secret passageways that lead through a series of tunnels and caves to several outlets a few miles away. It's a perfect escape route if a zombie ever gets in here."

"Have you ever had a zombie get in here?"

Quinn shook his head. "No. We're pretty secluded out here. We didn't really even know there was a zombie outbreak until we heard it on the radio. They tend to stick to the major cities. That's where the food source is." He turned to the soldier. "C'mon. I'll show you around."

The man followed Quinn as he introduced him to the other survivors. I walked to the barn. The smell of fresh hay and dirt swirled in my nostrils, and a Bay horse met me at the corral. I gently placed my hand on the animal's nose. It huffed out a breath of air. Tears welled up in my eyes. The last time I had been around a horse was when I was thirteen—my parents took me on a horseback adventure through Yellowstone National Park. It was a four-day three-night trip that involved camping in the backcountry. We had a guide so we wouldn't get lost or hurt, even though we didn't really need one. The horses had done the trip so many times, they would've walked back to the ranch. I remembered how quiet the place was and how many animals we saw. It was my first time on a horse, but the guide said I was a natural.

After the trip, I begged my parents for a horse of my own, but since we lived in the city, it wasn't feasible. As a compromise, they allowed me to join the local country club and I took riding lessons there. I didn't own the horse, but I was allowed to ride it whenever I desired. I would still have the horse if the zombies hadn't attacked, and I wondered if it survived the outbreak.

"You ride?" Quinn's voice broke through my thoughts.

I wiped the tears quickly away and shook my head. "I haven't for a long time."

Quinn made his way to the gate. "You want to go for one?"

I frowned. "We really should get back on the road. We have supplies to get."

Quinn flicked open the latch. "Why? We don't have a schedule. Liet won't know you were here riding horses instead of getting supplies."

I hesitated.

"C'mon. It'll be fun."

I took a deep breath. "Why not?"

We stepped into the barn and readied the saddles and bridles. I was amazed that after so many years I remembered how to do it. I swung into the saddle and held the reins loosely in my right hand. I waited for Quinn before we headed down the canyon floor.

The red rocks rose for miles above us, and the sun beat onto the dry ground. My stomach was in knots. We would be sitting ducks if a zombie horde found us. We had nowhere to run. I placed my left hand on my gun, glancing around nervously. Quinn looked over his shoulder.

"You don't have to worry about zombies here," he called to me. "We have scouts placed in various lookouts up there." He pointed to the top of the canyon. "If anything is coming our way, we'll know about it. Besides, we haven't had a zombie attack here in years. Like I said, we're too far out of their way."

I tried to find comfort in his words but couldn't. We rounded a bend in the canyon and it opened up into a valley. My hand dropped to my side. Rolling hills surrounded the green landscape on either side, and white and red wildflowers dotted the land. Cows grazed freely. I could see a few of the lookouts on the tops of the hills, but they lounged in the grass, chewing on stalks like they didn't have a care in the world. As we approached the valley, my horse started to shift uneasily from one foot to the other and snort in the air. At first, I assumed he smelled something he didn't like, like a zombie, but then I realized he wanted to run. I grabbed the reins with both hands and stood in the stirrups. The horse took off like a shot, bolting past Quinn. I glanced over my shoulder and noticed his smile as he encouraged his animal to follow.

 I faced forward again and felt the wind rush through my hair. The air was sweet and smelled of grass and soil. I closed my eyes. The steady rhythm of the horse's hooves filled my ears, and for the first time in years, I felt at peace. I didn't have to worry about zombies or Liet or the workers. There was just the breeze on my face, the sun on my back, and the horse beneath me. I opened my eyes again and directed the horse toward a stand of willows. Quinn caught up with me, and we headed toward the creek.

 I dismounted and found a spot in the grass next to the water. I propped myself on my elbows and lounged in the shade. Quinn tied the horses to a small tree, then took a seat next to me but an arm's length away. The conversation about boyfriends and girlfriends entered my mind. It must have been true. He probably didn't like me. If he did, he would have sat right next to me.

"Have you ever lost any cows to the undead?" I tried to keep the disappointment out of my voice.

"A couple. They're pretty easy to cut down when they're feeding, though."

"Have you ever had any cows turn into zombies?"

He shook his head and turned to face me. "No. Whatever causes them to be that way doesn't work on animals."

I turned my gaze to the stream of water. "Huh. I wonder why."

Quinn stood and picked some dead leaves off the tree next to him. "I doubt anybody knows. That's one thing I'd like to change. Instead of building a wall, we need to figure out how, what, and why this plague started. If we know that, maybe we can stop it from happening again." He tossed the leaves into the water. "Do you think Liet will let you go to Florida?"

I shrugged. "It's possible. I'm sure I can convince him, though."

Quinn sat back down. "Do you think your friend will help us out?"

"I don't know. Like I told you before, it's been a long time since I've talked to her. All I can do is go down there and hope for the best."

Quinn nodded. "I hope it works out."

"Me too."

We sat by the creek until the sun dipped below the horizon. On the way back to the house, a cool breeze blew across the valley. I looked up and stared at the stars. Somewhere in the distance, a zombie moaned, but it was so faint I was able to convince myself that it was the wind.

CHAPTER 15

Liet summoned me to his chambers as soon as we got back into town. We had gone back to the Walmart in Casper and loaded everything that was salvageable. I wondered how many more places we were going to be able to plunder before there was nothing left. I knew we couldn't keep depending on existing supplies, we would eventually have to create our own.

I yawned as I stepped into his office. My back was sore from sitting for so long, and my eyes were tired from driving. I was also freezing from the inspection shower, my hair still dripped. My butt was sore from the saddle, but that was a pain I didn't mind. Liet looked up from his paperwork as I approached.

"I've decided to take your advice," he said softly. "I think you should take a truck down to Florida."

The exhaustion drained, and I perked up. "That's great. You're doing the right thing here."

"Of course I am. The only way I'm going to get anything from those jerks in Florida is if I bribe them with stuff from here. How soon can you leave?"

I shrugged. "Let me get a couple of hours of sleep and a real shower, and I'll be good to go."

Liet nodded. "All right. Take Pam with you."

"You don't want Quinn to go with me?"

Liet stared at me for a moment. "Why would I want him to go with you? There is nothing on this side of the wall that concerns him. He can take care of his own business on the other side. We'll take care of ours."

I held my hands up defensively. "Fine. Whatever you desire."

"Be ready in four hours."

I mock saluted, then headed up to the apartment.

After I got up from a two and a half hour nap, I took a shower. I threw the curtains back and grabbed a towel off the counter. I wrapped it around my body and headed into my room. I jumped when I noticed Liet sitting on my bed. I hurried to the closet and pulled on some clothes.

"Is there something going on between you and Quinn?" Liet's voice was low.

"I don't believe that is any of your business." I stepped out of the closet and went to grab my brush off the dresser.

He grabbed me by the arm. "Of course it's my business. I'm your guardian!"

I jerked out of his grasp and stared at him. "You may be my guardian, but you're not my parent. You have no right to tell me what I can or can't do." I stormed into the bathroom. Who did this guy think he was?

"Krista, I'm not playing around here. I want to know. You're too young. You have no idea what you're getting yourself into."

I tugged the brush through my hair. "I'm old enough to go into zombie-infested lands to get your supplies, but I'm not old enough to have a boyfriend? That makes a lot of sense." I stopmed to the door, but Liet grabbed me by the back of my shirt and pulled me back into the room.

When he let go, I spun around and punched him in the mouth. I don't know what came over me. It just happened. All I could think was that I wanted to get away and he wouldn't let me. It was instinct. His hand came up to his lip, and he licked the blood away. He raised his hand to slap me across the face, but I blocked it and landed another punch, this one next to his eye. Again, it was instinct. If I had actually been thinking, I would've known that was probably a bad idea. He stumbled backward and fell. I didn't wait until he got up. I grabbed my stuff and ran downstairs, climbing into the truck that waited for me. Pam sat in the driver's seat, and I told her to step on it. Liet came running after us, but Pam put the truck in gear, and we headed down the road. I heard him calling my name as we turned the corner.

Pam furrowed her brow. "What was that all about?"

I leaned my head back on the seat, closed my eyes, and took a deep breath. "He thinks I'm dating Quinn."

"And?"

"We got into a fight about it and I hit him."

"What? Why?"

"I don't know. It just happened. He grabbed my shirt and I hit him in the mouth. It was a reaction. He thinks he's my father. He thinks he can control me. He can't."

"You might want to think about getting that temper of yours under control."

I didn't answer. Maybe Liet needed to think about treating others with respect. Maybe I hit him for all of those who wanted to but couldn't. Maybe if he wasn't so creepy and I didn't feel like my life was in jeopardy every time he came into the room, I wouldn't have to punch him.

After a few minutes, Pam asked, "Well, are you?"

I raised my head and stared in disbelief. "Dating Quinn? No."

Pam shrugged. "Well, you should be."

"Why?"

"He seems like a nice kid. And you deserve to be happy. Do you like Quinn?"

I frowned. "I've never really thought about it." Of course I thought about it. All the time, but I wasn't going to let Pam know that. I wasn't comfortable talking to her about my personal life. Besides, Quinn made it pretty clear he wasn't interested.

"Well, from what I can tell, there's a lot there to like. He's tall, handsome, and caring."

I shook my head. "I don't even think he's interested in me."

"Have you asked him?"

"So, why did you send that soldier into the zombie wastelands?" I was desperate to change the subject.

"Did you find Jerry? How's he doing?"

"Yeah, we found him. But you're lucky we did. Anything could have happened to him, you know."

Pam smiled. "I knew you weren't far behind. I told him if he stuck to the highway, he would be fine."

"Why didn't you kill him like you were ordered to do?"

Pam stared at me, anger flashed in her eyes. "Because he didn't do anything wrong."

"Yeah, but you've killed workers for less."

Pam focused back on the road. "Have I? Have you ever seen me kill a worker?"

I thought for a moment. When was the last time I saw Pam kill someone? Had I ever? I couldn't remember any particular instances, and then my stomach turned. I stared at Pam.

"So instead of killing the people you were ordered to kill, you set them free to possibly be devoured by zombies? How is that better than a quick, painless bullet to the head? You're sentencing them to death either way."

"Maybe. But at least this way they have a fighting chance. You know as well as I do that there are groups of people in the West who have survived, maybe they have too. My hope is that they find these groups and live long prosperous lives."

I shook my head, averting my gaze out the window. Did Pam really believe that life was so much better on the other side of the wall? It was tough in North Platte, there was no denying that, but at least they had weapons. She sent them into the world unarmed with the hope that someone would pick them up. I knew from firsthand experience that groups in the West were very particular about letting outsiders in. I hoped Pam was right and they fell in with a crowd like Quinn's that was willing to help.

"What did you want me to do?" There was an accusatory tone to her voice.

I turned to face her. "I don't know. Maybe you should have tried to stand up to Liet."

"Then I would have been the one with a bullet in my head. At least I'm trying. At least I'm not running away."

"Running away? Is that what you think I'm doing? I'm trying to do my part for society. Besides, you don't live with Liet. If you did, you'd take every opportunity to get as far away from him as possible."

Pam sighed. "I know, I know. I don't even know why I'm fighting with you about this."

We were silent for several minutes.

"If you could change it, would you?" I asked.

Pam stared at me. "In a heartbeat."

That night, we stayed at the military station in St. Louis. We were both so tired from the drive that we ate and went straight to bed. We got up early the next morning and continued on our way. We didn't speak much, only commenting on things we saw on the trip, and I wondered how much I could trust Pam. From the beginning, she had always been there to take care of me and teach me new things, but she was still one of Liet's soldiers. I knew she was sincere when she told me she wanted to change things, but I wasn't sure if she would follow through. Yeah, she let some prisoners go, but I wasn't convinced that was the best course of action. Just because they dodged a literal bullet didn't mean they dodged the figurative one. Pam's wishful thinking didn't lead the condemned to safety. I guess it was better to lie in bed with the hope that they were safe than with the image of someone's head exploding because of your gun. I was convinced Liet could scare Pam into giving information. I would have to wait and see what happened.

When we reached Florida, the guards at the border gate let us pass without a second glance. I was shocked we didn't have to be examined. It had become so routine to me, I almost felt dirty when it didn't happen. I drove, and it seemed not much had changed since the last time I was there. There seemed to be a few more people, but poverty and a low sense of moral still pervaded the populace. We decided to stop in Tallahassee for the night. We were only a few hours away from our destination, but we weren't on a time schedule, and if we arrived too late, we would have to wait until morning anyway to deliver the goods. We drove a little way outside of the town and found a place to camp. It had been so long since either of us had been able to sleep under the stars, we decided to take full advantage. Plus, it was so hot and humid in the truck, there was no way we would sleep. We could at least breathe outside. Sort of.

We were both up with the sun, and after a quick breakfast, we climbed into the cab. Pam drove the four hours to Orlando, and I stared out the window, wondering what it was going to be like when I finally saw Pearl again. I imagined all kinds of scenarios, from a tearful embrace to a cold shoulder. I tried to remember if we had left on good terms, but it seemed like a lifetime ago, and my experiences since then clouded my memory. My stomach fluttered with butterflies and my palms began to sweat.

We pulled up to the Disney Contemporary Resort, which had been renamed the Johnson High School, and it looked the same as I had left it. For some reason, I expected it to be rundown and falling apart. I guess that was what I was used to. I could tell they applied a new coat of paint, and the grounds were still immaculate. Teenagers roamed around, and I wondered if all of them were orphans. They couldn't be. There were too many. All the kids were probably required to go to school there. That made the most sense. I took a deep breath and stepped inside.

The front desk was still there, and I approached the woman behind it, who smiled and asked how she could help us.

"We're here to see Olivia Johnson."

"Do you have an appointment?"

I smirked. "Sort of. Liet sent us."

The woman smiled and picked up the phone. When she was finished, she pointed to the elevator. "Go up to the penthouse."

"Thank you."

When we reached the top floor, a man in a dark suit waited for us. I recognized him as the security guard from when I was there, and he nodded in my direction. He took us to the sitting room where Olivia waited. She smiled as we approached and held her hands out to embrace me.

"Krista, darling, it has been so long." She took a seat on the couch and patted the space next to her. "You must tell me everything."

I took a seat where she indicated, and Pam sat across from us.

"There's really nothing to tell. We supervise the workers as they build the wall, and we fend off any attacking zombies."

Olivia waved her hand in the air. "Nonsense. I'm sure you have plenty of adventures to regale me with. How's Liet?"

I forced a smile. "Fine."

"Oh, I'm sure he is. Now who's this?" She directed her attention to Pam.

"This is Pam. She is one of Liet's colonels."

Pam nodded in the woman's direction.

"Very nice to meet you. So tell me, what is it that brings you back to Florida?"

"Liet wanted me to bring you a gift."

"Really? What is it?"

"A truckload of supplies from the West. He figured you might be running low on things, so he sent stuff to replenish your stores."

"Wasn't that thoughtful of him? What is it that he wishes in return?"

I cleared my throat. "He needs some different workers. Preferably ones that are not the dregs of your society."

Olivia's mouth opened in mock horror. "Is he insinuating that I would send our criminals and undesirables to him? I assure you, those that make the trip to North Platte have every intention of working hard for their country."

I shook my head. "No, no. He's not accusing you of that. He wants a few more…professionals to work with. Say, some of your engineers."

Olivia glanced from me to Pam and back to me. "I'm not sure we can give up any of our engineers. We need all of them here. Give me a couple of days to confer with the other families. I will let you know."

I smiled. "Thanks."

"Now, what can I do to make your stay more comfortable?"

"I was wondering if you knew where I could find Pearl."

Olivia smiled. "Of course, dear."

Since I left, they converted the rooms on the second floor into apartments. Most of the teachers lived there, along with the Johnson family servants. I found the number on the door and hesitated before knocking. Again, all the different scenarios of how Pearl would react ran through my mind. I imagined she would slam the door in my face. Pam stood next me. I felt her breath on my cheek.

"Well, are you going to knock?"

I took a deep breath. I raised my hand and tapped quickly on the door. I heard the shuffling of feet, then the door swung open, and I was face to face with Pearl. At first, Pearl stared at me blankly, then realization hit, and she threw her arms around my neck. I was so relieved, I let out the breath I held and hugged her back.

"Oh, my god," Pearl spoke as she pulled away, "I would have never guessed in a million years that you would be standing at my door." She turned and held out her hand. "Please, come in."

We stepped into the apartment.

"Pearl, this is my friend, Pam."

Pearl shook her hand. "It's nice to meet you." She placed her hands on her cheeks and stared at me. "I still can't believe you're actually here. I know it's only been several months, but it seems like forever!"

"It's been a while."

Pearl stepped forward and embraced me again. "I've missed you so much," she whispered.

Tears stung my eyes. I missed Pearl, too, way more than I imagined.

Pearl pulled away. "Let me get you two something to drink." She stepped into the kitchen while Pam and I took a seat on the couch. "I want to hear everything that you've been up to," Pearl called from the kitchen. She brought out lemonade and handed the glasses to us.

"No, you first. I want to hear what you've been doing."

Pearl grimaced. "Oh, not much has changed since you left. Obviously, I'm still living in the same place and I still have the same job. But I was reunited with my uncle."

"Really?"

Pearl nodded enthusiastically. "Yeah, my dad's brother. It's been great. We both miss the rest of the family, but at least we have each other."

"What does he do?"

"He's an electrician. He and his company pretty much keep Florida running. He's hoping they will approve our application so we can go with the first wave and start colonizing the East Coast."

My forehead wrinkled in confusion. "Why do you have to apply? Why don't you go?"

Pearl took a drink. "Because it's not safe. Just because the majority of the zombies have migrated West, that doesn't mean all of them have. The Families send out crews to make sure the cities are safe, and they come back with reports all the time that there are still zombies out there. As soon as they come back and say it's clear, The Families will send out engineers and architects to rebuild the U.S., starting with the East Coast. Tom, my uncle, hopes to be a part of the original colonists."

I knew it was possible a few zombies might linger behind, but nothing that one person couldn't handle. I couldn't believe it. Quinn was right. Not that I really doubted him, but I had to hear it with my own ears. Fear kept these people in Florida. I wondered what other lies they had been told.

"But that's enough about me. I want to hear about you now. Tell me everything."

I did.

CHAPTER 16

It was almost midnight by the time the three of us went to bed. Pearl's uncle was away on business, so she insisted that Pam and I stay. We had nowhere else to go, so we agreed. The next morning, I stood out on the balcony, enjoying the sun and watching as the students made their way to school. Pearl brought me a cup of coffee.

"So is it as bad as they say it is?" Pearl cradled the cup in her hands.

"Is what as bad?" I blew on the coffee before taking a sip.

"North Platte. They say zombies attack daily, taking at least three people with them."

I shrugged. "Well, it's not paradise, for sure. But it's not that bad either."

Pearl shook her head. "I can't even imagine. I know you've been through a lot, but I can't imagine why you stay out there. I mean, look at you. You've always been skinny, but you look downright starved. If it weren't for your muscles, I'd think you were about to waste away to nothing!"

I set my cup down. "Life is difficult, Pearl, but it's not impossible. Like I told you last night, there are survivors on the other side of the wall. You just have to be cautious."

Pearl shivered. "I heard that even if they touch you, you become one of them."

I got angry. Pearl was a smart girl, why was she falling for their lies? "Who told you that?"

"The Families. They receive reports all the time from North Platte and air them on the TV and radio. It's because of those reports that I don't really want to go colonize the East. I want to stay here where it's safe."

My eyes widened. "You have TV and radio down here?"

"Of course. How do you communicate with the world?"

"CB radios if we're lucky."

"So, it's not true? How do you turn into a zombie?"

"I don't really know, but I know that it takes more than a touch."

"Have you ever seen anyone change?"

I hesitated. "No."

"Then how do you know?"

"Quinn, the guy I told you about last night, has seen people change. He says that it takes twenty-four hours."

"Then how do you know a touch won't do it?"

I put my leg up on the rail and pulled up my jeans, exposing the deep purple scars caused by the zombie's nails. "Because I was attacked, and I haven't turned yet. That was weeks ago. Plus, there are these checks we have to go through. Even the doctor wasn't worried about these marks."

Pearl visibly paled, and I pulled my pant leg down.

"So, we didn't really talk about it last night because we were busy catching up, but tell me about these crews that get sent out to the cities."

Pearl drank of her coffee. "They are basically cleanup crews that go in and destroy any zombies that are still in the area. According to them, there is still a serious threat out there."

I scowled. "The only zombies that are left behind were probably trapped in something. There are no longer roving bands in the East."

"You don't know that."

"I know a lot more than you do. I've been East, Pearl. We used to get our supplies from there. Trust me, it is nothing like the West."

Pearl lowered her eyes to her coffee, and I stared out to the horizon. I set my jaw. I wasn't really mad a Pearl, but I was frustrated that she took The Families' word as gospel. I guess following them blindly was better than actually living your life. That required risks, and risks could be scary. I knew she wasn't the only one. I knew there were a lot of people out there who believed everything they were told. There had to be or else society couldn't function. If everyone was a leader, there would be constant wars. Followers kept the world balanced. It was too bad they were following the wrong leaders.

Not that I thought Quinn and his friends were necessarily better, but at least their plan called for action. They weren't driven by power but a desire to see the human race survive. That was at least a noble cause. Could The Families claim that?

"So," I interrupted the silence, "when is Tom supposed to be back?"

"Oh, he won't be back for a couple of days. One of the transformers in Miami went down, so he'll be there until it's fixed."

"When are you hoping to head to Georgia? I mean, when is he?"

Pearl stared at me, a small smile on her face. "He wants to go as soon as possible, but I'm trying to postpone it. I want to stay here where it's safe. But, he is my uncle, so what can I say?"

I turned back to my cup. Pearl hadn't changed at all since I left. It became painfully apparent that we didn't have anything in common and that I couldn't count on my friend to help distribute the firearms. We were going to have to figure something else out, but I didn't know what, and I was sure Liet wouldn't let me come back to Florida.

A soft knock resounded through the room, and Pearl went to answer the door. While she was gone, Pam joined me on the balcony. We looked at each other but didn't say a word. Pearl returned a few minutes later and told us that Olivia was ready to open her package.

I handed her the coffee mug. "Well, I suppose we'd better get down there. Thanks for everything."

Pearl looked shocked. "You're leaving? I was hoping you could stay a couple of days and I could take you around and show you the new Florida."

I grimaced. "Unfortunately, we have to get back. Liet is short-handed."

Pearl raised her eyebrows. "I can't believe you are going back to that awful place."

"We all do what we have to do."

Tears formed in Pearl's eyes. "I'll miss you." She stepped forward and embraced me.

I wrapped my arms around my friend and laid my chin on Pearl's shoulder. "I'll miss you, too."

That wasn't a lie. I did miss sitting up and talking to her. I thought if I could tell anyone about Quinn and my feelings, it would be her. But I also knew it wouldn't take long for us to run out of things to talk about. She had her vision of the future and I had mine. It was a shame they weren't the same.

We let each other go.

"If you're ever back in Florida," Pearl wiped the tears from her eyes, "make sure you look me up."

I smiled. "I will."

Pam and I made our way downstairs where we met Olivia and her entourage in the lobby. We walked to the semi, and I opened the back. Olivia smiled with satisfaction.

"I believe that the other families can be persuaded to fulfill Liet's request." She snapped her fingers, and her men got to work unloading the trailer. "You can expect them in the next couple of weeks."

"I'm sure Liet will be ecstatic."

Olivia smiled, then headed back into the hotel.

As Pam and I watched the men work, I heard someone call my name. I turned and scanned the area, and a girl with blonde hair ran toward me. I stared in disbelief.

"Krista, is that really you?"

"Tanya?"

Tanya giggled. "Yeah, it's me. What are you doing here?"

I was stunned, and it took me a minute to collect my thoughts. "We're dropping off some supplies."

Tanya continued to smile. "I know, I know, you're surprised I'm speaking to you."

I nodded. "Yeah, a little."

"All of that stuff that happened at school is in the past. Things have changed since you've been gone. How's everything going?"

"Fine."

"Oh, we really should catch up. When you're finished here, do you want to meet me at the coffee shop over there?" She pointed across the street.

"Sure."

"Great. See you in a bit." She turned and headed back to the shop.

"You sure are popular down here," Pam remarked.

"I guess," I replied.

When they finished unloading the truck, we went to the shop. Tanya stood behind the counter and smiled as we walked in. She grabbed some coffee, gestured to one of the tables, and we all sat down.

"Have you seen Pearl yet?"

I nodded. "Yeah, we stayed with her last night."

Tanya clicked her tongue. "She hasn't changed much, has she?"

I shook my head. "Nope."

"You know, I used to believe if I pretended the zombie attack wasn't happening, then it would stop happening or just happen to other people. When they started migrating west, I thought it was the best thing that could happen to us. I didn't realize there were far worse things. Unlike Pearl, my eyes were open."

I furrowed my brow. "What do you mean?"

"She believes all the hype. She thinks that if we leave Florida, we are sacrificing ourselves. Lambs to the slaughter, if you will. But I know she's wrong. She has to be. I mean, you're still alive."

I drank as she spoke and almost choked on the liquid. I decided to probe further and played a little dumb.

"What hype are you talking about?"

"Oh, the crap The Families bombard the airwaves with. They tell us if we leave, we are going to wind up dead. Or worse, undead." Tanya leaned forward and lowered her voice. "They tell us that so they can keep control. If everyone spreads out into the East Coast, they lose their grip on society. They don't want to leave Florida. It's their only safe haven."

"Eventually they're going to have to go somewhere," Pam interjected. "Florida can't sustain population growths forever."

"I know that, and they know that. They don't want to make it easy. Until they can figure out how to enforce their power outside the Florida border, they're going to keep us here as long as they can." She turned to me. "But you were smart. You got out of here when you got the chance."

I laughed. "Yeah, my life has been a cakewalk since I left here." I glanced at Pam, and we both chuckled.

Tanya shrugged. "Maybe not, but at least you're doing something. Most people here are biding their time and waiting to die."

"Isn't that what Florida's always been for?" Pam smiled.

Tanya either didn't catch the sarcasm or chose to ignore it. "I think it's wonderful you've gotten out and decided to do something."

"It's not too late for you to leave, you know." Tanya was really weirding me out. What happened to make her change her mind?

Tanya shook her head. "I'm not going anywhere. I've been reunited with my dad, and he wants to stay here. After watching my mom and sister die, he's *extremely* overprotective. I can't blame him, though. I don't really want to leave his side, either. There's no way I can go to North Platte. He started this business, and everything has been great. It does make me sad, though, to think that I'll never be able to experience the world like we used to."

"You can't change the fact that zombies attacked. The world is different no matter how you look at it."

"I know. But it would be nice to once again experience what it's like to live free. To not be ruled by tyranny. If I could change that, I would."

Pam stood abruptly from her seat. "Coffee's going right through me. Where is the bathroom?"

Tanya pointed to the other side of the room. I waited until the door closed, then leaned forward and folded my hands on the table.

"How far are you willing to go to ensure change?"

Tanya lowered her voice to a whisper. "I shouldn't say anything because if someone overhears me, I'm on a one-way trip to Nebraska, but I would love for The Families to be taken out. We can't live in fear. If we are going to reclaim the land, then we need to get off our butts and do something about the zombies."

I heard the bathroom door open and close. "I know of a way you can help."

I straightened up as Pam came back to the table.

Tanya smiled. "How much longer are you two planning on staying?"

"We should really head back," I said. "There's nothing here for us."

Tanya stood from her chair and held out her hand, which both Pam and I shook. "It was nice to see you again."

Pam headed for the door.

"Hey," I called after her, "I'm going to stop by the ladies room, I'll meet you at the truck."

Pam nodded and headed out. I turned toward Tanya.

"There are people who feel the same way you do in the West. Although I find it weird that you even feel that way. If we ever get the chance, you have to tell me what changed your mind. We want to arm the people so they can overthrow The Families and help destroy the zombie horde. Can I trust you with this?"

"On my dad's life."

"I hope so because he will be the first person I come after if you double cross me. The only way we can transport the weapons is by hiding them on the trucks. If we can get you the weapons, do you have a means to hide them and get them to the people who can use them?"

Tanya nodded.

"How are you going to get to the trucks?"

"My dad owns a storage unit here in town, so a lot of the supplies will be brought there."

"That's convenient."

Tanya smiled. "I know. It's strange how fate crosses the paths of those who need each other the most."

"There will be another truck in a couple of weeks with instructions under the passenger seat."

"I'll be waiting for it."

I glanced over my shoulder out the front window. I then proceeded to the bathroom. On my way out, I stopped once more at the counter.

"There will be no way for us to contact each other, and for safety's sake, we probably shouldn't. I know you are taking on a great risk, especially with your family, but I appreciate your help in this matter."

Without waiting for a response, I turned and left the coffee shop.

CHAPTER 17

I took the first driving shift and fretted the entire time I was behind the wheel. Did I make the right decision? Would I be able to trust Tanya? I hadn't talked to her for two years, then in the months I was gone, she completely changed her outlook on life. It wasn't unheard of, just odd, especially with Tanya. I was pretty sure Tanya wasn't a spy and there was no way Liet or The Families knew what we were up to. *I* just found out. Even if they did, Pearl would be the better mole. I trusted her and she followed The Families' every word. But they couldn't know. I didn't know what Tanya hoped to gain from the situation. She claimed she wanted a better world, but who didn't? Unfortunately, I didn't have any other options. I had to get the weapons to Florida.

It was unnerving for me to hear that The Families had taken on a dictator role, though I wasn't really surprised. Even in my short time there I was able to see that they were power hungry. Although crises can bring out the best in people, it usually brings out out those who are looking to gain something. The Families had the money and the ability to protect the citizens and make sure they lived in comfort, but once that was gone, they had to keep the people in line with fear. Money didn't mean anything anymore. Food, clothing, and weapons were what made an individual rich. If they could control the commodities, they could control the masses.

Eventually, though, the population would grow and supplies would run low. I saw it firsthand in North Platte, and I could only imagine Florida would experience it on a grander scale. Although it was obvious they had trades people and professionals. Without raw material, they wouldn't be able to produce their wares. Once the supplies dwindled, blind faith in the leadership would no longer be enough. Groups would form that would question The Families' authority, maybe they already were, I didn't know. What I did know was that The Families would quash any uprisings. I was sure most of the rebellious people were sent away to labor on the wall, even Tanya implied that, but a few wouldn't be able to disappear so easily. That would explain why crews were being sent into the neighboring states. Eventually, The Families would have to allow a few people out to colonize.

In a sense, Liet had it a lot easier; he at least had the zombies to back him up. If someone irritated him enough, he could exile them. If they really pissed him off, he could say they got bit and shoot them in the head. Either way, it was a win win for him. Yet, he and his troops were outnumbered by workers by five to one. If the people decided to revolt, there wasn't much he could do about it, which is why he kept them overworked and half starved. They didn't have the energy to fight. If it came down to it, though, I bet it wouldn't take much to get the workers and some of the guards to riot. There seemed to be some dissention in his ranks. Pam stopped following his orders exactly, and he had condoned another to death for giving out more food than was rationed. I hadn't been there a lot in the past weeks, but I was sure it was only going to get worse.

I also wondered if The Families were going to hold true to their promise of sending professionals. Even though Liet never really claimed that is what he wanted, I was sure that was his intention. I was going to have to lie and tell Liet they needed supply trucks sent down every month so I could get weapons into the state, and I knew Liet wasn't going to be happy, but he would do it. The Families wouldn't question it, they would think Liet was being friendly. This would ensure that I would be able to keep going to the West and keep seeing Quinn.

I thought about how Liet reacted right before leaving for Florida—how he had wondered if I was dating. Why did I have to explain myself to him? Why would he care in the first place? I was entitled if I wanted to. Then, when Pam asked me the same thing, it got me wondering. Did it look like I was dating Quinn? From his words and actions, we were friends and probably always would be, but it apparently had people talking.

Quinn didn't think of me in that way, anyway. He never made a move on me, or even hinted that he might be interested. He even suggested I date Kyle. I wished he was interested in me. He was attractive, and he was my age. Given the circumstances, I could do worse. A lot worse. Like Pam said, I deserved to be happy, and I was pretty sure he could do it.

Pam stirred next to me. She extended her arms out in front and arched her back. "How long have I been asleep?"

"A couple of hours."

"Geez, you'd think with all the coffee I had this morning, I wouldn't be so tired. You ready for me to take over?"

I shook my head. "Not yet. I'm okay."

Pam sat up in the seat. "You still thinking about Pearl?"

I shrugged my right shoulder. "Kind of."

"At least she's happy."

"I guess. I don't understand why she is so complacent."

"That's how the majority of people live their lives. They don't want to make the world a better place, they want to exist in it, and if someone tells them how to do that, then they're happy. Not everyone has a sense of adventure like you do."

"Pfft, yeah, look where that got me."

"It could be worse; you could still be in Florida." Pam smiled. "North Platte might not be the best place to live, but at least we're far away from The Families." She shivered. "God, could you imagine? I doubt they can go to the bathroom without someone knowing about it."

I couldn't believe those words came out of her mouth. Did she live in the same North Platte I did?

"Liet's not much better. In fact, he's a lot worse."

"Only if you're a worker. And they don't have it that bad. They have food and shelter."

I stared at the road for a few minutes. What in the hell was Pam talking about? I decided I probably didn't want to know. My guess was she was justifying things in her own mind, trying to convince herself she wasn't as bad as The Families. I knew if we got into a debate about it, I might let the rebellion slip, so I played it safe and kept my mouth shut.

We rode in silence for a few more hours, then Pam took over driving responsibilities. We stopped again in St. Louis, and headed out early in the morning. When we made it back to North Platte, Liet waited at the storage yard. My heart jumped into my throat, and I hesitated getting out of the truck. I thought for sure he was going to punish me for hitting him before I left. Maybe smack me then like he wanted to in my room. When Liet approached, I flinched and readied myself for a fight.

"It's about time you got back. Complete hell has broken loose since you left."

I stared at him in confusion. Was he waiting to get to the punishment part? Was he trying to make me sweat?

"We came back as soon as we could," I said. "What's going on?"

"A fire destroyed half the storage yard. Didn't you notice it when you pulled in?"

I shook my head. "The sky is always filled with smoke. Adding more to it really isn't that noticeable."

"I need you ready to go as soon as possible to replenish the supplies."

"Can I have a day?" I was tired. It had been a long couple of days. I wanted to spend one night in my own bed and listen to my CDs.

"Sure. It will probably take that long for Quinn to get here anyway."

"Thank you."

I still waited for him to blow up any minute. It was possible he cooled off in the few days we were gone, but it was always hard to tell with Liet.

I walked toward the courthouse, my mind already lying on my pillow and my body snuggled under the covers. Liet fell into step with me.

"I assume your trip went well?"

My vision of heaven cracked and I glared at him. "It was fine. They said some new recruits will be coming in the next couple of weeks."

"They better. We're running real low on quality workers."

I stared at him, hoping he would burst into flames. "Maybe it's not the quality of worker, maybe it's the quality of leadership."

I figured by this point in time if he hadn't gotten angry, he probably wasn't going to. I was exhausted and everything he said and every breath he took grated on my nerves. I didn't care how angry I made him anymore because I knew I had a way out.

Liet narrowed his eyes to slits. "If you were in my shoes, what would you do differently?"

"Maybe try to show a little compassion."

"Compassion?" Liet spit the word out like venom. "Do you think the pyramids were built with compassion? Or the Great Wall of China? Compassion gets you nowhere."

"Yeah, well, slave driving doesn't seem to be getting you anywhere either."

"There is no happy medium, Krista. It's either the hard way or the highway."

I rolled my eyes and hurried to the apartment. I wanted to stay and argue, maybe claw his eyes out, but I knew that would get me nowhere. I knew I would have my chance soon enough.

I took a hot shower. The water felt good as it splashed on my back. When I finished, I dressed in sweats and climbed into bed. The soft pillow enveloped my head, and I instantly fell asleep. I dreamt that I was back at Quinn's ranch. We rode the horses through the field when the cows suddenly started stampeding. We couldn't do anything, so we moved out of the way and watched as the animals streamed by. After the cows entered the canyon and the dust settled, we noticed a group of zombies following them. I tried to get my horse to move, but its hooves had sunk down into the dirt. I turned to Quinn. His mouth was open in a silent scream, and half-rotted hands pulled him off his horse. He reached out for me, and I tried to grab him, but a zombie jumped in between us and bit my arm. I pulled it back in surprise. My heart stopped for a brief second when I noticed Dad standing before me. Someone grabbed me from behind and pulled me to the ground. Mom chewed on my hair, and Dad moved forward to bite my neck.

I jerked awake. I went to the bathroom and splashed water on my face. On my way back to bed, someone sat in the chair on the opposite side of the room. I clicked on my lamp. It was Liet.

"What are you doing in here?"

He steepled his fingers and took a deep breath. "I was born and raised in Oregon and lived there until I was fifteen."

I took a seat on the edge of the bed. "I know. We talked about this in the truck on the way up here. Remember?"

"After my fifteenth birthday, my mom divorced my dad. She claimed that it was because he drank too much, but the real problem was her. She didn't like to stay faithful. My dad was a trucker, so he was gone a lot. My mom claimed to get lonely, so she found other men to keep her company.

"The court asked me who I wanted to live with, and I told them my father. But because of his profession, they wouldn't allow it. I had to stay with my mom. We moved to Louisiana right after the family reunion. My dad told me he would come and visit me all the time, take me on his trips when he could. Since the school year was starting, he said he'd see me at Christmas. He never showed up. When I called, he told me things were too crazy at the moment, so we'd have to wait until things settled down. He told me this for two years. By the time I was eighteen, he quit promising to come get me.

"My mom wasn't around much, either. Since she was a single mom, she worked all day and spent her nights in the local bars, picking up men. She found some real winners. I won't bore you with the details. The nights she came home with her boyfriends, I would make myself scarce. As you can imagine, I got into a lot of trouble roaming the streets.

"My mother wanted nothing to do with me when they sent me to juvie and then to prison. My parents left me, Krista. They abandoned me. All I ever wanted was a family. Someone to love and care for. I have that now, and I'm not going to let anything take it away." Liet stood and crossed the room to me. He wrapped me in a hug. "I let you go into the West because you'll go crazy if you stay here.

You're just like me. You need to roam. I don't like it when you leave, though, and a part of me dies every time you drive through the gates. He can't take care of you like I can, and he won't. I will continue to let you collect supplies as long as you promise to keep your relationship professional. But don't mistake my compassion for weakness." He released me and left.

Between the dream and waking to find Liet in my room, I couldn't go back to sleep. I turned off the light and threw on some clothes, heading to the guard tower.

The searchlights scanned the field in front of me, and I took out a dozen zombies before the sun rose. Their moans penetrated the cool air and sent a shiver down my spine. Images of my dream were still fresh in my mind, and I wondered if my parents were out there roaming the earth. Would I ever run into them? I was sure that if I did, I would have no problems putting a bullet between their eyes. Of course, I might let them wander in their own personal hell. After all, they brought it on themselves. I needed them more than ever, and they went and got themselves killed.

I buried my face in my hands. I hated that I was so mad at my parents, but I hated it even more that they weren't here. I knew I shouldn't blame them for what happened, but it was nobody's fault but their own. It certainly wasn't my fault. I told them not to go. I told them to stay. They didn't listen. I wiped my hands down my face and stared at the horizon. More moans echoed through the morning air. A few silhouettes appeared, and I grabbed my rifle. I focused down the sight. The half rotted flesh of a zombie filled the optics, and I squeezed the trigger. The creature fell over backward, and another walked right over it. I chambered another round.

"Stupid morons," I whispered under my breath before taking another shot.

The sun popped over the horizon, and another soldier stepped into the tower. I collected my weapons and went back to the courthouse. A Jeep Wrangler was parked on the street as I made my way to Liet's office. Quinn was there with Bill and Kyle, and they smiled as I entered the room. I smiled back and had to refrain from running up to them and giving them a hug. They were the most welcome sight in North Platte. I stood in front of Liet's desk and placed my hands on my hips.

"Two trucks, as usual," he said without looking up from his paperwork. "And we need more building supplies. See what you can do."

I turned and headed out of the room with the guys when Liet stopped me. He stepped from behind his desk and wrapped his arms around my shoulders.

"Sorry I scared you last night," he whispered so only I could hear. "I really don't know what I'd do without you."

I tried to pull out of his grasp, but he pulled me tighter and nuzzled against my neck.

"Things are going to be different from now on. I promise." He planted a kiss on my cheek, and I was finally able to squirm out of his grasp.

I wiped my face as I headed to the truck. Every fiber of my being was grossed out. I would rather have endured an entire day of inspection showers in the dead of winter than have to experience that again. I almost preferred that he would have hit me. This killing me with kindness crap was killing me. I visibly shuddered when Liet followed me.

"Quinn, you'd better take good care of her. She's all the family I have left." He winked and closed my door.

I turned to Quinn, hoping he could somehow take the ickiness away.

"What's that all about?"

"He thinks you and I are dating. I think he's trying to show that he's the dominant male."

Quinn chuckled.

He thought I was joking, so I stared at him.

"Seriously?"

I nodded.

Quinn glanced out the window at Liet, then turned on the engine. "Why would he think that?"

I shrugged. "Your guess is as good as mine."

Quinn went to put the truck in gear when gunshots echoed through the streets. We looked at each other.

"That sounded close," I said.

We both glanced out the window and watched a soldier run up to Liet. His arms flailed as he explained what was going on. Liet's face turned red as he yelled at the man and pointed to something behind him. My stomach knotted, and I pushed open the door.

"What's going on?"

Liet stared at me for a moment, his jaw clenched. More shots were fired, followed by a loud boom. I fell to my knees and covered my ears.

"We've got zombies in the city."

CHAPTER 18

I followed Liet and some other soldiers to the worker's housing a few blocks away. A small fire raged in the front yard of one of the houses, and several soldiers fired into a crowd of five zombies—a male and a female, both looked like they were in their early thirties, and three kids ranging in age from six to fifteen. I was sure they just turned—their skin hadn't had the chance to decompose. The only indication they were undead was their pale skin, sunken eyes, and unseeing stare. My best guess was that someone in the family had been infected, brought it back, and infected everyone else. I pulled my weapon. Liet surveyed the scene with his hands on his hips and a scowl on his face.

The zombies were taken down quickly, and a few soldiers worked on putting out the fire. I holstered my weapon. Quinn, Bill, and Kyle made their way to the scene. I took one step forward, when something grabbed my hair. At first, I thought it was the wind or maybe someone running by, but when they started pulling, that made me angry. I reached over my head and grabbed the person's wrists. I went to throw them over my shoulder, to teach them a lesson about grabbing people from behind, but they slipped out of my grasp as their skin peeled freely from their bones. I ducked and pulled away as the creature was about to chomp down on my shoulder, leaving a hunk of my hair in the zombie's hands. The creature moaned, and I flipped out my arm sword. With a swift movement, I took off the creature's head. I glanced around. Movement behind the house caught my eye, and I took off running. I jumped over the waist-high pickets and scanned the area. Nothing. I turned to my right and headed through the gate that connected the neighbor's yard and stopped in my tracks.

The grass was stained red with blood, and a group of seven zombies crouched next to their latest kill. Half of the body had already been consumed, but the head, chest, and arms still lay on the ground. The eyes of the man stared blankly at the sky, and his intestines were strewn between three creatures. I grabbed my weapon and started firing. I took down two before the rest of them noticed me and converged on my position. I moved to the back of the house, and with a quick jump and some help from a tree, I was on the roof. The zombies followed me, but since they couldn't climb, they moaned and pounded on the side of the house. I took the opportunity to pick them off one by one.

When I finished, I did a quick survey of the area. From my vantage point, I couldn't see any more creatures, but that didn't mean they weren't lurking in a house or some other enclosed space. I hurried to the front and climbed off the roof. Liet yelled at another soldier as I approached.

"And get the bodies to the pyre!" His face was red with exertion. He glared at me. "Where did you go?"

I pointed at the house. "I was taking care of some undesirables in the backyard. What happened?"

Liet shook his head. "I don't know. But when I find out, there'll be hell to pay." He averted his attention to someone behind me. "What are you doing? I said quarantine the entire area."

I turned to see a soldier helping a family carry some belongings.

"Nothing goes. Drop that stuff right now!"

The woman did as she was told and escorted the family down the block.

"What are you doing with them?" I wondered.

"Everyone within a three block radius is being taken to holding pens on the other side of the wall. If someone else turns, they'll be shot on sight. Everyone else is on strict lockdown. I won't have this epidemic spreading through my town."

"You can't lock them down. You don't even know where the plague started."

He stared at me. Rage burned in his eyes. That was the Liet I knew. Surprisingly, he spoke in an even tone. "I'll do what I have to do. What are you still doing here anyway? I thought I sent you to get more supplies."

"You needed my help."

"I didn't need anything! My soldiers could have handled it fine. You just thought we needed your help."

My face flushed with anger. "Oh, yeah, who destroyed seven zombies in a backyard that your soldiers didn't even know about? Without me, they could still be wandering the street."

Liet stuck his face inches from mine. "Why do you think it's all right to go looking for danger? Don't you realize you could have been killed? We would have found them eventually."

"Yeah, but by then it might have been too late."

"Why is everything a constant battle with you?"

"Why can't you see I don't need you to protect me?" I screamed. "Why can't you see that I can take care of myself?"

Liet's jaw muscles tightened. "I know I said you could go on the trip, but I've changed my mind. You're grounded. Get to your room right now." He grabbed at my arm, but I backed out of his grasp. My foot caught on an uneven part of the street, and I fell onto my butt.

"Hey!" A voice called off to my right.

Quinn approached at a fast pace. I jumped to my feet and stood between the two guys, holding my hands out in front to stop Quinn.

"Here comes your boyfriend to save the day."

"Quinn, stop, please. I'm fine."

Quinn stopped, his hands on his hips and his teeth grinding together.

Liet grabbed me by the arm and spun me around. "I told you to go to your room." He pushed me toward the courthouse. "You, hero, get out of my sight."

I stormed off, but I didn't go to my room. Instead, I climbed into the truck with Quinn and headed west. I stared out the window, avoiding Quinn's gaze, as he sat in the driver's seat, fuming.

"Stupid jerk! I wish I could take him out now. Put one between his eyes." I slammed my fist into the side of the door.

"Even if you take him out now, Florida would send another to replace him. We have to time this perfectly if it's going to work."

I glared at him. "And what were you doing? What were you expecting to do to Liet on the street back there?"

Quinn shrugged. "I don't know. It upset me to see him do that to you."

"Do what? I tripped. I don't need you to fight my battles for me either."

Quinn opened his mouth to say something, thought better of it, and took a deep breath. "You're right. I'm sorry. Liet's going to be pissed when he realizes you're gone. I hope he doesn't take it out on the workers."

I hesitated for a moment. I hadn't thought about that. All I was worried about was proving to Liet that he didn't control me. Maybe that explained why he was so calm when I got back from Florida. Maybe he had already taken all his anger out on some poor innocent victim. It softened my mood and made me feel slightly guilty.

"Besides, if you had attacked Liet, he would've killed you." I shrugged. "Well, maybe not him, but his soldiers would have." I folded my hands in my lap and stared at them. "Thanks for trying to come to my rescue." I smiled feebly at him.

He smiled back. "Sure."

We traveled for a while in silence. How did the zombies get into the city in the first place? They had such stringent rules about checking the workers, someone should have noticed a bite mark. Whoever dropped the ball on that one was going to pay dearly. I felt sorry for those who were being quarantined. If someone else did turn, then everyone who was in the cage with them was fair game. Being in a cage alone had to be scary and stressful. I couldn't imagine also having the extra worry if one of your friends was going to turn. What else could they do? It wouldn't be very cost effective to build separate cages for all of them. It was a shame that it had to come to this.

The truck bumped on the road and pulled me out of my thoughts. I looked out the window and noticed a herd of undead crossing the street. Quinn pressed down on the accelerator. I stared at him.

"You enjoy this way too much."

Quinn smiled. "I enjoy watching you wash the truck." His mouth snapped shut after he spoke, and his face turned red.

I did my best to hide my smile. "Oh, so now the truth comes out. What part do you enjoy the most? Seeing me get covered in undead crud or how I react when a zombie attacks my leg?"

Quinn pressed his mouth shut and shook his head. "I shouldn't have said anything. I'm sorry."

"No, no. I want to know. You've piqued my interest."

He cleared his throat. "I like to watch you. Since the moment we first met, I haven't been able to get you out of my mind. When you told me earlier that Liet thought we were dating, the first thing that popped into my head was that you would date me to validate his feelings."

I was stunned silent. My intention was to tease him a little to lighten the mood. I had no idea it would take an even more serious turn. It made me wonder if Pam and Liet noticed Quinn watching me, if that was what tipped them off to the fact that we might be together. I always caught myself staring at him, wondering what it was like to kiss him and if we would ever be a couple. But now that the topic actually came up, I was too embarrassed to talk about it.

Quinn forced a chuckle. "Hey, whatever you want to do is fine. I couldn't go another trip without saying anything. At least you know where I stand."

I wanted to tell him that I felt the same way, but the words stuck in my throat. All I could do was stare out the window, smiling to myself. Quinn ran into another zombie and blood and pus flew over the hood, coating the windshield like someone threw a bucket of the goo. Quinn turned on the windshield wipers and smeared the viscous fluid all over the glass. He pulled the trigger to release the cleaner fluid, but nothing came out.

"Crap," he muttered under his breath.

Quinn slammed on the brakes. I braced myself against the dash.

I took a deep breath and steeled my nerves. "Quinn, I want you to know that I feel the same way. But I don't know how well things will work out with Liet."

He looked at me, a serious expression on his face. "I'm not afraid of Liet."

I stared at him for a silent minute. "I know, but I think maybe we should keep this between us. A secret. Just for a little while."

"If that's what makes you comfortable."

I nodded. "It does."

We stared at each other for a long time.

"What changed your mind?" I finally asked.

"What do you mean?"

"Last time we talked about boyfriends and girlfriends, you told me that Kyle was available."

Quinn laughed. "I was trying to gauge your interest. I didn't know if you liked me, and I was too embarrassed to say anything, so I told you that so I didn't look like an idiot."

A horn honked behind us. We broke our gaze and glanced out the window. In the rearview, the horde we passed on the road was slowly limping to our location.

"I suppose I should take care of the windshield." Quinn sighed. "I'm sure Bill and Kyle are wondering what's going on."

"Looks like it's going to have to be a quick clean job from the roof."

Quinn shrugged. "I have to be able to see. Will you watch my back?"

"Of course."

Bill and Kyle pulled up next to us.

"What are you doing?" Bill yelled.

Quinn grabbed the cleaning fluid and a rag. He turned toward the other truck and pointed at the bottle.

"What is taking so long?" Bill snapped.

"I couldn't find the rag," Quinn said. He turned to me. "Oops."

We both chuckled, then I climbed onto the roof. I waved at Kyle.

The zombies were pretty far back, so I knew we had some time. I stood with my gun out, keeping an eye on the area, while Quinn wiped off the windshield. I thought about the fact that I had a boyfriend, something that had never happened before, and Quinn was so involved with cleaning, we didn't notice the corpse clinging to the side of the cab. It reached forward and grabbed Quinn by the ankle. I noticed him look back, but I didn't follow his gaze to see what he looked at. When he yelped and started kicking, then I turned to see what happened.

The creature's mouth latched onto the bottom of his shoe, and Quinn couldn't get him off. I flipped out my arm sword to take off its head, but before I could get there, Quinn rolled off the top of the truck, taking the zombie with him. I dashed over to the side. He got the undead off his foot, but that gave it the perfect opportunity to moan, alerting the others in the area. I turned to see a new horde coming over the hill on the left and moving toward us. This one was close. It would be at our location in a few minutes. There were even a few of them in the ditch on the side of the road. They must have been hanging out, unaware of our presence, but they knew we were there after the moan. Bill and Kyle climbed out of their truck and shot into the crowd. I took out a few who were closest to me, then turned to see what happened to Quinn.

My heart stopped when I looked over the edge and he wasn't there. I fell to my hands and knees and scanned the area, calling his name. A zombie came around the front of the truck and grabbed at my face. There was no way the creature could have gotten me, it was instinct that I jerked back.

"Kyle, have you seen Quinn?" The panic rose in my chest.

Kyle quit firing and stared at me. "What?"

"Have you seen Quinn?"

"I can't hear you!"

Something clanged on the opposite side of the truck. I turned to look. A group of zombies pounded on the side and somehow opened the passenger door. I realized at that moment that zombies could climb into trucks.

"Krista, jump!"

Kyle waved his arms for me to jump to the truck. Close to two hundred zombies came into our location, and I knew we had to leave. I took a deep breath and a couple of steps and jumped onto the top of the other cab. We all climbed in, and Bill threw the truck into gear. I glanced out the window and watched as the zombies covered the truck. My heart sank as I imagined Quinn being devoured. My bottom lip quivered and I bit it so no one would notice.

Bill looked over his shoulder. "You all right? You get bit?"

I shook my head, dumbfounded. "No. I don't think so."

"What about you, Quinn? You bit?"

I turned in surprise and looked into the sleeper cabin. Quinn was pale, covered in blood, and grabbed his arm. Relief flooded into my body.

"I don't know," his voice was soft, shaky.

I climbed in next to him.

"Don't worry, we'll get you to the cabin as quick as we can," Bill said.

I cradled his head in my lap. Tears flowed freely from my eyes. "You'll be okay. We'll get you some help."

"I think I broke my arm."

"You'll be fine. Don't worry." The words caught in my throat. I wanted to believe it, I really did, but I knew the odds weren't in my favor.

It took us an hour to reach the ranch. By then, some color returned to Quinn's face and he was able to climb into the house of his own accord, but he didn't look good. Bill took him into the bathroom and helped him clean up. Kyle, I, and the others at the ranch paced the front porch until Bill came out. He stared at us somberly.

"There are a lot of wounds. It's hard to tell if any of them are bites. He didn't break his arm, but his wrist is sprained." He met the gaze of the others. "He's resting comfortably right now. I'll take the first shift, Kyle you take the next. If he turns in twenty-four hours, you all know what to do."

I chewed on my thumbnail. I felt nauseous, and my hands shook uncontrollably. It was going to be the longest twenty-four hours of my life.

CHAPTER 19

I sat on the couch next to the fireplace and stared off into space. My palms were sweaty, my mouth was dry, and I still felt nauseous. What would I do if I lost Quinn? I really liked him. He was the first boy that I didn't think had serial killer tendencies. And he was the first boy who liked me back. Why was it that the good ones always died early, but jerks lived forever? Why wasn't Liet laying in that bed? If it was Liet, I would haul his butt out into the desert. If he made his way back, then he wasn't a zombie. I knew life wasn't fair, that became painfully evident after my parents died, but I didn't know why it felt like it had to make me completely miserable. Hadn't I suffered enough?

Kyle sat next to me and offered me a plate with a hamburger, chips, and baked beans. I shook my head, and he set it on the coffee table in front of us.

"You doin' all right?"

I shook my head again. "Have you ever seen anyone change?"

Kyle nodded.

"What's it like?"

"We really should try and focus on the positive. He's going to be fine."

I stared at him. "What's it like?"

"It starts out kind of like the flu. They get a really high fever, they throw up a lot, and then they drift into a coma. Their skin takes on a gray tone, and the area around the bite turns black with black streaks leading away from the wound. Once they wake up from their coma, they lash out at anything near them."

My stomach tightened. "Has Quinn exhibited any of those symptoms?"

Kyle shrugged. "I don't know."

"How long after the bite does it take for the symptoms to appear?"

"Depends. But everyone turns within twenty-four hours."

Bill came into the room at that moment and asked Kyle to join him upstairs. My heart sunk, and I buried my face in my hands. This was part of my life. There was no denying that eventually someone close to me was going to turn into a zombie. I had been lucky that I never saw anyone turn, but luck always ran out. Why did it have to be Quinn? What did he ever do to anyone? For that matter, why did it have to be any of those innocents living in North Platte? It was one thing for an adult, but children? It was almost unfathomable. It was like we were being punished, but for what? I drove myself crazy thinking about it.

I stood from the couch and walked onto the porch, hoping some fresh air would relieve my nausea. A slight breeze blew, and I folded my hands across my chest to ward off the chill. A few people still milled around the ranch and finished their chores, but the majority of them were in their homes eating dinner. They had families to take care of. I didn't have anyone. There was one point in time I thought it was better to be alone, especially when the alternative was Liet, but Quinn changed all that. A dark depression fell over me, and I sat on the porch swing.

Ever since my parents died, I refused to get close to anyone. I had friends, but how close was I to them? I didn't talk about my feeling to anyone. I lashed out at Liet, but he deserved it. Somewhere at the back of my brain, a voice told me not to get too close. It was supposed to be easier that way. Make it simpler if they were ever turned into zombies.

But it didn't make it simpler. In fact, it made it worse. There was so much I could learn from Quinn. If he turned into an undead, I would spend the rest of my life regretting I didn't get to know him better. And what if he were the one? What if he offered me complete happiness? We decided in the truck to start a relationship, but why didn't we talk about it sooner? Why did we have to be so stubborn and shy?

Night crept in, and I stared at the sky. All of the lights from the other houses were turned off, and the faint moans of zombies carried on the wind. I shivered and stood to go back inside. Someone started a fire, and I sat on the couch next to it. I stared at the flames, my eyes growing heavy from the heat, and I eventually fell asleep.

Boots clumped on the hardwood floors and jerked me out of my slumber. For a brief second, I thought I was back in the lookout tower with my parents. The smell of bacon bombarded my nostrils, and I turned, expecting to see my mother. When I looked over the couch and saw Bill, realization of where I was sank in. I sat up and asked about Quinn.

Bill smiled. "He's fine. Like I suspected, they were scratches." He let out a sigh. "Tell you what, that had to be the scariest night of my life."

"Yeah, but it hasn't been twenty-four hours yet. There still might be the possibility that he could change."

"Nah. There weren't any of the warning signs like with the others. He's fine."

My stomach unknotted and a weight lifted from my shoulders. I suddenly realized I was very hungry. I stepped into the kitchen and looked over Bill's shoulder as he cooked. I made short work of the eggs, bacon, and coffee I was handed.

When I finished, I went outside. Work on the ranch continued like nothing ever happened. Quinn stood by the corrals and I walked to him. His left wrist was wrapped in a brace, and cuts and scratches covered his face. He smiled as I approached. Without saying a word, I grabbed his face and kissed him hard on the lips.

When I pulled away, I expected to see surprise on Quinn's face, but he just smiled.

My face flushed and I went to turn away, but he gently wrapped one arm around my waist and the other around my neck and kissed me passionately. My knees buckled, and I threw my hands around his neck to keep from falling. When he pulled away, I couldn't catch my breath.

"I, uh, I…" I took a deep breath. "I wanted to let you know that I'm glad you're all right."

"I don't go down that easily."

"I'm glad."

We kissed again.

One of the horses whinnied and nudged Quinn on the shoulder. He turned and chuckled.

"I should probably feed them."

He released me, and I placed a hand on the fence to steady myself. He reached for the pitchfork and studied it, trying to figure out how he was going to throw the hay.

I smiled. "Here, let me help you with that." I reached for the tool, but he moved it out of my way.

"I can figure out how to do it."

I grabbed his arm and playfully jerked the pitchfork out of his hand. "We don't have a year to wait. We need to head back out and fill the trucks. Hopefully the zombies have left the area so we can get the other truck running." I scooped up some hay and tossed it into the horse's feed bucket. "Will you be coming back out with us?"

Quinn leaned against the fence and watched me work. "Of course. I want to make sure you're going to be okay."

I rolled my eyes. "I can take care of myself."

"I know."

When we finished feeding the horses, we headed back to the house and gathered our supplies. Bill insisted Quinn stay behind and heal, but he wouldn't hear it. The four of us climbed into the semi and headed to the other truck.

The area was clear when we arrived, but we hesitated getting out. We knew a group of them could be over the hill, in the ditches, or hiding inside the truck. I shuddered as I thought about the creatures climbing inside. Part of me wanted to leave the vehicle there, but Liet would be extremely angry if I did. I already ran away, even though I planned on going back, and I didn't need to add anything else to Liet's mood. The thought did run through my mind that Quinn and I could disappear and never return, but then who would help the workers?

Something moved in the cab and everyone froze. Our breaths came in soft puffs. If we breathed too loud, the zombies would hear us. At least that's what I thought. As if they could hear our breathing over the idling diesel engine. After a few minutes, when nothing else moved, we relaxed a bit.

"Too bad we can't cut our losses," Kyle said.

"Yeah, too bad they aren't our losses to cut. A lot of good people are waiting on these supplies." I swung my legs into the front seat. "We've procrastinated long enough. I'm going over there."

Quinn grabbed my arm. "It only takes one moan to sound the alarm. If there is one still in the truck, you'll be a sitting duck."

"Sitting here isn't getting the zombie out of the truck or the truck fixed. We need to get moving. I don't see anyone else volunteering." I glanced at Bill and Kyle.

"We'll give you support from the top of the truck." Bill opened his door.

Kyle opened the door and climbed onto the roof. I slid down into the dirt, my gun drawn, and cautiously walked to the other truck. My heart pounded in my ears. I did a quick sweep of the trailer, making sure nothing was on top or beneath, then stepped around to the passenger side door. The truck was covered in blood, puss, and body parts from the road, so I didn't want to lean against it. I took a deep breath, closed my eyes, then turned so my gun pointed into the cab. Nothing. Skin flakes and bits of tattered clothing that had fallen off the creatures coated the interior. The smell of rotting flesh bombarded my nostrils, and my stomach jerked. I covered my nose to block out some of the smell and keep from puking. A breeze stirred some papers that had been scattered, and I assumed that was what we saw from the other truck. Cautiously, I climbed the stairs and parted the curtain to the sleeper cab. Nothing. The zombies moved on.

I jumped out of the cab and holstered my weapon. Walking around to the front of the truck, I signaled the all clear to the others. Bill and Quinn refueled the vehicle while Kyle stood watch.

"With any luck, this will be all the semi needs." Quinn squinted at the sun, keeping his eye on the horizon for undead.

When they finished, Quinn climbed into the driver's seat. "Oh my god!" He cried, and we all ran to see what was wrong. Quinn looked at us, his nose wrinkled. "Are you sure there aren't any zombies in here? It stinks!"

I rolled my eyes and turned my attention back to the hills.

"Eww, there's something gooey on my seat."

I tried to refrain from laughing, but I couldn't. When I searched the truck, I noticed a layer of clear fluid covering the seats, and I succeeded in covering my jeans with the stuff. I didn't feel sorry for Quinn.

The truck roared to life, and I pushed Quinn into the passenger seat. "You really should rest your wrist," I explained. "Just tell me where we're going."

He pointed toward the highway. "Get back on I eighty and head west. When we hit I twenty-five, we'll head down into Colorado and see what we can find."

I pulled the truck onto the highway and followed his directions.

By nightfall, both trucks were loaded with supplies, and we camped in Fort Collins's jail. Several propane-powered lanterns were distributed throughout the room, and our camp stoves were lit and cooked canned vegetables and chili. Quinn kept readjusting, arching his back and rubbing his shoulder. More than likely, he was stiff and sore from sitting in the truck. Even though his wrist was the most serious of his injuries, he had bumps and bruises from the fall.

"Are you all right?" I eventually asked him.

He rubbed his shoulder. "No, my shoulder is killing me."

Bill reached into his bag and pulled out a First Aid kit. "Here, take a couple Ibuprofen." He handed the pills to Quinn.

"Thanks." He popped them in his mouth and chased them down with bottled water.

"If you need any more, let me know." He grabbed a lantern, stood, and looked at his brother. "C'mon, Kyle, it's time for bed."

Kyle bid us good night and followed Bill into the cell.

I looked at Quinn. He still rubbed his shoulder.

"Would it help if I massaged it a little?"

"It might."

I positioned myself behind him and placed my hands on him. The muscle underneath was hard and sinewy, with a small bulge at the base of his neck. I rubbed, and he flinched away from me.

"Sorry." I started again, more gently.

The muscles loosened as I worked on them. My face flushed and I became a little uncomfortable at the silence. Is that why Bill and Kyle left? Were they purposefully trying to give us some time alone? I didn't know why it made me uncomfortable, we were officially a couple. Maybe it was because I didn't really know how to act. Or give a massage. It was all so new to me.

Quinn's fingers gently touched mine, and he looked at me over his shoulder. "Are you all right?"

"I don't know. I'm still a little nervous about you and me. To tell you the truth, Quinn, I've never had a boyfriend before. I'm not sure how to act."

Quinn turned to face me. "The last girlfriend I had was in first grade. I'm not really sure what to do either." He placed his hands on my knees. "We can figure it out together. But one thing is for sure, I'm still your friend. That doesn't have to change."

"Except now we are friends who get to kiss." I smiled.

"Mmm, speaking of…" He leaned forward and our lips connected.

We kissed for several moments before Quinn pulled away. He arched his back.

"I hate to break this up, 'cause I'm really enjoying it, but I think I need to get an ice pack from Bill." He stood and gave me one last kiss. "Good night, Krista."

"Good night, Quinn."

I lay in bed for a long time thinking about him. Just as I was about to drift to sleep, disappointment enveloped me because I didn't have anyone to tell about my new boyfriend.

CHAPTER 20

After we filled both trucks, we headed back to the ranch and hid the guns in the supplies. Then, we went back to North Platte where Liet waited for us. He stared at Quinn as we approached. I prepared myself for his wrath.

"What the hell happened to you?"

"I fell off the top of the truck."

"You fell off? How did you fall off the top of the truck?"

"We were up there cleaning off some zombie blood, and I didn't know there was one behind me, so as I wrestled with it, I rolled off the side."

Liet stared at him for a moment, his eyes flicking up and down. "At least you didn't turn into a zombie. I guess you should be thankful you didn't get more hurt. That's a pretty long fall from the top of one of those."

"Tell me about it."

The breeze changed direction, and Liet wrinkled his nose. He glanced at Quinn and me. "You guys stink. Didn't they make you shower before you came in here?"

"Yeah, but they don't wash our clothes. We had some issues with zombies." Quinn rubbed the back of his neck. "If you think we're bad, you should smell the truck."

"I'll pass." Liet turned on his heel and headed into the courthouse, the four of us followed behind. Liet went to his desk and glanced at a file.

"We're going to need medical supplies. After that little debacle with the zombies in town, we've depleted most of our resources."

"What did you find out about that?" I expected Liet to explode in anger at any moment. In fact, I would have preferred it. His calmness creeped me out. I thought back to the hug he'd given me. I couldn't endure another.

Liet leaned back in his chair. "Apparently, one of the workers who had corpse cleanup duty stepped on a zombie that wasn't quite dead." He paused for a moment. "That's probably not the right choice of words, but you get my meaning. From what I could gather, he stepped on its torso, and it flipped up and bit him on the thigh. Since he was covered in blood and guts from moving bodies, no one noticed his leg was bleeding. The soldier on duty that day decided to forego the mandatory strip search because it was beginning to rain, and he waltzed right into his home. Obviously, he turned and sought out other victims."

"How many people were turned?"

"About forty."

Forty? That was a lot. No one noticed one or two people getting sick? I knew the disease spread fast, but it was odd no one reported it sooner. I knew the carrier wouldn't say anything. I didn't when I had to go through the line and all I had was scratches.

"Who was the soldier?"

Liet smirked. "You don't need to worry about that. It's been taken care of."

I shivered. I knew the incident led to the soldier's death, perhaps even a little bit of torture. I witnessed how mad Liet had been when we left, so I doubted the man got off easily. Knowing Liet, he probably fed him to the zombies.

"I suspect you'll want to leave first thing in the morning."

I nodded. "Of course."

The four of us headed up to the apartment, and I was never happier than when I took off my jeans and T-shirt. I thought about throwing them in with the other dirty clothes, but then tossed them into the fireplace. I shampooed and soaped up twice in the shower.

After dinner that night, I snuck into the storage yard where the trucks were parked. Most of the supplies had already been unloaded, so I set to work recovering the guns we'd hidden. I stashed them in a storage shed, and was about to head back, when I ran into Liet.

"What are you doing out here this time of night? Are you planning on running away again?" He glanced over my shoulder, as if looking for someone.

"I thought I left my sweatshirt in the truck."

Liet frowned. "Why would you want it if you did?"

"It's my lucky sweatshirt."

Liet walked past me to the truck. He opened the door and closed it just as quickly. "Was it in there?"

I shook my head. "No, I must have left it somewhere."

He leaned against the truck and placed his right foot on the step. "I'm sure this truck will have to be cleaned before you take it out again. How did you stomach that smell?"

"We rode with the windows down."

"Isn't that dangerous?"

I shrugged one shoulder. "Not any more so than heading into the West."

Liet pushed himself away from the truck and approached me. He moved a piece of hair from my shoulder and slid his hand down my arm, resting it above my elbow.

"I'm relieved you came back. You had me worried sick." He hugged me tight. "I think Quinn has served his purpose."

I pulled away from him. "What do you mean?"

"I mean, we don't need him anymore. He taught you what you needed to know. You know how to survive in the West, you can train others."

Panic gripped my chest. If I said that I still needed Quinn, Liet might figure out that we were actually together, but if I said it was fine, I might never see Quinn again. I could always visit him on the ranch, but then I risked other soldiers knowing how to find it. I knew the only reason Liet brought this up was to punish me.

I needed to think of something fast so I could still gather supplies with Quinn.

He stared at me. "Look, I know that I'm not your father, but I am older and the only family you have. You're still young, someone has to protect you."

I had to keep myself from visibly shuddering. "You're right, Liet, and I'm sorry I ran away. I promise it won't happen again." I forced a smile. The words were like acid on my tongue, and I suddenly felt like I needed another shower. "You know, I'm kind of tired, and we have a long day ahead of us tomorrow. I think I'm going to go to bed." I squirmed out of his grasp and made my way back to the courthouse.

"This is the last time, Krista. The very last time," Liet called behind me.

I cringed.

I didn't sleep very well that night. I worried that Liet would change his mind and make me stay behind. I also worried he would show up in my room again. There was also the fear that he would hurt Quinn, who slept on the couch in the living room.

A sense of relief washed over me as the pink hue of morning shone through my bedroom window. My eyes felt like sandpaper, but I was going to leave in a few hours. I got up and went to make a pot of coffee.

Bill, Kyle, and Quinn were still sleeping as I made my way to the kitchen. I tiptoed past the living room and tried to be as quiet as possible while preparing breakfast. I was in the kitchen for two minutes before I turned to see Quinn standing behind me. He smiled and said good morning, and it took every ounce of self control to keep from kissing him.

"Why are you up so early?" He yawned.

"I couldn't sleep." I scooped some coffee into the filter. "You?"

"I always get up this early. Work on the ranch starts as soon as you can see."

I clicked on the coffee pot, and it hissed to life. "We might have a problem," I whispered.

"What kind of problem?"

"I'll tell you about it later."

Kyle and Bill stirred, and I moved to grab some eggs out of the fridge.

When we finished, we headed downstairs to climb into the trucks. As usual, Liet waited for us, but this time he had two soldiers with him. He smiled as we approached.

"I was thinking," he said, "that you could take Wilks and Anderson with you. Show them the ropes."

I pursed my lips. "Where are they going to sit?"

"I figured one of them can ride with you, and the other one can ride with Bill."

"What are Quinn and Kyle going to do?"

"They can take Quinn's Jeep."

"It seems a little silly to be taking so many vehicles." I pointed out.

"Not really. One of the trucks you are filling with supplies will be going to Florida, so when it's full, Wilks can take it straight down there. Since Quinn will have his Jeep, he can take Bill and Kyle back home. Then you will come back here." He folded his arms across his chest, daring us to question his authority.

I shrugged. "Whatever." Then walked to the truck. Maybe I wouldn't come back. Maybe I would get into Quinn's Jeep. Liet wouldn't know where to find me. I just had to worry about those soldiers.

Anderson climbed in next to me, while Wilks and Bill climbed into the other truck and Quinn and Kyle got into the Jeep. We pulled out of North Platte and headed down the road. When we were a few miles outside of town, I pulled over onto the side of the road. Quinn pulled up next to me.

"Where are we going?" I called over the roar of the semi's engine.

"Follow me."

I nodded, and we headed to Cheyenne. We parked in front of the hospital, and Kyle and Quinn climbed into the cab of the semi.

"This has got to be the most dangerous mission yet."

Anderson stared at Quinn. "Why?"

"Think about it, when people first started getting sick, where do you think they went?" He waited for an answer that never came. "To hospitals. Once they turned into zombies, they were trapped inside and had a free lunch. This place is going to be infested."

I looked over my shoulder. "How do you want to do this?"

"Carefully. What exactly do we need?"

"A little bit of everything."

"Perfect."

Quinn removed his wrist brace and took his Kahr TP45 out of its holster to check the magazine. He grabbed some extras out of my bag and tucked them in his belt before sheathing the katana that was under the driver's seat in the truck. Kyle grabbed a shotgun and a fireman's ax, then nodded at Quinn, who looked at me. I opened my door and pulled out my gun. Anderson stumbled out of her door, weapon drawn, and waited for instructions. The four of us slowly walked toward the building. We stopped outside the glass doors and pressed ourselves against the wall.

"What about those two?" Anderson whispered as she pointed to Bill and Wilks.

"They stay outside. Keep the trucks clear." I whispered back, then placed my finger on my lips.

I peered around the corner into the foyer, didn't notice any undead, so Kyle and I pushed open the doors. It was dark as we stepped into the building, and the smell of alcohol, bleach, and rotting flesh permeated the area. Anderson gagged. I clicked on my flashlight and shone the beam around the room. Gurneys and chairs lined the walls, along with blood, body parts, and half-consumed corpses.

I side-stepped methodically down the hall, checking every corner, underneath every gurney, and in each room.

We were about to turn the corner to head down the hall to the supply room when a shuffling sound stopped us. I signaled for everyone to press against the wall, and I peeked around the corner. An undead patient, whose hospital gown had come undone and was wrapped around his ankle, ambled down the hall. I couldn't see any other creatures, so I assumed it was alone. Although, it only took one moan to send the others flocking. I flipped out my arm sword and waited. Sweat beaded on my forehead, and some ran down my back. It took the creature *forever* to make it to the end of the hall. When he finally reached my position, I swung my arm. He didn't even know what hit him, and his head fell to the floor with a sickening crunch. We continued to the supply room.

We opened the door and were confronted with five undead. The creatures didn't notice us, and we would have been fine and could've taken out the threat, but Anderson let out a small squeak of horror. They turned and let out a long moan. Quinn, Kyle, and I cursed under our breath before opening fire. We backed away from the supply room and headed back to the front door. Anderson led the way, running. We turned into the main hall only to find it infested with undead. We were trapped. Anderson fired wildly into the crowd.

I glanced around, trying to find somewhere to go. All the rooms around us were closed and I heard the creatures banging to get out. I fired a few shots. We probably could've taken out most of the creatures, but the quarters were too tight, and Anderson kept moving into the line of fire. She shot wildly into the crowd, missing targets and wasting ammo. Quinn jumped onto a gurney and worked on removing a ceiling tile.

"Krista, c'mon."

He grabbed my hand and pulled me up next to him. I grabbed the ceiling and hoisted myself up. When I was secure, I reached down to help Kyle. Quinn called for Anderson, but her ammo was gone and she panicked. She ran blindly toward the nearest room. I pulled Quinn into the ceiling, watching as Anderson opened the door, only to be swarmed by more zombies. I didn't have to keep looking to know what happened next. The three of us crawled to the front of the building and kicked out a tile over the front door. We jumped into the sun and sprinted to our vehicles. The front door caught on a rock, and zombies streamed out of the hospital. I floored it, and we drove to safety.

When the truck stopped, Wilks flew out of his cab and jerked open my door. "Where's Anderson?"

I shook my head. "She didn't make it."

"What do you mean she didn't make it? Did you leave her there to die?"

"No," I kept my anger in check. How could he even imagine that?

Wilks turned around and pulled on his hair with both hands, muttering, "No, no, no."

It was odd, but everyone reacts differently. I set a hand on his shoulder. "I'm sorry. There wasn't anything we could do."

He collapsed onto the ground and cried. I turned to the other guys. They shrugged their shoulders.

"I say we give it an hour, then head back to the hospital." Quinn put his wrist brace back on, a look of pain pinched his face, but he tried to cover it up.

Wilks jumped up from the ground. "Go back? Are you insane? We'll be eaten alive!"

Bill shook his head. "Now, Wilks, everything will be fine."

"How is it going to be fine? Did you see how many zombies were in that place?"

Bill nodded. "I did. But think about it, most of them came streaming out of the hospital. In an hour, they will have wandered to other parts of the city. The hospital will be mostly clear."

Wilks pointed a finger at him. "You don't know that. How could you know that?"

"We've been doing this for a while," Kyle chimed in.

Wilks shook his head and pounded his fists on the side. "I don't care. I'm not going back. You can't make me!"

Bill placed his hands in his pockets and spit on the ground. "You're going back. But you can wait in the truck."

Wilks paced in a circle as he muttered incoherently.

I rolled my eyes and approached Quinn. I jerked my head to the right. "You got a minute?"

"Always."

We moved to the other side of the truck so the others couldn't hear.

"As I'm sure you've deduced, Liet is trying to faze you and your people out."

He placed his hands on his hips, a look of concern crossed his face. "Do you think he knows about us?"

"I doubt it. Besides, he was suspicious before anything happened. He just needed an excuse. I think my running away may have pushed him over the edge."

"What do you want to do?"

"I don't know. I'd like to attack now. We have enough guns to equip the majority of the workers in town."

Quinn shook his head. "It won't work. Like I told you before, even if we get rid of Liet, Florida will send someone to replace him. We have to attack simultaneously."

I sighed. "Maybe things will change when we take Wilks back. I mean, how many soldiers do you think are going to volunteer when they find out Anderson was killed on her first time out and Wilks has turned into a raving lunatic?"

He scoffed. "I doubt they volunteered."

"Either way, this still might work in our favor. Liet does have a finite pool of humans to send out. Someone has to stay behind and watch the workers."

"Let's see how it works out." He stepped forward and wrapped his arms around my waist. "Perhaps after we fill these trucks, you and I can spend some quality time on the ranch."

I smiled and placed my arms around his neck. "I would enjoy that."

He leaned forward and kissed me.

We walked back to join the others. Wilks sat on the step to the cab, rocking back and forth and staring into space. Quinn looked at Bill.

"Don't you have a sedative you can give him?"

"I sure do." He grabbed the First Aid kit out of the truck and handed a pill to Wilks, who took it without question.

After an hour passed, we jumped back into the trucks and headed to the hospital. The sedative took effect, and Wilks lay in the sleeper cabin, watching his hands. Quinn, Kyle, and I headed into the hospital and filled half the truck with supplies. A few zombies still milled around, but we took care of them easily. I thought about looking for Anderson's body, thinking maybe that would help Wilks, but then

I thought better of it. Wilks was already dangerously close to the edge, I didn't need to push him over.

CHAPTER 21

We filled the truck with supplies from local pharmacies and the other truck with food without incident. When we finished, we headed toward Quinn's ranch. There was some concern Wilks would remember the way, so Bill gave him a sleeping pill so we didn't have to worry. As we pulled into the canyon, a sense of peace washed over me. I loved not having to worry about anything. Quinn and I headed into the house while the others stowed guns on the truck. I sat at the table and composed the instructions for Tanya while Quinn made us some coffee.

"How long do you think it will be before we're ready to attack?"

He sipped his drink. "I don't know. A couple of months at least. I want to make sure everyone is properly armed."

I scribbled the notes on the paper. "I hope it's sooner rather than later. I don't know how much longer we're going to be able to keep Liet in the dark."

Quinn pulled a chair up next to me and sat down. He leaned forward and placed his hands on my knee. "Then stay with me now. The more times you go back, the more chances he has of keeping you there."

I placed my hands over his. "I would love to stay here with you, but I still have a lot of work to do. Who's going to pass out the guns?

I have to go back to make sure they are in the right hands."

"What about Pam? She seems trustworthy."

"I don't know about that. I think that if it came down to it, she would do anything to save her own butt."

He touched my cheek. "I hate to see you have to go through all that crap with Liet."

"It won't be for much longer, I promise. Like you said, it should only take a few more months before we're ready to attack. After that, I will follow you to the ends of the earth." I kissed him on the tip of the nose, then finished my letter to Tanya.

As early evening fell over the ranch, Quinn and I took the horses for a ride. We came back in with the cowboys and the herd of cattle. After a light dinner, we cuddled in front of the fire. When it was time for bed, Quinn let me have his room, and he settled onto the couch. It didn't take long for me to fall asleep. It had been a long day.

A shard of light pierced through the curtains and hit me right in the face. I slowly opened my eyes and smiled as I took in the surroundings of Quinn's room. I extended my arms over my head and arched my back in a long stretch. When I finished, I stared at a picture of Quinn kneeling next to a calf, then got dressed. I headed downstairs to see Quinn in the kitchen cooking breakfast. I walked up to him and stood next to him, my butt resting on the counter. He leaned over and gave me a quick kiss.

"How'd you sleep?"

"Great. I haven't slept that well in months."

"It's the country air. It'll do that to you." He smiled.

I wrapped my hands around his waist. "I love the fresh country air." I kissed his chin.

The back door opened and closed with a bang, and I quickly released Quinn. I glanced up, it was Kyle, and he smiled at us knowingly. He continued through to the living room.

"Hey, what happened to Wilks?"

Quinn nodded toward the couch. "He woke up about midnight, freaking out because he didn't know where he was and screaming about zombies. I'm surprised you didn't hear him. Bill gave him another sedative and sleeping pill. He's awake now, but he's not all there."

I walked to the couch. Wilks stared at the ceiling and mumbled about zombies under his breath. I took a seat in the chair across from him. I had been around a lot of people, and I knew everyone reacted to the undead differently, but I never saw anyone freak out as bad as Wilks. Fear was a powerful emotion, and it had the power to drive someone insane, but it usually took more than one incident. Maybe there was something there before. Maybe that was why Liet chose him for this particular mission. Whatever the case was, he wasn't going to be able to take the truck to

Florida. He was useless, and Liet hated that more than anything in the world.

"What do you want to do with him?"

"I don't know. If we leave him here, we risk the possibility that Liet will accuse us of killing them both and sentence us to death. If we take him back, we run the risk of Liet killing him for not carrying out his orders. He won't be good to anyone no matter where we take him."

Quinn folded his arms across his chest. "He might snap out of it eventually." He stared at him for a minute. "Why don't we take him back, and if Liet threatens to reprimand him, I'll intervene and bring him back here. Either way, he'll be out of Liet's hair."

"You can try. I can't guarantee it'll work for you."

"Let's worry about that later. C'mon, let's eat."

After breakfast, we got into the trucks and headed back to North Platte. When we were a few miles from the gate, I had a revelation. I turned to Quinn.

"I think I have an idea of how we can save Wilks and make it so I will be able to continue going with you."

The right side of his mouth pulled into a smile. "Yeah? What is it?"

"You'll see. I'll want you to wait at the truck. If things work the way I'm hoping they will, we'll be going back out soon."

"I hope so."

* * *

I stormed into Liet's office and threw the doors open with force. A woman sat on his lap, and he pushed her to the side when I entered the room.

"What were you thinking?" I yelled. I didn't wait for an answer. "Do you think it's some kind of joke to send me out with rookies?"

He pushed his eyebrows together. "What are you talking about?"

"Anderson and Wilks."

"Oh, yeah. What happened to them?"

"What happened to them? You want to know what happened to them?" I placed my left hand on my hip and pointed at him. "Let me tell you what happened. The first sign of zombies, they flipped out. Anderson got killed, and Wilks is a raving lunatic. If you want me to be safe out there, you have to give me people who know what they're doing. Are you trying to get me killed?"

Liet stood and held his hands out to his sides in defense. "Of course not. I just thought—"

"What? That you were being helpful? It's a good thing Quinn and Kyle were close, or we would have been in a lot of trouble."

"Look, I'm sorry. I just wanted—"

"Sorry isn't going to bring Anderson back. How do you expect them to get supplies if they can't even stay alive?"

"I expect them to do the same thing you do."

"Well, it obviously didn't work."

Liet placed his hands on his hips. "And why is that? Why is it that you're the only one who seems to have the skills to survive in the West?"

I hesitated. Why did I survive? I wasn't any more skilled than the two soldiers who went out. We all trained the same. I wasn't as afraid as the other two, that was obvious, although I was when I first went out. It was luck, that was the only thing that could explain it, but I couldn't tell that to Liet.

"Because I have something to come back to." It was the first thing that popped out of my mouth.

Liet folded his hands across his chest. "Really?"

"Yes, really. I know you're always here waiting for me. I know the supplies I'm collecting are going to make your life easier, so I'm more careful than Wilks and Anderson were." I stepped closer to his desk. "The only thing that keeps me going is your faith in my abilities." I gagged, but I don't think he noticed.

Liet lowered his arms, his mouth curled into a smile. "Fill two more. I want to see Wilks. See what happened to him."

"He's outside with the trucks. Trust me, he's worthless. You'll need to find someone else to take the truck down to Florida."

Liet moved around the desk.

We both left the office. A smug smile of satisfaction crept onto my lips, and I fought to keep it under control.

We stepped into the sunlight and Liet walked up to the vehicle, pushing Bill and Quinn aside. He climbed into the truck and pulled Wilks out by his collar. The sedative Bill gave him wore off hours ago. His skin took on a pasty white pallor, and he fidgeted with his fingers. He didn't even notice Liet.

"What did you do to him?" Liet growled at Quinn.

"What did we do? We did what you asked us to." Quinn clenched his teeth and placed his hands on his hips.

Liet released his collar and pushed Wilks aside. "Useless. Utterly useless. Take him with you. With any luck, the zombies will take care of him."

Wilks's eyes grew wide at the word zombie, and he visibly began to shake. A look of disgust crossed Liet's face.

"Zzzzombies." Wilks stuttered. "Zzzzombies are everywhere. They got Anderson." He glanced over his shoulder. "They're going to get you, too." He grabbed Liet by the arms and shook him.

Liet pushed him away, and Wilks fell to the ground.

"I won't go back out there. You can't make me go out there!"

"Get him out of my sight."

Bill moved to help Wilks to his feet. Wilks moved like he was electrocuted out of Bill's grasp and pulled his gun out of the holster. He pointed it at the guys.

"You stay away from me. All of you."

"You'd better use it or put it away, son." Liet's eyes flashed with anger.

Wilks trained the gun on him. "I won't go back out there." He turned the gun on himself and pulled the trigger.

My mouth dropped open, and I watched his body fall to the ground in slow motion. Bits of brain matter and skull clanked onto the ground, and tears flowed involuntarily from my eyes.

"Well, I guess that problem solved itself." Liet stepped over his body. "I still need my two trucks." He snapped his fingers, and soldiers from the courthouse came down and grabbed the body.

It took me a while to catch my breath, and Quinn helped me into the truck. I couldn't understand why Wilks's death affected me so much. I saw people torn apart and skinned by zombies, and I didn't give it a second thought. I personally took out hundreds of zombies, and it didn't faze me. But watching Wilks take his own life shook me to my soul. Maybe it was because I thought I had seen it all. Maybe I thought we as humans had to do everything to survive, that we owed it to ourselves and the race. Maybe I thought no one was really that weak. I didn't know. What I did know was that the image of his mushroomed head and brain matter oozing onto the ground was going to be burned into my mind's eye for the rest of my life.

CHAPTER 22

I stared out the front window, trying to get the vision of Wilks out of my head. The tears stopped flowing and were replaced with a numb realization. I tried to remember my psychology stuff. I thought that would help me understand why he did it. What type of personality was needed for suicide? I was pretty sure Wilks wasn't depressed. Although he could've been. North Platte wasn't exactly a vacation destination. It could have been the same thing my parents had. What was that called again? Some stress disorder. Of course, it was possible he was crazy. I didn't know. I just met the guy. I would probably never know why he did it.

"You all right?"

I turned to Quinn but looked through him. "Why didn't you do anything to stop him?"

"What could I have done?"

"You could have rushed him. Taken the gun away. I don't know. Anything."

Quinn sighed and placed his hand on my knee. "Krista, if he didn't shoot himself, he would have shot us. He had completely lost his mind. There was no way we could have talked him down."

He was right, of course, but it seemed like someone should have done *something*. "Have you seen this happen before?"

Quinn nodded. "People lose hope. They're afraid of becoming the living dead, so they take what they believe is the only way out. Sadly, it's more of a common occurrence than you can imagine."

"But, there is hope. Look at what we're doing."

Quinn rubbed my knee. "It's okay for you to grieve for him. In fact, it's healthy. And it makes you human. But when people get to that point, not much is going to change their minds."

Anger flared into my chest, and I turned away from Quinn. I doubted he was purposely being condescending, but that didn't make me feel any better. I didn't need to be talked to like I was five. Of course it was all right for me to grieve for him. Why wasn't Quinn grieving? Had he seen it so many times that he was callous to the situation? But why was I grieving? I didn't know him. In the grand scheme of things, he was one less person I had to worry about saving. But he was also one less person in the world, and we were already low on population. I was sure we would be on the endangered species list if there still was one.

We drove the rest of the way in silence. After we loaded the trucks, we headed to Quinn's ranch to rest for the night. I had a difficult time sleeping. Every time I closed my eyes, I saw Wilks shoot himself. I got up and decided to get some fresh air. As I passed the couch, Quinn didn't seem to be faring much better. He twitched and made low moaning noises. At one point, he twitched so bad he kicked the arm of the couch. I shook his shoulder gently to wake him up, and he shot straight up.

"Don't do it!" He screamed.

I sat down next to him. I put my arm around his shoulders, and he buried his face in my neck. As I sat on the couch staring at the ceiling and stroking his hair, I felt the anger melt out of my body. I knew Quinn wasn't being callous earlier in the day, he was dealing with the death the best way he knew how. As I thought about it, it was actually really sad he saw that happen before. No one should have to witness that. I hoped it wasn't family or a close friend. I would've asked him about it, but I figured he would have told me if he wanted to. He wasn't immune to feelings, he just didn't show them.

The next day, it was difficult for both of us to get out of bed. I went back upstairs around midnight, then tossed and turned. At ten, I forced myself downstairs. Quinn was still on the couch, but he got up and joined me in the kitchen. He brewed us a pot of coffee.

"Why don't we stay one more day before we take the trucks back to North Platte? I mean, there's no rush to get the stuff back. Liet has more than he needs, and nothing is going to Florida for two weeks anyway."

I nodded. "Okay."

"Do you want to go for a ride?"

I nodded again.

It was noon before we had our horses saddled and trotted down the canyon floor. The sun was warm and a slight breeze blew, but I didn't find comfort. I stopped my horse at the end of the canyon before we entered the field.

"Quinn, I've been thinking."

He turned in his saddle so he faced me.

"I don't think the people of North Platte have a few months. If we're going to attack, we need to do it soon."

"How soon is soon?"

"Within the next few weeks."

"What about Florida though? Once word gets out that the workers of North Platte have rebelled, they'll send in reinforcements."

I shook my head. "I don't think they will. I think they will insulate themselves even more. If they are concerned with keeping order and control, this will give them more reason to keep people in the state and in line. I don't think we have to worry about them."

"So what are we supposed to do once we take over the city? We're still grossly outnumbered by zombies, and we need the people from Florida to help us fight them."

"We barter. We have supplies they need, and they have the people. We'll work out a trade."

"And if that doesn't work?"

"It has to work. We can't keep surviving this way. We have to take our country back."

"Okay. Let me talk to the others. See what they think."

I nodded, then nudged my horse into the field.

We stayed out until the sun set, then headed back to the house. I was exhausted by the time we finished dinner, and slowly climbed up to the room. Quinn called the others to the house to talk about my new plan. I hoped they would agree to it, but if they didn't, I was going to take matters into my own hands. I knew it wouldn't be easy, but I was sure I could convince some of the worker's to rebel. We had the weapons and the ammunition there in North Platte, it was just a matter of getting them into the right hands. After Wilks, I knew if we procrastinated any longer, it might be too late. We had to act. I pulled the blankets up to my chin and drifted to sleep.

Quinn woke me a few hours later.

"Sorry," he whispered as he knelt on the floor. "The others agree with you. They think that if we wait too much longer, either the zombies will destroy the workers or Liet will. We'll try to attack in two weeks."

I smiled. Quinn kissed me on the forehead, and I drifted back to sleep.

I awoke refreshed and optimistic the next morning. I heard Quinn in the kitchen making breakfast, so I pulled on some clothes and joined him. After a meal of eggs, bacon, and toast, we took the horses out for a ride. The rising sun bathed the valley in soft hues of yellow and orange. The sound of lowing cows filled the air, and the scent of wet grass tickled my nose. My horse was content at a steady trot, and we made our way to the creek. We dismounted and tied the horses to the tree.

I found a spot on the bank in the sand and took a seat. Quinn sat in front of me and laid his head on my lap. I ran my fingers through his hair.

"Just think," I said, "someday this will be a daily occurrence, not a fleeting moment."

Quinn looked up at me. "I can't wait."

I kissed him gently on the forehead before leaning back on my elbows.

We stayed in the shade until noon, then headed back to the house for a quick lunch. When we finished, we got ready to head to North Platte. I hesitated climbing into the truck, and I stared at the ranch for a long time. My horse walked to the fence and bobbed his head a few times, as if waving. I sucked in a breath of air. The scent of soil, hay, and manure lingered in my nostrils for a while. I couldn't wait until I could stay forever.

As we traveled down the highway, I tried not to let anything dampen my spirits. The scene of the sun bathing the valley muted the horrors of Wilks's death, although it was still in my mind. Even the zombie hordes that splattered on the road couldn't break my spirit. I looked over at Quinn. Leaning my head back on my seat, I took in the curve of his jawbone, his lips, his dark eyes, and the lobe of his ear. A smile crept onto his face, and I sighed with content.

"You all right over there?"

"I'm getting there."

I turned to face front. The trench that would eventually hold the stone wall dominated my field of vision. Dust clouded the sky and was mixed with the inky black smoke from the funeral pyre. We approached the gate and stopped. The guard glanced at us briefly before we climbed out of the cab and headed toward the inspection area. I shuddered.

"I can't wait until this place is gone."

"You and me both, darlin'."

"Same here," said Bill.

"No argument from me," Kyle agreed.

We reported to our respective lines and waited to be hosed down. We met up later on the stairs to the courthouse. I hesitated. I stared at the building, wishing I never had to see it again. Just a few more weeks, I told myself. Until then, I had to tough it out. Quinn touched my arm.

"We can leave. Right now. Take a truck and never come back."

For a brief second, I was tempted. "No. Too many people need us."

We proceeded up the stairs and into Liet's office. As usual, he sat behind his desk, going through paperwork. He barely looked up as the four of us entered the room.

"Two more trucks?"

Liet looked at us. "No. We're fine on supplies for a while. But I will need you to take the truck to Florida."

"I thought you were going to find someone else to do that?"

He sighed with exasperation. "I don't have any men to spare right now. You're always willing to go to the West, what's wrong with Florida? Is it because Quinn isn't there?"

I held my hands up in defense. "All right. I can be ready to go in the morning."

"That's what I thought." He tamped the pages of his file together, then turned back to his work.

The four of us went up to the apartment, and I made dinner. When we finished, we sat in the living room and talked about the next places we would go for supplies. We had been there for an hour when Liet came into the room. He grabbed a plate of dinner and sat on the couch between Quinn and I. We all stared at him, waiting.

He shoveled a bite of chicken and beans into his mouth. "What are you talking about?"

"We're figuring out what other towns in eastern Wyoming we can pillage for supplies before we have to move to the central part of the state." Quinn said.

Liet nodded. "Sounds like a good plan. What did you come up with?"

"We're still figuring that out," Bill explained.

Liet looked at the map on the coffee table. "Are you planning on marking them on here?"

Quinn cleared his throat. "We weren't going to, but we can if you want us to."

"Why don't you do that? That way, if anyone else needs to go out there, they'll know where they need to go."

Exasperation flooded through me. "What are you talking about? You said earlier that we have all the supplies we need."

Liet stared at me. "That's true for now, but eventually we'll need to go back out."

"When that's the case, we'll know where we need to go. You don't need to send anyone else out." I tried to keep my anger under control.

Liet set his plate on the table and wiped his hands on his pants. "Actually, I believe we will start sending others out. Quinn, Bill, Kyle, I appreciate all that you have done for us, but I don't think we will be needing your services any longer."

I moved so I was on the edge of the couch. "What are you talking about? They're the only ones who know the West. You saw what happened when you sent rookies out...they died."

Liet's eyes narrowed to slits. "Others can learn the nuances of the West. I'm sure these men have families they would like to be with. We can take care of ourselves."

I opened my mouth to protest, then thought better of it. If Liet had his mind set that we didn't need Quinn anymore, nothing was going to change it. My jaw ached from clenching it. I stared hard at Liet, hoping he would burst into flames or his head would explode. He didn't even notice. He ignored me, so I turned back to the map. The four of us marked the cities and towns that we believed would be the best to pillage for supplies. After an hour, we all decided it was time to turn into bed.

My heart stopped for a moment when Liet followed me into the room. I turned to face him, my arms crossed over my chest.

"I told you, this was the last time you were going out. I need you here. I need to know you're safe. I expect them to be gone before ten."

"That shouldn't be a problem." I spoke between gritted teeth.

He stopped with his hand on the doorknob. "It better not be." He closed the door behind him.

I lay in bed and stared at the ceiling. What was Liet's problem? One minute he was like, "Yeah, go to the West. Be free, but be safe." Then, the next he wanted me locked in my room. His mood swings were exhausting and potentially deadly. I wanted nothing more than to remove him from his position of power, get out of his house, and ride off with Quinn into the sunset. Even if he didn't let me go back out when I returned from Florida, I was still going to leave. I knew where all the keys to the vehicles were. And we had more than semis. I rolled onto my side and closed my eyes, but sleep did not come easily.

When I woke up the next morning, the guys already loaded Quinn's Jeep. Liet stood over them, watching intently. I was a little disappointed no one woke me up, but I'm sure Liet planned it that way. I asked if they needed any help, but they told me they were fine. I embraced each one of them and told them how much I appreciated their help and how much I was going to miss them. I tried not to linger longer on Quinn, but I found it difficult to let him go.

"Don't worry," I whispered. "I will see you again when I get back."

"I hope so." He glanced at Liet over my shoulder. "I'll see you soon."

I waved at them as they pulled away, and a tear dropped onto my cheek. I wiped it away quickly so Liet wouldn't notice. I turned toward him.

"I'm ready to go whenever."

He scowled. "You're not going anywhere."

I stared at him in confusion. "But, I thought you said you wanted me to go to Florida."

"Do you really think I'm that stupid?" He snarled. "You put on a great performance the other day, but actions speak louder than words."

I was dumbfounded. "What are you talking about?"

He pointed a finger at me. "I see how he looks at you. And the way he escorted you to the truck after Wilks killed himself. Don't tell me nothing is going on between you two."

My stomach knotted, and I turned to follow the Jeep down the road. Liet grabbed me by the arm and jerked me backward. I turned to punch him in the face, but he blocked it and backhanded me across the cheek. The pain burned through my eye socket, but I wasn't going to give up. I pulled and struggled against Liet. I even kicked him in the shins a couple times, but he dug his nails into my arm.

"No!" I screamed. "Quinn!"

Liet got his free arm around my neck and applied pressure. I clawed and scratched his arm, but the oxygen was slowly being cut off to my brain. My knees buckled. The tears flowed from my eyes, and I grabbed at the air, hoping to magically pull Quinn back. I was sure Liet was going to kill me.

CHAPTER 23

I regained consciousness a while later. My head pounded and my throat was sore. I sat up and noticed I was in a cot in the women's house. I swung my feet off the side of the bed and a chain clunked onto the floor. I lifted my right foot and examined the Master padlock that connected the two ends of the chain. I jerked on it angrily. I glanced up and noticed Pam sitting across me. She smiled feebly.

"You feeling all right?"

What the hell kind of question was that? Of course I wasn't all right. "I'd be doing a lot better if I wasn't chained up."

Pam nodded. "I know. I wish I could do something for you, but I can't."

I stared at her for a moment. "You could let me go."

Pam shook her head. "Liet has the only key. He's wearing it on a necklace."

"You could try and contact Quinn. He'll know what to do."

She shook her head again. "Liet's monitoring the air waves. Anyone who uses the radio without authorization will be shot on sight."

I balled my hands into fists. Why did she even bring it up? If she wasn't going to do anything she should've kept her mouth shut. I guess she was *trying* to look good.

"If you're not going to help me, what are you doing here?"

Pam's eyes widened in surprise. "I want to help you, Krista, but what you're asking me to do is impossible. Besides, where would you go if I set you free? To Quinn? How are you going to get there without a vehicle?"

My eyes narrowed to slits. "I can get a vehicle. Don't you worry about that."

"You wouldn't make it past the gate. You know what sharp shooters we have in the tower."

"Being dead might be better than being a prisoner."

"Don't say that. You know that's not true."

I held up my hand to silence Pam. "You don't know. You're not the one chained up."

Pam's face turned red. "You got yourself into this mess. I'm trying to make things a little easier on you."

Anger boiled in my chest. "How did I get myself into this mess? Because I followed your advice? You're the one who told me I deserved to be happy!"

"Then you should have stayed in the West! Why did you come back?"

I stared at her. I wanted to tell her it was because we were planning a war, but I couldn't. If Pam wouldn't help me escape now, I was sure she would take the information directly to Liet. That was probably the only reason she talked to me. She was trying to get information.

The door to the house flew open, and Liet stepped into the room. He stood at the end of my bed, his hands on his hips. He stared at me for a moment, then swung his gaze to Pam.

"I need you to get four soldiers. Preferably ones who know how to drive a semi and don't scare easily."

Pam saluted before heading out the door. Liet sat in her place.

"You know," I said softly, "there's a lot more to gathering supplies than just knowing where they are."

"You mean like dating your guide?"

I clenched my jaw. "What does it matter to you?"

"It matters a lot to me! *I* wanted to be the one to provide for you. *I* wanted to make sure you were safe. I'm your family, not him." He took a deep breath. "I told you before, Krista, I don't like to be abandoned. Especially for another guy."

I clicked my tongue on the roof of my mouth. "I don't know why I'm the only person in this entire camp you care about. What about the workers? What about that girl, Megan? Why do you have to focus all your attention on me?"

"Because you can't take care of yourself."

The heat rose into my face. "Can't take care of myself?" The question came out as a whisper. "I've been taking care of myself for almost three years now. I don't need you."

"Of course you do. Where would you be if it weren't for me? Still in Florida? Waiting on the Johnsons? Maybe married to some loser. I gave you this life, and I can take it all away."

I grabbed the chain. "I can guarantee I wouldn't be chained to this bed!"

"I didn't want it to come to this, Krista, but you left me no choice. I tried being nice, I tried grounding you, but nothing worked. You either physically attacked me or ran away. This was my last option."

I shook my head. "You're crazy. Why didn't you just kill me?"

"You know I can't live without you. We have to take care of each other. You can't do that if you're in the West with him." He stood and caressed my cheek.

I turned my gaze to the kitchen to keep from spitting in his face.

"You'll come back around eventually." He turned and headed out the door.

I threw myself back onto the bed and placed my fists on my forehead. If only I could get a hold of Quinn, but he thought I was going to Florida. He would be suspicious when he didn't hear from me in a couple of days, but he wouldn't come looking for me. He couldn't. Liet told him that they no longer needed his services. If he came back to the city, he would be killed, and he knew that, too.

I had to escape. That was my only way out. But how? I was chained to the bed, and the only key was with Liet. I could try and cut through the metal, but with what? There was nothing in the house I could use, and I was sure no one would help me. My only chance was to appeal to Liet's sentimental side. I was screwed.

Weeks passed. Well, it felt like weeks, but it might have only been days. I didn't have a calendar so I wasn't really sure. I was completely miserable and convinced I was going to die chained to the bed. Liet never came to see me again, but Pam made sure I had food and water. The chain was long enough to allow me movement around the house, but I couldn't get out through the door or windows. My ankle bled from where the chain rubbed. The only thing that kept me going was knowing Quinn and his people would attack any day, but that hope was slowly dwindling. From my calculations, they should have been there a week ago.

I was surprised when Pam came to the house with the key to my chain.

"What's going on?"

"Liet wants to see you."

"Why?"

"The trucks we sent out haven't come back."

"So send out some more."

"No one else will go."

I scowled. "So he's expecting me to clean up his mess."

That pretty much clinched it for me: Liet was insane. That was the only way to explain his actions.

Pam unlocked the chain and escorted me to the courthouse. As I stepped through the threshold, I took a deep breath. Pam stayed behind at the door.

Liet looked up from his work and smiled as I approached the bench. I stopped a few feet from his desk and tucked my hands in my back pockets.

"Liet."

"Ah, Krista, I'm glad you could make it." He stepped around his desk and wrapped his arms around my shoulders, gently kissing the top of my head.

I suppressed the shiver that ran down my spine. "What do you want?"

He pulled back and went to his desk. He shuffled through his papers until he found what he looked for. He stared at it for a moment before placing it back on the desk.

"Looks like we need fuel."

I sucked in a deep breath and pulled my hands out of my pockets. I wanted to ask him what his problem was, if maybe he was dropped on his head as a child, but I knew that moment might be my only chance. I didn't want to anger him.

"Why didn't you call Quinn?"

Liet waved his hand dismissively in the air. "He wouldn't return my summons. I think he's afraid I'll hurt him."

"Would you?"

Liet responded with a smile.

I rolled my eyes. "How many trucks?"

"We only have one that we can spare right now. Will you be able to fill it up?"

I glanced up to the ceiling and thought for a moment. When I came to a conclusion, I folded my arms across my chest and focused my sights back on my cousin. "I might know of a place. But it's been a while since I've been out. How soon do you need it?"

"As soon as you can get it here. And I doubt things have changed that much in ten days." He leaned back in his chair and fiddled with a pencil on his desk. "Of course, I wouldn't expect you to go alone. In fact, I downright forbid it." He nodded to the man who stood behind him. "This is Ben. He will accompany you on your mission."

I looked the man up and down. His faded green fatigues hung loosely on his small frame, his cheeks were covered with a few days worth of stubble, and his dirty brown hair stuck out in multiple directions. His dark eyes were sunken in, and his shoulders slumped forward.

"You running out of men out here? This one looks a little green."

"He is a bit new, but he can handle himself."

"He'd better. I don't want another Anderson or Wilks on my hands."

Ben's face paled.

"I need you to leave as soon as possible," Liet said.

"I'll need my weapons."

"You can have them as soon as you leave the city." Liet motioned toward Ben, and he came from behind the desk.

He joined me, and we turned and left the room.

As the sun set, we walked to the other side of town where the vehicles were kept behind locked gates. I climbed into the passenger seat of the tanker truck and placed my foot on the dash. Ben pulled onto the highway.

Ten days? Was that all? It seemed like so much longer. It made me feel better, though, because I was convinced Quinn forgot about me. Written me off as a lost cause. But it wasn't true. Not enough time passed. I was sure Quinn still planned on attacking, and he would have saved me, I know it. But this situation worked, too. Either way, I was free.

Liet must really have a screw loose. I mean, he had to know I wasn't coming back. If he thought Ben was going to stop me, he's really dumb. Thank goodness for his stupidity. Without it, I'd still be chained to that bed. I think luck played a big role, too. I glanced out the window and up at the stars. Yep, I was the luckiest girl I knew.

We were about an hour away from North Platte when we ran into our first zombie. The truck was cruising at 65 miles per hour, with Ben zoning at the wheel, when the figure emerged in the headlights like a ghost. By the time he realized what was going on, the creature splattered all over the front of the truck. Under reflex, he slammed on the brakes and pulled over to the side of the road. I stared at him. His eyes were wide and his knuckles were white as he gripped the steering wheel.

"Are you all right?"

He turned slowly to face me and nodded mechanically. "I think so." His voice was barely over a whisper.

I undid my seatbelt. "Get up." I motioned with my hand for him to move. "I'll take it the rest of the way." A moan echoed outside and I glanced over my shoulder. I grabbed his arm. "C'mon. We don't have much time."

Ben undid his seatbelt and moved to the other seat. I put the truck in gear and took off down the road as two more zombies crawled on the cab. I watched in the rearview as their bodies thumped onto the pavement and rolled into blackness. His face went white.

"Are you sure you're all right?"

Ben took a deep breath and closed his eyes for a moment before nodding. "Yeah. I'm okay. I'd never seen a zombie before. I thought I hit a person."

I snorted. "Never saw a zombie before? How long have you been in North Platte?"

"I got there five minutes before I met you in the office."

"Well, you'd better get used to it out here. The undead are everywhere. They may be slow and easy to kill, but they are like cockroaches, where there's one, there's several." I nodded toward the gun on his belt. "Best to keep that handy."

He touched the gun briefly and nodded. "I will."

Great, I thought, more fresh meat for the undead. I hope he doesn't drag me down with him.

I drove on I-80 until I was so tired I could barely keep my eyes open. Ben snored next to me. I glanced at the dash, and the clock read 2:00 a.m. I pulled the truck to the side of the road, and as soon as the tires hit the rumble bar, Ben jerked out of his sleep.

"What's going on?" He wiped the drool from the corner of his mouth.

"I need a break."

He straightened up and glanced nervously out the window. "Are you sure it's okay to stop here?"

I put the truck in park and shrugged. "No. But I have to pee." I opened the door and stepped out. Before closing it behind me, I stuck my head back into the cab. "You're driving."

I hurried around to the back of the tanker drum, out of Ben's sight and undid my pants. I kept one ear open for the sounds around me, but could only hear the howling wind. When I finished, I turned to head to the passenger side of the truck and came face to face with a half rotted corpse. The creature wore one sleeve of a red and black-checkered shirt and a pair of tattered Dickies. Its ribs were exposed under black rotted flesh, and one eye was about ready to fall out of the socket. One work boot was securely on its foot while the other was attached by its shoestrings that twisted around its ankle, slowing the already snail-paced creature down. I went to dodge away from it under the truck, but noticed another zombie, this one just the top half, was in my way. I pulled out my gun and squeezed one round each into the creatures' heads. Running, I went back to the cab and climbed into the seat.

"Let's go."

Ben hesitated for a moment, who knows what ran through his mind, but I imagined he tried to figure out what was going on. It wasn't until a creature banged into the side of my door and knocked him back into reality that he put the truck in gear and headed down the highway. I gave him directions of where to go before crawling into the sleeper cab and falling into an uncomfortable sleep.

I woke as the sun came over the horizon. I stretched and looked over at Ben—his mouth gaped wide open in a yawn.

"We almost there?" I asked, suppressing my own yawn.

Ben nodded. "I think so. Do you have anything to eat?"

I shook my head curtly. "There'll be food when we get there."

Half an hour later, the truck pulled into the deserted town that was our destination. The gas station sat on the edge, next to the highway, and I had him pull up to the nearest pump.

"Okay, we have to do this quickly and efficiently." I scanned the area. "I don't know how many undead are in the area, but once they catch wind of us, they'll be here in no time."

Ben glanced nervously out the window.

"Here's the plan." I explained to him we would get the pumps and hoses in place first, then he could head to the station and collect the food. I told him I would watch his back while he unscrewed the gas cap from the cement.

He placed a hand over his weapon protectively. "Why can't I watch your back?"

I pushed my eyebrows together and huffed. "I'm five-foot-two and weigh a hundred and ten. Do you really think I can get the cap off?"

Ben frowned. "How do I know you're not going to shoot me and leave me out here to die?"

"Ben," I kept my voice as calm as possible, "if I wanted to harm you, I could have pushed you out of the truck when you were sleeping."

He stared at me for a moment, his eyes wide.

It took a little convincing, but I finally got him out of the truck. It took us fifteen minutes to get the hoses set up and another couple of hours to fill the tanker. Ben ran into the building during that time, and we feasted on beef jerky, canned meat, warm soda, and stale chips. We sat in the cab and kept our eyes out for the undead. Luckily for us, we only saw two, and that was as we finished the job. I put a round in their skulls before heading on our way.

When we were a quarter of a mile down the road, Ben let out an ear-piercing holler. It was so unexpected, I jerked the wheel and almost flipped the tanker.

"WOO-HOO! That was exciting!" He punched the dashboard a few times with both of his fists in rapid succession. "You never knew when those SOBs were going to strike, and when they did, POW, POW, you took care of them. How'd you learn to shoot like that anyway?"

My heart pounded in my chest, and I took a couple deep breaths to calm down. "Practice."

"It was amazing. I've never seen anyone shoot like that before." His mouth opened into a wide yawn and he shook his head. "Uff, I'm tired."

I looked at him out of the corner of my eye. "Why don't you get some sleep? We've a ways to go, and I'll wake you when I need you to drive."

Ben's head bobbed forward, and he caught it before his chin hit his chest. Sluggishly, he crawled into the back.

I turned the tanker truck onto a secondary highway, which we followed for another hour, then turned down a dirt road. The landscape changed from the flat desert into rolling hills covered with juniper trees, then into steep cliffs with pines and red rocks. My stomach fluttered with excitement, and I tapped my fingers on the steering wheel. I had the truck going as fast as I safely could, but it seemed to be taking forever. I wanted to squeal when the gates to the ranch opened, and I pulled the truck inside.

Quinn waited for me on the porch as I exited the truck. I wrapped my arms around his neck and told him how much I missed him. He squeezed me back so hard, I lost my breath. Our gaze met for a brief second before we locked lips in a hard, long kiss. When we released, I buried my face into his chest and he placed his chin on the top of my head.

"He gonna be out for a while?" Quinn nodded toward the truck.

I didn't look up. "He should be. I slipped some sleeping pills in his drink while we filled the tanker."

He pulled back and lifted my chin with his hand. Smiling, he planted another kiss on my lips before we walked through the house. We went into the back room and opened the secret door that hid the entrance to the cave. Generally, the stone room was filled with boxes of Christmas decorations and clothes that no longer fit, but those had been moved out and replaced with boxes of ammunition, rifles, shotguns, handguns, and any other weapon we could get our hands on. A few of the others followed in behind us, and we grabbed as many weapons as we could carry. Heading back outside, the group hid the weapons on the truck.

When we were done, I kissed Quinn and headed back toward I-80. Ben snored behind me. By the time he woke, the truck was pulled onto the shoulder and pointed east, the sun directly overhead. We placed him in the driver's seat and handcuffed his hands to the steering wheel.

"What the…?" He screamed and jerked at the cuffs, attempting to free himself.

I opened the driver's side door. "This is as far as I go."

Ben pulled at the cuffs again. "What do you think this is going to accomplish? I don't know Liet very well, but I'm sure he'll come after you."

"No he won't. He doesn't know where to look for me."

"He's going to kill me for letting you go. He specifically told me to never let you out of my sight."

I shook my head. "You'll be fine. Just deliver the fuel. Nothing will happen to you."

"You know that's not true. You know he'll torture me to find out where you are."

"Well, luckily for you, you have plausible deniability. He knows who he's dealing with. You'll be fine."

"How do you know that?"

I shrugged and closed the door.

The window rolled down and I turned. Ben poked his head out.

"What am I supposed to do?"

"Well, I would suggest not lingering for long. There are a few zombies roaming around over here." I jumped into the Wrangler, and we waited for Ben to head down the highway before turning around and driving west.

CHAPTER 24

By the time we made it back to the ranch, the radio had been blaring with obscenities from Liet for fifteen minutes. I chuckled to myself as I sat down and picked up the hand mic.

"I'm sorry, Liet, you're not coming in too clear. Can you please repeat that last thing you said?"

"I will rip your head off the next time I see you. You fu—"

I turned the radio off. "We'll give him a couple of hours to calm down."

We went to the living room where Bill, Kyle, and a few others gathered. I sat on the couch, and Quinn stood in front of the fireplace. He placed his hands on his hips.

"We have a mission, and I think it's time we attacked North Platte." He cleared his throat. "The original plan was to have simultaneous attacks in both Nebraska and Florida, but that's impossible to accomplish. There's no way to communicate with Krista's contact down there, and the worker's don't have much time left. If we can take control of the city, we can barter with The Families and eventually topple them. Here's the plan."

We were up the next morning before the sun. We traveled in four vehicles, three of which carried four passengers each, and they headed to North Platte. The fourth car was occupied by Bill and Kyle, and they were going to Florida to let Tanya know what was happening. We didn't want her to hear about the uprising and think that was the sign for her to attack.

The temporary chain link fence extended almost seventy miles both north and south from North Platte, and we were going to enter the area on the far end. It was pathetic, really, since crews worked twenty-four hours a day that they hadn't made it past the towns of McCook and Thedford. I suspected since Liet was such a control freak there would be guards at both areas. I was sure he didn't want anyone sneaking into North Platte without him knowing about it. But I assumed if anyone was dumb enough to sneak out, they let them go.

Once we got past the wall, though, the real challenge would start. North Platte was surrounded by another chain link fence, guard towers, and land mines. The majority of the towers were empty because Liet didn't have the soldiers to fill them, and the mine fields were relatively new. After the zombie incident in town and the lack of soldiers to fill the towers, Liet put the fields in. Only he and a few of the workers knew exactly where the mines were. I didn't even know they existed until I heard some of the female soldiers talking about it while I was chained up. It made our plan more dangerous, but not impossible.

It took us two hours to make it to Casper. From there, we traveled on I-25 to US 20 and made our way to Valentine, which took another five hours. It was a straight shot south from Valentine to Thedford to North Platte, and it only took two hours, but we had to be cautious. We were going to hit the city near midafternoon, and that meant we would be very conspicuous. The plan was to park a few miles outside of the city and walk in. A few zombies lurched around on the road, but they would be easy to take care of. Out of all the obstacles we were going to face on that trip, the roaming zombies were the least of my worries.

We pulled over a few miles outside of Thedford and scanned the area. Through the binoculars, I saw a crew of five workers and two guards. I handed the glasses to Quinn.

"We'll need to get over there quietly," I whispered. "The guards have radios, and we don't need them spoiling our surprise party."

Quinn lowered the binoculars. "One of us should approach head on, while the others sneak around the back. I'm sure they won't call in a lone straggler, and that will keep their attention so the others can get into position."

I nodded. "Okay. Who's going to walk right up to them?"

"Anyone but you."

"You know, it might be a better plan if it is me. I know most of the guards, and they probably know what Liet did to me. It might be enough of a surprise for me to show up that it will take them off guard."

"Or they might have been instructed to shoot you on sight."

I scoffed. "By the time I'm close enough for them to recognize me, it'll be too late. At least it better be. I expect you to get yourself into position quickly." Without waiting for a response, I pulled the handkerchief out of Quinn's back pocket and covered my face. Running, I headed toward the guards and workers.

I was winded by the time I made it to the guards and workers, and I placed my hands on my knees to catch my breath. I played up my tiredness a little, hoping the guards wouldn't see me as a threat. They kept their guns on me and the workers slowed their work to see what was going on.

"What are you doing here?" One of the guards asked.

I pulled the handkerchief off my face. "I was...I was being pursued."

The guard lowered his weapon and squinted. "Krista? Is that you?"

I took my chance and stomped down on the barrel of the gun. Yeah, the guy was dumb enough to walk right up to me. The weapon clattered onto the ground, and the other soldier readied to fire. I pulled my gun out of the holster and pointed it at the guard's head.

"I would drop it if I were you."

With hesitation, he set it on the ground and put his hands up. The worker's stared at me wide-eyed. If they had any intentions of harming me, they were quickly diffused as the rest of the caravan pulled up behind them. They were completely surrounded. Quinn jumped out of the vehicle and bound the guards' hands with some rope.

"That was easy," he commented.

I placed my hands on my hips. "Unfortunately, getting into North Platte won't be."

I watched as the worker's dropped their tools and approached the group.

"What's going on?" one of them asked. "Are you going to liberate the city?"

I stared at him for a moment. "That's the plan."

"What can we do? We want to help."

I glanced at Quinn, then turned back to the man. "Some of these guys here will go with you. Take the guards and head back into the city. Gather as many people as you can, and tell them to meet you at the storage shed. We'll have weapons waiting for you."

The worker's nodded enthusiastically and jumped into the trucks. When they were out of sight, we climbed into our vehicles and continued south. I hoped they would be smart enough to gag the soldiers and keep them tied up in the truck while they went through the inspection line like normal. If they weren't, it was going to make our job that much harder. I was sure they were that smart. They had to be. We had enough to worry about with the land mines.

According to the stories, land mines were scattered all around town. Where they got them and how many there were, I didn't know. We had to be careful. We pulled our Jeeps off the road and continued south at a snails pace. One of the men sat on the hood and poked the terrain in front of him with a stick, looking for mines. We hadn't traveled very far when the man signaled for us to stop. Quinn and I were in the Jeep behind him, and I poked my head out the window.

"Find something?" I called.

The response came in the form of a cloud of dust and rocks that exploded from the ground. I'd never seen a mine explode, so I didn't know if that was normal. I stared out the windshield, waiting for something—anything—to happen. After a few seconds, the dust settled. I opened my car door, surprised there hadn't been a loud bang that would indicate explosives. Cautiously, I tip-toed to the front vehicle, my gun in hand. As I rounded the back of the Jeep, a moan resounded from the front of the car. A zombie clawed furiously at the man on top of the hood, and I noticed the gaping hole in the ground with a board that was attached to a spring. I raised my gun. My first shot hit the creature in the chest. It knocked it away so the man could get away, then I placed a round in its skull. I was about to ask the man if he was all right when the ground rumbled. Hands and heads poked through the soft earth, and I looked around in horror. I grabbed the man by the arm and jerked him to his feet.

"Get in the Jeep!" I ran back to my vehicle and climbed into the passenger seat.

Bodies bounced out of the ground as the springs were activated. It literally rained corpses. Several of them hit the Jeep, with the vast majority landing back in the field. As soon as they could get on their feet, we were going to be surrounded by hundreds of zombies. The Jeep in front took off like a rocket, and Quinn followed behind them. Several creatures smashed into the side of the vehicle and were crushed under the tires. It only took us a few minutes to outrun them, but no one drew an easy breath until the zombies were spots on the horizon.

"Oh, my God," I breathed. "He buried zombies instead of mines."

"Well," Quinn commented, "it would definitely deter someone from approaching on foot."

I started to chuckle when four small bangs resounded and Quinn slammed on the brakes, cursing under his breath. I looked out the windshield as the front Jeep skidded to a crooked stop. All of the tires were flat, and I looked out my window at the ground. Barely visible under the dirt, twinkling like glitter in the sun, was buried razor wire. I looked at Quinn.

"And that would deter anyone from approaching in a vehicle."

The people from the first Jeep piled into the back of Quinn's. We crept across the razor wire. We made it through, but had to change two of the tires. Thank goodness Liet was shorthanded. If he had guards in the tower, we would have been dead in the zombie field. If they really wanted to toy with us, they could've shot us while we changed the tires.

"What else do you think he has in store for us?"

"I don't want to know," Quinn replied.

The caravan drove for thirty minutes before we encountered Liet's next obstacle. The field before us was strewn with pike fences, razor wire fences, and zombies tied to stakes. We stopped on top of a hill and surveyed the area.

"Well, I can tell you right now we're never going to get the Jeeps through there." Quinn sighed with exasperation.

"Then we hoof it," I said. "We didn't come this far to turn back now." I turned to the others. "Grab as much ammo as you can carry, and make sure you have something to chop the zombies' heads off." I headed to the trunk of the vehicle and grabbed supplies.

As I loaded extra magazines into my belt, someone gently touched my arm. I looked at the man who had been on top of the Jeep.

"I'm afraid I'm not going to make it to North Platte with you," he said softly.

I furrowed my brow. "Why?"

He held up his arm and showed me the bite wound. I sighed and looked at him with sympathy. I opened my mouth to speak, but I didn't know what to say.

"I'm glad I could make it this far," the man said. "Good luck."

Before I could speak, he made his way over the hill. I felt nauseous when I heard the gun shot, but I knew it was the best way for him to go. I gave him a moment of silence and in my mind, thanked him for his sacrifice. Then, I took a deep breath and focused on what lay ahead. We still had a job to do. I finished loading up with supplies.

We stood at the top of the hill as a group and looked down at the obstacle. We turned to each other, nodding our readiness, and headed into the field. The first things at the bottom of the hill were pikes set together in an X-shape with barbed wired running between the Xs. They were too close together to step over or slide under, so we had to cut them. Zombies were tied with leashes right behind the wire, and they strained to get at us. Their moans reached deafening levels. We cleared a spot and Quinn got to work cutting the wire. When he finished, we moved through the fence one at a time. Those who went through first took care of the next wave of creatures, taking down as many of the undead as they could.

The next level of the field was a ditch filled with muddy water. More zombies were tied to stakes, but since the ground was so soft, some of them pulled the stakes out and moved toward us. We gathered into a group, our backs to each other and moved through the water as a circle. We fired as the walking dead came near us, trying to conserve as much ammo as possible. Someone behind me screamed, and I glanced over my shoulder. A zombie latched onto her thigh, and blood soaked through the jeans. She pounded on the creature with the butt of her gun, but it didn't let go. I turned to fire, but the group kept moving, pushing my arms up and out of the way.

"She's gone," someone shouted. "Keep moving."

I turned to face the next onslaught of undead. I fired until my magazine ran dry. I went to grab another, but my belt was empty. I holstered the gun and flipped out my arm swords. Several others ditched their guns and grabbed their blades. The final part of the field was razor wire stretched taught over thorn bushes. Zombies were strapped in the laying position under the wire, but they reached for us, slicing their arms to shreds on the barbs. We stopped and surveyed the area.

"We'll have to use them as stepping stones," Quinn said.

My heart leapt into my throat. I wasn't about to step on a zombie. "What?"

"We kill them first, then we use them as stepping stones. If we go one at a time, we'll be fine."

He stepped onto the chest of the creature closest to him and whacked off its head.

Unsteadily, he made his way to the next and repeated. I followed behind him, watching my footing and the creatures next to me. One of them grabbed my ankle, almost throwing me off balance and into the razors below, but I steadied myself. I chopped off the hand and continued on.

We made it through the field and up a small hill. I collapsed onto the ground panting. I thought we would be in North Platte by noon, but after running the gauntlet, it was early evening.

"Maybe we should camp here for the night. Finish the siege in the morning."

Quinn lay next to me and scanned the area with the binoculars. When he was done, he handed them to me. I rolled over and put the binoculars up to my eyes, scanning the fence and guard towers. My arms were so tired, they shook under the weight of the glasses. Nothing. We would be able to get into the city undetected. From there, we had to make it to the storage yard, get the guns, and hand them out to the workers. Easy.

"Looks like fortune is on our side," I whispered.

Quinn smiled. "It's about time."

"You remember what storage shed I told you the weapons were in, right?"

He nodded.

"Okay. See you soon." I gave Quinn a quick kiss before heading into the city.

I cautiously walked down the street, but I didn't try to hide. No one knew I was there, so I wasn't expecting to get caught. I walked right into the courthouse without any problems. Outside of Liet's door, I pulled my gun out of the holster. I hesitated for a moment, then kicked the door open. Liet sat behind his desk and jumped at the sound. He reached for his weapon.

"I wouldn't do that if I were you."

His hand froze in midair. "What are you doing here?"

"Something that should have been done a long time ago." I motioned with my gun for him to put his hands up.

He scowled. "What are you going to do? Take over the city? You think your compassion is going to get the wall built faster?"

I shook my head. "It's not about the wall. It's about taking back what's ours."

Liet scoffed. "You can't kill them all. There are too many. You start hunting zombies and you're going to lead a lot of people to their deaths."

"That's what they want you to believe." I stepped around the desk and grabbed the gun out of his belt. I placed it in my waistband and motioned for him to move.

He stood from his chair and walked toward the door, his hands raised in the air. I followed behind him, smiling to myself, when someone slammed into me from the back and jerked on my hair and clawed at my face. I grabbed the person by the back of the head and flipped them over my shoulder. A woman I didn't recognize landed in front of me. Angry, I pointed the gun at her. I wouldn't have shot her, I couldn't. I didn't have any ammo, but they didn't need to know that. Liet took the advantage and kicked it out of my hand before punching me in the face.

I stumbled and fell to one knee, but I quickly recovered. Liet went for the gun he knocked out of my hand, so I grabbed the one I had in my waistband. I pointed it in Liet's direction, and the woman tackled me. She was really starting to irritate me. It didn't take much effort for me to get on top, and I smashed my folded arm sword into the woman's temple. The woman went limp and lay unconscious. I turned my attention back to Liet. He pulled a revolver out of his boot and pointed it in my direction.

"Drop your weapon."

I did as I was told and put my hands in the air. I stood and turned to face him. "You can shoot me, but you won't make it out of here alive. Quinn and his men are taking out the soldiers as we speak. Once he sees me dead, he will kill you."

Liet's face crunched in anger. "At least I'll have the pleasure of seeing you die. You abandoned me, just like everyone else. If I can't live with you, no one can." He squeezed the trigger.

I watched the hammer fall, and the bang of the gun was deafening. Hot pain seared through my shoulder, but I wasn't dead. I jumped to the side as he pulled the trigger. If I hadn't, it probably would have hit me square in the chest. I fell to the ground, and Liet aimed to shoot again. I rolled toward him and smashed into his legs. He lost his balance, but didn't go down. I took the opportunity to whack him in the knee with my folded arm sword, and that took him down. I kicked the gun out of his hand and sprung to my feet.

Liet lunged forward and caught me around the waist. He tried to tackle me, but I drove my elbow between his shoulder blades. He loosened his grip and stepped back. I flipped out the blade on my right arm. I tried to raise my left, but the pain was unbearable.

"I don't want to kill you, but I will if I have to," I snarled.

Liet smirked and rounded his desk. He pulled a bat out and circled the room. "Is that how you want to play, huh? I'll play. And I'll enjoy bashing your head in!"

He swung the bat at my head, and I had to spin to block it with my right. The shockwave rattled up my arm, and I almost lost my balance, but I pushed it out of the way and swung at his midsection. He jumped back, and I missed him by inches. He hoisted the bat over his head and came forward again, planning to smash the top of my head in. I blocked the attack and twisted the blade so it cut into the wood. Liet jerked it back and pulled me off balance, but I didn't go down. I regained my footing and turned slightly, using all of my strength to pull the bat down. Liet came forward, and I sliced at his stomach again. This time I was successful.

Liet stumbled backward in surprise, the bat falling from his hand. He stared at his stomach, then glanced back at me. His face turned red and his lips pursed into a line. With a shout, he charged me. I spun out of the way and arched my sword through the air. I flipped the blade closed, and the metal contacted the back of his skull. His body moved a few more steps forward, then he collapsed onto the floor.

My knees gave out. Blood leaked from the bullet wound in my shoulder, and my arm was on fire. My eye was blurry from Liet's punch, and I could feel every scratch on my face. Sweat dripped from my nose, and my breathing came in rasps. A soft moan caused me to jerk my head upward. The woman who attacked me earlier was coming to. I forced myself to stand up. If she wanted to attack me again, I was going to make sure that was the last thing she did. She sat up groggily and covered the lump on her head. When she saw me, her eyes filled with fear and she backed away. I watched her leave the room, and then I grabbed Liet's arm. I dragged him to the jury box and handcuffed him to the heat register. When I was sure he was secure, I went to join the others.

Gunshots echoed through the buildings, and people ran toward the wall. I joined the group. They had the majority of the soldiers cornered in their towers, firing into the crowd. I watched a few workers fall, but most of them took shelter behind the building supplies and in the houses. I saw Quinn and company behind a pile of concrete barriers. I fell to the ground next to him, out of breath and fighting to stay conscious.

"Kristal" He grabbed my arms and helped me sit up. "Are you all right?"

I winced. "Yeah. Liet is chained up in the courthouse."

"Do you have the key?"

I leaned back so I could reach into my pocket. "What are you going to do?"

"Maybe if we bring him out here, we can get the others to stop firing." He grabbed the key from my hand and took off running toward the courthouse.

A bullet whizzed over the barrier, while another smashed into the concrete above my head. Dust drifted into my eyes, and I ducked further down. A worker approached and handed me a magazine. I nodded my thanks, and he focused his gaze and the barrel of his weapon on the guards in the tower. I unholstered my weapon and slid the magazine in, waiting for an opportunity to fire, but my shoulder ached so bad I wasn't sure I could hold my gun up. The guy next to me popped over the barricade and fired a couple shots before squatting back down. I glanced back toward the courthouse.

Quinn returned with Liet a few minutes later, though to me it had seemed like hours. Liet's hands were cuffed behind his back, and Quinn attached a chain around his neck. He led Liet like a dog on a leash. As they got closer, I could see Liet's desperation to get away. He dodged to the right in an attempt to break free of Quinn's grasp, but Quinn jerked the chain and pulled him back in line. He wrapped the chain around his hand to shorten it and placed the barrel of his gun against Liet's head. He marched him past the safety of the concrete and into the line of fire.

"Hold your fire! Hold your fire!" A voice rose above the blasts of the guns.

I picked myself up and looked over the barrier. Pam made her way down from the tower. She stopped a few feet in front of the pair, her gun pointing to the ground.

"Drop your weapons," Quinn shouted.

"Don't you listen to him," Liet said.

Quinn pulled the chain so tight, Liet had to arch his back to be able to breathe. "If you don't drop your weapons, I will shoot the General." He cocked the hammer on his gun.

Pam dropped her gun onto the ground. The other soldiers followed suit.

"You cowards!" Liet screamed. "You worthless—"

Quinn smacked him in the back of the head with his gun, and he fell unconscious onto the ground.

The soldiers were lined up next to the fence, their hands behind their heads and their eyes averted to the ground. Workers paced around them with weapons, daring them to step out of line. A few went so far as to thrust the butt of their guns into the soldiers' stomachs or smash a fist into their nose, but Quinn always pulled them back.

I relished our victory, despite the pain in my shoulder and the overwhelming desire to pass out. Part of me was actually surprised it worked. I wanted to see the workers' smiling faces and the looks of defeat on the soldiers', so I attempted to ignore the pain.

"I see it didn't take much for you to convince the workers to rebel," I said.

"Are you kidding?" Quinn chuckled. "When we got into town, the workers who had been in Thedford already recruited half the city. They were waiting for us to show up so they could get their guns."

"What about McCook? Did you send someone up there so reinforcements don't find us?"

He nodded his head. "Yeah. Some of my men took a group of workers down there. They should be back by nightfall."

"How many were killed?"

"I don't know. We still don't have a number on that yet. There are some wounded who've made their way to the hospital. I suggest you do the same. C'mon. I'll help you." He wrapped his arm around my waist and pulled me close.

I smiled and leaned most of my weight against him. We hobbled to the hospital. A few people waited for treatment, but not nearly as many as I expected. A nurse grabbed me immediately and placed me in a wheelchair. Quinn kissed me gently before they took me inside and placed me on a gurney. I stared into the large examination light and let unconsciousness take over.

CHAPTER 25

I awoke later that night in a bed connected to IVs. My shoulder had been bandaged, but it was still sore. Quinn sat on the chair across from me. He came forward and sat on the edge of the bed. He pushed the hair out of my face, resting his hand on my cheek.

"Did you get in a fight with a cat?" He chuckled.

I pushed his hand away playfully. "At least I have some battle scars. Were you even involved in the fight?"

"Hey, that's not fair. My wrist still hurts." He held up his arm so I could see the brace.

I rolled my eyes. "It would mean more if it had been injured in the battle." I grabbed his hand and held it in mine. "How many were killed?"

"About ten. And that's including soldiers."

"Not bad. It could have been a lot worse."

"I think most of them were tired of the life anyway. I mean, you saw how quickly they surrendered once Liet was captured. I think fear kept them motivated."

"What are we going to do with them?"

Quinn shook his head. "Nothing. Those who want to will be integrated back into the population. We'll figure out what to do with those who don't want to integrate later."

"Have you heard anything from Florida yet?"

He shook his head. "No. We won't let on that there has been a rebellion. If they come looking for Liet, we'll tell them he's busy."

I smiled. "Where is Liet?"

"We locked him in one of the holding cells in the jail." He leaned forward and kissed me on the forehead. "Get some rest. I'll see you tomorrow."

I lay back on my pillow and sighed. After Quinn left, I drifted into a deep sleep, dreaming of horses and western sunsets.

* * *

Life in North Platte became more tolerable. The soldiers that could be integrated into the community without incident were, while the others were placed in holding cells in the courthouse. We still didn't know what we were going to do with them, but we had a while to figure it out. Both soldiers and civilians worked together to continue building the wall. They no longer worked on the wall in twenty-four hour shifts, but guards were in the towers at all times, and everyone was responsible for killing any zombies that came near the city. Quinn and his crew trained those who wanted to learn fighting techniques and marksmanship so they could head into the West and kill zombies. For the first time in a while, there was a sense of hope.

I had been out of the hospital for three days. I learned that I was in surgery for two hours while they dug out the bullet. My shoulder blade had been broken, but the bullet missed the major arteries in my arm. The doctor said I was lucky. I was going to be in a sling for six weeks. I had to spend four days in the hospital. They wanted me to stay longer, but I had stuff to do.

I sat at Liet's desk and looked through a pile of papers. I squinted, shook my head, then set the folder down and grabbed another. The door at the end of the room swung open, and Quinn walked in. I smiled, then directed my gaze back to the file.

"How's it going in here?" Quinn asked as he stepped up behind me.

"Look at this," I showed him the information. "Liet documented when they went to the bathroom. Can you believe it?"

Quinn shuffled through the folders. "How many of these are there?"

"One for every person who has ever come through North Platte."

"I thought you were looking up the supply manifests."

"I did. Liet kept count down to the can. It didn't take very long to go through those."

"How are we looking for supplies?"

I shrugged. "If we continue to ration, we should be fine, but I don't think we want to anymore. Most of these people are starving."

Quinn nodded. "I can get a group together and we can make a run. We should be able to stock the shelves pretty well." He sat on the desk. "I also wanted to let you know we fixed the fences at the north and south ends of the city and placed guards in the towers. We're set if anyone tries to get in."

I frowned. "I still think you're being overly cautious. I don't think Florida will send anyone to attack us. It's been a week. Don't you think they would have sent someone by now?"

He shrugged. "I don't know. I have no idea what kind of communications they have. Did you find anything in Liet's files about talking to The Families?"

I shook my head and rifled through some files. "There were some random communications, but nothing major. Unless he did things secretly, I think we should keep doing things the same way we have been. If we keep building the wall, no one will get suspicious, and no one will come to investigate."

"Well, even if they do, we have precautions." He stood from the desk and kissed me on top of the head. "I'll get a team together so we can get supplies."

"You know, I'd really like to come with you."

"I know, but you're in no shape to go. Your arm is still in a sling. I'll only be gone for a couple of days."

I stood and threw my good arm around his neck. I held on for a few minutes before kissing him on the mouth. He smiled, then left the courthouse.

Quinn was gone for two days when the first envoy from Florida showed up. The East Gate Guards alerted me to their presence, and I informed them to let them pass. I waited for the visitors in the courthouse. I hoped no one would come from Florida, but a little voice at the back of my brain told me to expect it. This wasn't normal. Florida never sent people up unless they were workers. They knew. I was sure of it. My palms started to sweat and my stomach knotted. In a few minutes, I was going to find out if they were willing to barter or if they were coming to eradicate the entire city. They didn't know about Liet; they couldn't. Perhaps I could still convince them everything was all right. I held my breath as the door opened.

Pam escorted three men into the room. I recognized one of them as Olivia's personal bodyguard. He nodded as they approached the bench.

"What can I do for you, gentlemen?" I leaned forward and folded my hands on the desk, trying to portray an air of casualness I didn't feel.

"Mrs. Johnson was expecting a shipment of supplies last week. When she didn't receive it, she tried to raise Liet on the radio, but no one answered. She sent us here to make sure everything was all right."

My stomach knotted even further. Olivia knew they weren't going to get another shipment until they sent up the engineers, which they hadn't done. Plus, we monitored the communications the entire time after the uprising, and nothing came through from Florida. My suspicions were confirmed. I took a deep breath.

"Liet's been really busy lately." I lowered my head, acting as if I had to regain my composure. "We had a little incident."

The bodyguard folded his arms across his chest. "What kind of incident?"

"A soldier, some crazed soldier, broke into our house a week ago. I think he was trying to kill Liet, but I was the only one home at the time. As you can see, I was lucky, but not lucky enough." I rubbed my shoulder.

The man clicked his tongue. "That's awful. What happened to the soldier?"

"I don't know. Liet has been obsessed with finding his whereabouts. He doesn't sleep and he hardly eats. He won't rest until justice is served." I pounded my fist on the desk for emphasis.

The man nodded. "I understand. Do you need any assistance from us?"

I set my jaw and shook my head curtly. "No. We can handle it. Thank you." I sniffed. "Is there anything else we can do for you?"

The man shook his head. "No. I think we've got all the information we need." He turned to leave.

"Do you still need that truck of supplies to take back to Florida?"

The bodyguard turned and smiled. "That would be helpful."

By the time they got the truck loaded, it was midafternoon. I was never so happy to see the men leave, and Pam waited until they were out of sight before we headed back to the courthouse. I paced the floor and chewed on my nails.

"That was weird," Pam commented.

I stopped and stared at her. "They know."

Pam scoffed. "How could they know?"

"I don't know how they know, but they know. They have *never* sent anyone up here to check on supplies."

"True. But how could they have found out?"

I paced again. "I don't know. Maybe they captured Bill and Kyle. Maybe someone got out and told them."

Pam knitted her eyebrows together. "Who would have told them? The majority of the soldiers couldn't wait until Liet's reign was over."

I stopped again and pointed a finger at Pam. "*Most* of the soldiers, but not all. What if one of them went to Florida?"

She shrugged. "It's possible. What should we do?"

I glanced at the desk with the folders of all the people in the city. "Someone got out. I need to talk to Liet."

Pam shook her head. "I don't think that's a very good idea. Let me ask around, see what's going on. If I don't find anything, then you can talk to him."

I hesitated. "Fine. But I'm only giving you one day."

"Okay. I'll have something by tomorrow morning."

I tried to busy myself the rest of the day by inventorying what was left of the supplies. My stomach was so upset I couldn't eat, and when night rolled around, I couldn't sleep. I went down to Liet's office and went through the files. If it wasn't one of Pam's soldiers, then it had to be a civilian. Visions of the woman who attacked me in Liet's office ran through my mind, and I tried to remember what she looked like. I wondered why we let the men go back to Florida. If they were checking up on North Platte, then we sent them back to confirm what they suspected. Of course, if they didn't go back, that would also confirm what they suspected. Either way, we were screwed. I hoped they were willing to barter.

I jumped when the door to the courtroom opened, and I fumbled for my gun. When I realized it was Quinn, I took a deep breath and continued to examine the files. My eyes felt like sandpaper, and it was hard for me to focus. I didn't look up when Quinn kissed the top of my head.

"What are you doing?"

"We had a visit from Florida. We're trying to figure out who squealed."

Quinn knelt next to me and turned the chair so I faced him. "Who came from Florida?"

"One of Olivia's bodyguards and two other men I didn't recognize."

"What did they say?"

"They wanted to know why Liet hadn't sent the supplies."

Quinn stood and thought for a moment. "This is exactly why I wanted to attack both places at the same time. Now, it will be impossible to get supplies in."

"What's done is done. We have to figure out what we're going to do."

He stared at the pile of folders. "Why are you looking through the files?"

"I'm looking for someone."

"Who?"

"The woman who attacked me in Liet's office."

"Why?"

"Because she might be the person who escaped. If I know who she is and where she lives, then I can check to see if she's there."

Quinn pushed his eyebrows together. "What if it wasn't her?"

I opened my mouth to speak but was interrupted when the door slammed open. Quinn and I turned to look at Pam, who approached the bench with a grim look on her face.

"I think I might have our culprit." She waved a folder in the air before slamming it down on the desk. "All of the soldiers are accounted for except for one. Ben."

I opened the folder and stared at the picture. It took my exhausted brain a few minutes before I recognized the man. I stared at Quinn.

"I guess he really didn't like being handcuffed to the steering wheel."

"You sure about this?" I asked.

Pam nodded. "Things got crazy when the workers started attacking, but according to witnesses, he disappeared right after the first shot was fired. Some of the other soldiers cursed him for being a coward, but now we know where he was going."

My forehead wrinkled in confusion. "Why Ben? What ties did he have with The Families?" I flipped open the folder, but the only information in there was his transfer sheet.

Pam shrugged. "Who knows? It's possible he didn't have any ties at all, he was smart enough to get out when the gettin' was good."

I set the folder down and buried my face in my hand. I sat like that for a few minutes, then raised my head. "We have to find out what they know. We need to get some spies into Florida."

"How do you expect to do that?" Pam questioned.

Frustration squeezed my chest, and I slammed my fist onto the desk. "I don't know, but we had better figure something out. Bill and Kyle made it down there, we can get someone else in."

Quinn placed a hand on my shoulder. "Even if we get someone in, how are they going to communicate with us?"

"CB radio, telegraph, carrier pigeon. I don't care. Just make it happen."

Quinn held his hands up in defense. "All right. We'll figure something out. Right now, though, I think you need to head to bed. You've been awake for a long time, and I don't think you're thinking too clearly."

I stared at him and the heat rose into my face. I opened my mouth to speak, thought better of it, and stood from the chair. I stared at both Pam and Quinn for a moment before heading upstairs.

After I closed the door, I leaned against it for support. My head spun and I felt nauseous. It wasn't supposed to be this difficult. After North Platte fell, it was supposed to be a quick overthrow of The Families; no one would get hurt and everyone would be thankful for the freedom. All we were trying to do was make the nation a better place to live. We needed to get rid of the zombies.

My head ached, so I decided to take a shower and lay down. I stepped into the bathroom and turned on the water. The heat massaged the back of my head, and I tried not to think about anything. We had been lucky that North Platte fell so quickly. The people sent to work here had done something to piss

The Families off. They were probably decent people, but their ideas didn't mesh with their rulers. It wasn't hard to convince them to retaliate because they had nothing to lose. Those who still lived in Florida had everything to lose. They didn't know what it was like outside the state, they only knew what The Families told them. I realized we would run into more Pearls than we would Tanyas, and that made our campaign that much harder.

Plus, we were a threat to The Families, whose control was based on fear. Once that fear was gone, The Families were done. They wouldn't like that, and that's why they sent the scouts. They needed to know for sure what they were up against. Sending back a truck would be a nice gesture, but it would only buy us time. Eventually, we would have to face the army of Florida.

I stepped out of the shower and dried off. I pulled on a pair of sweats and a tank top, then headed for bed. Quinn sat on the edge and smiled feebly at me as I took a seat next to him. I wrapped my arm around his shoulders and buried my face in his chest. His warm breath on the top of my head comforted me.

"It was stressful enough when we had to worry about zombie attacks. Now, we have to worry about the living, too. What are we going to tell the workers of North Platte?"

"They knew what they were getting into when they revolted."

I took a deep breath. "What are we going to do?"

Quinn sighed and pulled me closer. "The only thing we can do is prepare for war."

Meet The Author

Bio

Pembroke Sinclair has had several stories published in various places. She writes an eclectic mix of stories ranging from western to science fiction to fantasy. Her stories have been published in various places, including Static Movement, chuckhawks.com, The Cynic Online Magazine, Sonar 4 Publications, Golden Visions Magazine, and Residential Aliens.

Her first novel, **Coming from Nowhere**, is also available at eTreasures Publishing and Amazon.com. Her story, Sohei, was named one of the Best Stories of 2008 by The Cynic Online Magazine.

If you would like to contact Pembroke, she can be reached at: pembrokesinclair@hotmail.com or pembrokesinclair.blogspot.com.

Made in the USA
Lexington, KY
20 November 2011